LONG
PORK

Behind the Bamboo Curtain

Mandy Partridge

First published in Australia by Aurora House
www.aurorahouse.com.au

This edition published 2020
Copyright © Mandy Partridge 2020

Typesetting and e-book design: Amit Dey
Cover design: Luke Harris
Map design: P. Brewer

ISBN number: 978-1-922403-15-5 (paperback)

A catalogue record for this book is available from the National Library of Australia

Distributed by: Ingram Content: www.ingramcontent.com
Australia: phone +613 9765 4800 |
email lsiaustralia@ingramcontent.com
Milton Keynes UK: phone +44 (0)845 121 4567 |
email enquiries@ingramcontent.com
La Vergne, TN USA: phone +1 800 509 4156 |
email inquiry@lightningsource.com

Tok Pisin – Pidgin English

Ami	army
Benetii	cassowary
Bigman	leader
Bikpela man	adult
Billum	string bag, dillybag
Biltong	beef jerky
Binatang	insect
Blakbokis	flying fox
Blakpela	black
Boipren	boyfriend
Brada	brother
Buk tambu	Bible
Bun I Brok	broken bone
Bus, bikbus	jungle, bush
Fowil draiv	four-wheel drive
Giaman	joke
Gol	gold
Gras bilong het	hair
Hamas?	how much?

Haus	home
Haus lain	long house
Haus tambaran	spirit house
I dai pinis	dead
Kaikai	meal
Kakaruk	chicken
Kalangal	parakeet
Kapul, cuscus	possum
Kiau	egg
Kiau bilong golip	pearl
Kilim	injure
Kilim I dai pinis	kill
Kina	cowrie shells, money, oyster, shell
Kindam	crayfish
Klos	clothes
Kok	penis
Koki	parrot
Kokomo	hornbill bird
Kuka	crab
Kukim	bake
Kulau	green coconut
Kumul	bird of paradise
Laikim	love
Laplap	cloth, sarong
Laulau	Malay apple
Lek bilong pik	leg of ham
Liklik	little
Liklik kindam	prawn

Liklik rat	mouse
Long pork	human flesh for eating
Luluai	chief
Maleo	eel
Mambu	bamboo
Manukau	sweet potato
Marita	pandanus fruit
Masket, raifol, gang	gun
Meme	goat
Moran	carpet snake, python
Motobaik	motorbike
Mumut	bandicoot
Naip	knife
Natnat	mosquito
Niuspepa	newspaper
Nogut	bad
Olgeta	all
OPM, Organasi Papua Merdeka	Free Papua Organisation
Paia	fire
Palai	goanna, lizard
Papa	father
Pato	duck
Pekpek blut	dysentery
Pekpek wara	diarrhea
Pikinini	baby
Pikinini bilong sipsip	lamb
Piksa	picture

Pis	fish
Plaua	flower
Ples	place
Ples nogut	dangerous place
Pok	fork
Poto	photo
Pupuk	crocodile
Raskol	rascal
Raunwara	lake (round water)
Ren	rain
Ring long telepon	telephone call
Rokrok	frog
Saksak	Sago palm
Sevis stesin	service station
Sikau	wallaby
Sikau bilong antap	tree kangaroo
Singsing	festival
Smokbalus	jet plane
Susa	sister
Susu	milk, breast
Taim bilong ren	rainy season
Tambu	taboo, forbidden
Trosel	turtle
Wantok	friend
Waswas	bathe
Welpig	bush pig
Wokabaut	walk
Yambo	guava

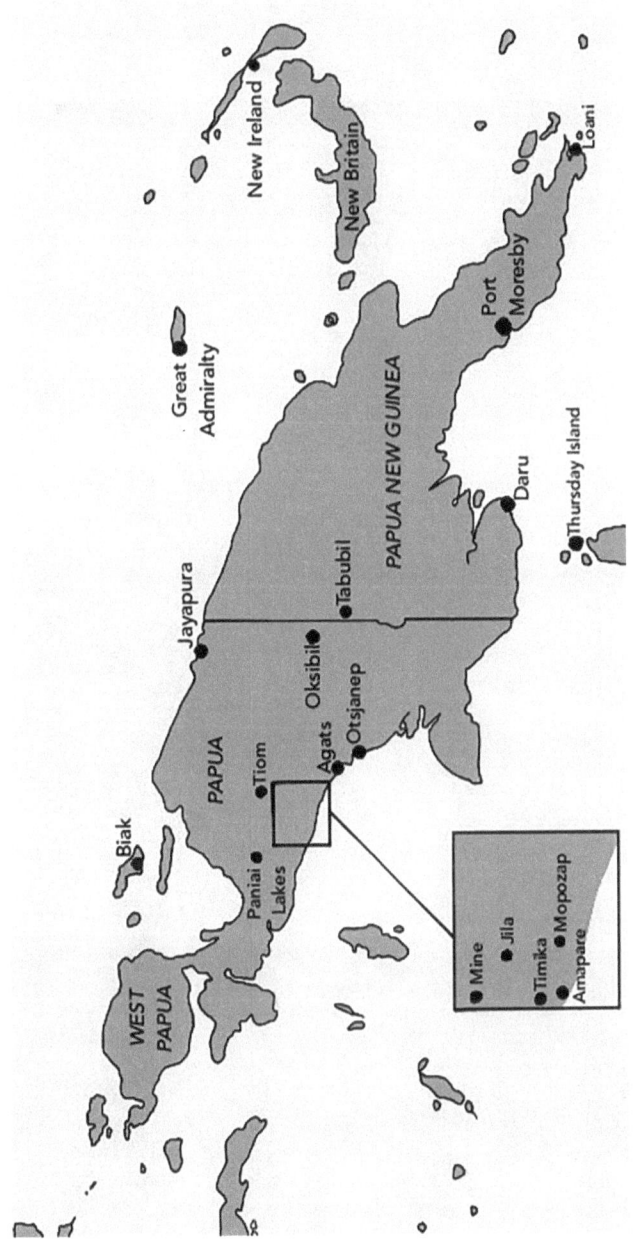

Map of Papua and Papua New Guinea

LIZA

Prologue

Ten days on, ten days off. It does my head in a bit, but I'm getting used to it. I miss my husband Mike, and my dog, walks on the beach and eating in cafés. My job at Freeport Mine in Papua is interesting, though – no two days are the same.

Miners are generally a robust lot with mostly minor injuries or the odd tropical sore, so I can usually fit them all into the first seven days of my roster, leaving me the last three days to visit the clinics for the local highlanders.

The locals are worse off than the miners, suffering from malnutrition, malaria, STDs, diabetes, domestic violence and alcoholism. I like treating the kids best – tiny kids, with big brown trusting eyes. Maybe it's because I don't have any of my own.

As I fly up to Papua, I like to look out the windows. It's a charter flight from Cairns, over the jungles of north Queensland to Timika, not far across the Torres Strait, on the south coast of Papua. Around the town of Timika are cleared farmlands. From there it's a helicopter ride up to Freeport Grasberg. After a while, the choppers seem just like minibuses; you see the same pilots, and you often know the passengers too.

I always need to remember to take a couple of pouches of White Ox with me from Cairns, or else I'm forced to smoke Indonesian cigarettes like Rajas or the nasty clove-flavoured Gudang Garams.

At the top of the mountains, nearly five kilometres above sea level, there are glaciers. The massive gaping mine cut into the mountain looms up ahead, ridges cut in concentric circles surrounding it, like some giant creature has clawed the rocks, and green valleys dropping away to the south. It's the biggest gold and copper mine in the world. Piles of mine waste spread for kilometres across the plateau to the north of the mine, while the smaller and older open-cut mine to the southwest, Ertsberg, holds the wastewater. The HEAT (Heavy Equipment Access Track) road cuts a zigzag path down the steep terrain to the Mill and the Ridge Camp, which is where there are portals to the underground shaft network. From there the road goes on to Tembagapura, literally meaning 'Copper Town'. This cluster of buildings perching on the southern ridges includes accommodation for nearly 10,000 workers, a cable car up to the mines, a canteen, helipads, and offices for admin, service workers and medics like me. Tembagapura clusters around a tiny school, shops, a church, a mosque, a power plant, water and sewerage works.

The mine operates 24 hours a day, and because the miners work a mix of both day and night shifts, the mosque doesn't make the amplified calls to prayer before dawn; instead they are the quieter, unamplified calls. Night-shift workers need their sleep too. In Tembagapura, workers' rights win over religious rights.

My clinic is near my digs. With the mine always working, so too the mine's doctors are on call 24 hours a day, seven days a week. Many of the Indonesian workers turn up to the clinic in town, some with their wives and kids. Everyone in Tembagapura either works for the mine or is related to a worker. To get to the other clinics I have to grab a lift in a chopper.

One of these clinics is in Tiom, high in the mountains, north of the Lorentz National Park, which really is wilderness. When I go there, I make sure I bring a good supply of medicines and dressings. The expats and Indonesians there wear high-vis work-wear, live in western-style houses, and drive four-wheel drives. By contrast the local Papuans still plough subsistence gardens with sharpened branches, wear laplaps, or sarongs, and *klos* – often T-shirts and shorts – live in huts with dirt floors and walk everywhere.

The locals visit my clinic, bringing with them their children and old people. So, I can communicate, I've picked up a bit of Tok Pisin, or pidgin. The highlanders have little by way of shoes or warm clothes, so I always try to bring blankets with me as well. When I see how well the expats and Indonesian settlers live, I find it shameful that none of this country's wealth trickles down to the locals.

LIZA

The crash landing

By mid-November the monsoon had started, lashing the south coast of Papua and causing choppers to be diverted from Timika to Jayapura in the north. Usually it was just me and the pilot heading up to Tiom, but this day John was carrying five workers past the hill village to the northern coastal capital of Jayapura, from where they would fly out on a plane.

The weather was bad, and the chopper heavy. With the clouds hanging low, the visibility was short and patchy – John was having trouble making visual contact with Tiom. To add to this the satellite navigator was playing up. The miners, usually joking and talking about plans for their leave, sat quietly scanning the jungle for tell-tale signs of smoke rising from the tribal fireplaces. As the wind started to pick up, the chopper was swept around. John rose in altitude, trying to get above the storm. Suddenly the miners spotted a mountain as it appeared above the clouds.

"Is that Angelmuk?" asked Ken, an engineer who'd been working at Freeport Grasberg for more than ten years.

"I dunno," replied John. "It could be Osua Trikora. We haven't seen the village yet. I don't think we've gone past it. Either way, we've blown off course."

"Is that sat nav still playing up?" asked Ken, sounding worried and trying to keep his voice steady.

"It's a piece of shit," said John. "Anyone's phone work up here?"

We all reached for our phones; most had sat nav, but the reception in the mountains in the middle of a storm was appalling.

"I'm getting on my radio to make a mayday call. I might have to do an emergency landing if this weather gets any worse," said John, sounding grim.

A chorus of swearing broke out.

"I can see a road," called Arthur, pointing towards the back of the chopper.

Everyone peered down to see a dirt track near a creek. John turned the chopper towards it.

"That's got to be the Tiom track," shouted John. "There's no other road round here."

"J Bird Ten to Grasberg control, over." John waited but there was no response.

"Mayday! Mayday! This is J Bird Ten, en route Grasberg to Jayapura. Sat nav is down and winds are cyclonic. Will attempt emergency landing on Tiom track. Grasberg control, can you hear me?"

The seven of us on board each held our breath as the chopper started to descend towards the trees. As we got closer to the ground, the wind strengthened, causing the chopper to get thrown around.

"No. It's too risky," said John emphatically, taking the chopper back up as fast as he could. "I'm going to forget about Tiom and carry on to Jayapura. It's just too dangerous to land in these conditions."

The chopper ascended into the clouds, the pilot using his compass to head northeast towards Jayapura on the northern coastal plain, and away from that mountain.

We were flying blind and we were all scared. The storm was interfering with both the navigation system and the two-way radio, and John was worried. He doggedly kept gaining altitude – Tiom was on a highland plateau between two high ranges that ran parallel to each other down the spine of Papua and New Guinea. Grasberg was on the southern range, and Angelmuk was on the northern range that was now veiled with clouds.

"J Bird Ten to Grasberg … Come in Grasberg … Aborted Tiom landing, repeat, aborted Tiom landing. Heading towards Jayapura in low visibility, repeat, heading for Jayapura. Are you receiving? Over."

Nothing but static came over the two-way, with the satellite screen showing waves of interference from the storm. Fighting the unpredictable wind, John concentrated on flying.

"This is Airport Amingaru. Is that J Bird Ten? Did you call mayday? Over."

"This is J Bird Ten. Amingaru, I am calling mayday. Over."

"This is Amingaru. I received partial transmission. What is your location? Over."

"This is J Bird Ten. Unable to locate Tiom, navigation is down, repeat, navigation equipment is down. Heading to Jayapura. Over."

"Amingaru here. Make landing if possible. Cyclonic winds … southerly …"

"Damn, they're gone," said John, who was sweating heavily now.

He kept the chopper level as we partially emerged from the clouds in time to see a string of peaks coming up on the left. He veered away and urged the chopper upward. At this altitude the jungle had evaporated, leaving bushes and grass. The ground was visible but steep. John turned the chopper and headed for a pass between the peaks.

A sudden blast of wind snatched at the helicopter, smashing it sideways into the mountain like a child's toy. It hit the rocks with a sickening crash, then slipped down the slope, coming to rest in the high valley between the two peaks, cliffs dropping away to both sides.

I was knocked out.

I came to as I was being carried away from the chopper by the older miner, Ken. Luckily, he's a big Aussie bloke, and I'm quite small. He put me down not far from the aircraft and explained the situation.

"Dirk and I are OK. Arthur and the other Dutch guy, Franz, are both injured. We think that John and Robert are both dead, but you'd better check."

I tried standing, but my legs weren't playing ball. "Can you help me? I think I've injured my back."

Ken and Dirk stood on either side of me and walked me over to where the other guys were lying. Dirk was tall and skinny with curly blond hair that made him look like a mad scientist.

"Can you grab the backpack with the red cross on it? And there's a sports bag with blankets in it somewhere, too."

Ken headed back to the wreck and pulled out my bags.

Arthur was moaning, his leg obviously broken; Franz was bleeding from the head. I quickly told Ken and Dirk how they could help, gave Arthur a shot of painkiller, and then cleaned and bandaged Franz's head wound.

"Find something that we can use for a splint, wood or metal, two bits would actually be good, you know, leg length."

I turned to Arthur. "Mate, this might not be perfect, and it might hurt, but we're going to have to straighten that leg out and wrap it up."

Arthur was a medium-sized guy. His muscles and dirty overalls told me that he worked with heavy machinery.

I got the two able men to hold his shoulders while I pulled his leg in a straight downward direction. Arthur made a noise like it hurt.

"Right, that looks pretty good, and seeing as how we don't have an X-ray, I'm going to splint it up like that."

I got Ken and Dirk to help position the splints – broken pieces of chopper – and bandage around them and the leg.

"Thank God we had Doctor Liza with us, eh mates?" piped up Arthur. "We were a bit worried there for a minute."

"Better show me the other guys now," I said, indicating the chopper, and the man lying near it.

Ken and Dirk picked me up again and helped me over to the chopper. Robert was an engineering graduate – American and quite young. Or at least he had been. It looked as if one of the chopper blades had folded into his side of the cabin, and slashed his neck, nearly severing his head. He was covered in blood, and definitely dead.

"We couldn't get John out of his seat," was all that Ken could say. The front of the cabin had taken the impact of the crash. The pilot was crushed between his seat and the instrument panel.

"What's that in his hand?" I asked. I had seen a bit of death in my life – all those cadavers at med school – so I was used to it. Ken made himself look again.

"I think that is an EPIRB device," Ken said. "A battery powered satellite locater."

"Better take it out of his hand, then, and set it off. It looks like he wanted us to use it," I said.

Shakily, Ken prised the device from John's dead hand and backed away from the wreckage. Taking the personal locator beacon from Ken, Dirk applied himself to working out how to use it.

We were the survivors. We huddled together with all the blankets we could find.

"Yeah, we were a bit worried there for a minute. As a matter of fact, I'm still pretty worried." A master of Aussie understatement, Ken summed it up.

As the clouds slowly cleared, we took in our surroundings. We were in the middle of nowhere, high on a mountain range, drenched in rain and blood. We had very little food and water, no phone coverage, and only the EPIRB between us and civilisation.

"Yep, it's not good," I agreed, before passing out once more.

LIZA

Rescued, sort of

I woke up some time later, hoping it was all a bad dream. It wasn't.

A fire burned in the centre of the clearing, throwing off choking clouds of smoke, as Ken and Dirk took turns feeding it with green brush. I was dying for a cigarette.

The men had been busy. A pile of our luggage was nearby, and someone had obviously gone through every bag looking for items of food and bottles of water. Robert's body had been dragged further away from our little camp, so we didn't have to look at him.

"We were worried that the chopper was going to fall down the cliff," said Dirk. "We haven't got ropes or anything to secure it to anyway. So, we've taken everything we could grab out of the cabin."

"Is that all the food?" I asked, eyeing the pathetically small pile.

"Yes, we'll starve if no one comes to find us," said Dirk.

Ken walked back to the camp carrying more uprooted bushes for the fuel stack. He looked grim.

"I can see for miles down there," he gestured. "But I can't see any sign of habitation. There's some smoke from a mountain, but I think it might just be volcanic."

"We've got that EPIRB sending out signals, and there are nine other choppers back at Grasberg," I said, always the optimist.

"And the Amingaru airport guys got at least a partial message from us," added Dirk.

"They'll come searching," said Ken. "They always do when a chopper goes down."

"How often do choppers go down here?" I asked.

"Well, there has been about one per year, in the time I've been up here. The Freeport people are always keen to pick up the workers before the Raskols have a chance to get to them," said Ken.

Dirk looked worried. "What happens if the Raskols find them first?"

"Well, you know, the locals aren't exactly thrilled that we're up here poisoning their water and stealing their land. One chopper full of guys got hacked up with machetes," said Ken.

"Oh, great," said Dirk. "They don't tell you that in the recruitment or training videos."

"What about the Asmat?" I asked. "Aren't the Raskols more westernised town dwellers? Would the tribal highlanders behave differently?"

"Well, the Asmat get on pretty well with the missionary mob. They've been down there in the Lorentz National Park for quite a while, like seventy or eighty years, running schools and clinics, and helping the locals. The Asmat might be kinder," said Ken.

"Do you mean, as in not kill us with machetes?" asked Arthur, clearly frightened now.

"Yeah," said Ken. "The Dutch missionaries helped to make the Taman forest a national park, so the Asmat could live their traditional life there. They've still got clean rivers and wildlife to eat. They don't hate us half as much as the Raskols do."

"I can actually speak a bit of Asmat," said Franz. Everybody turned to look at him. "My parents worked for the missionaries, and I spent a bit of time there as a kid."

"Wow, that's great, Franz," I said. "What are the Asmat like?"

"Well, I think they've changed a great deal," said Franz. "They used to be headhunters, you know. The missionaries taught them that cannibalism and polygyny were sinful, so they haven't really done that for, like, fifty years or more now."

"Terrific," said Arthur. "Headhunters!"

"No, really," said Franz, "it was mostly a lack of protein thing – the pigs were scarce in the forest and fishing was seasonal. Birds and monkeys are hard to hunt. Killing men was like a tribal vendetta thing. The next village raided yours last year, so you raid them this year. The men would kill the men and women, chopping them up into pieces to carry. But if they found a baby or small child, they would carry it home and give it to their wife. The infant mortality rate was very high here, before medicine, so they valued any baby and adopted it. They're doing different farming practices now. Every family keeps pigs. They have machetes and nets, so hunting and fishing are easier now too. And they've got markets. They don't need to eat people anymore."

"Jesus. Help me over to that cliff, and I'll just jump off now," said Arthur.

"Let me give you some more of that pethidine, Arthur," I said. "You're in a lot of pain, and we're in a frightening situation."

I found that I could stand up by myself now. I hobbled over to my backpack. "I'll also give you both some more antibiotics to fight off infection. Looks like we've got more medicine than food, but we'll ration everything."

"I'm dying for some water, actually," said Franz.

Ken took him a bottle and said, "Try to just have a couple of mouthfuls."

"I'm actually dying for a fag. Anyone else?" It seemed that Ken and I were the only smokers. He had a pack of Horizons, so I bummed one.

"Wouldn't have thought a doctor would smoke," smirked Ken.

"Spare us the lecture," I spat back.

At least the sun was appearing through the parting clouds. The fire warmed and dried us out, even if it did blow smoke at us as the winds changed. Our meal was a shared packet of rice crackers and seaweed paper. As we ate in silence, the wind again picked up. We watched the chopper rock precariously, teeter, then topple over the cliff. For a long while no one spoke.

Finally, Arthur said. "Goodbye, John, you were a good bloke, and you did your best for us. We'll make sure to tell your family that you died quickly and saved the rest of us. We're sorry you went so young Robert. Your life was only just beginning."

Everybody tried to stay positive for each other, hoping that we would not all end up like John and Robert. Ken decided he might as well pass the bottle of whisky around.

Later in the afternoon, we were rescued. Well, sort of.

A group twelve tribesmen, ranging in age from teenage boys to old men, approached us carrying spears. Naked except for penis gourds, vines and feathers, they advanced cautiously. I woke up Franz. He was the only one who might be able to speak to them. Franz spoke a few words to them, and in return they responded with lots of words and gestures. After a while the conversation slowed and Franz translated.

Franz pointed at Arthur and said, "Him bun I brok."

The tribesmen looked at Arthur and his bandages and nodded.

Franz said to us, "They said we should come with them, soon. It is a long walk to their village, and a hard climb. They want to do the climbing bit before the sun goes down. They'll help Arthur to walk. I suppose we should pack our bags."

We quickly divided up our belongings and decided who would carry what. Then we started walking.

The walk was indeed difficult, especially for Arthur who was struggling. We came to a steep scramble where one of the tribesmen unwrapped a vine that he'd been carrying over his shoulder and across his chest. He dropped it over the cliff, securing it to a tree and holding on fast. A younger man climbed down the slope using the vine, then some of the others followed, feet first, facing into the hill. Back at the top, one of them wrapped the free end of the vine around Arthur's waist, lowering him to the men waiting below. Not confident that I could tackle the steep descent, I also asked to be taken down that way, while Franz, Ken and Dirk managed alone. Finally, the tribesman – a strong young man – came down last, bringing the vine with him.

These tribesmen were Asmat – small but sturdy men, fit and muscular. Two of them appeared to be tribal leaders – one appeared older, one younger, so we assumed they were father and son. Their noses were pierced with boar's teeth. The men tucked their penis gourds into belts made of twine or vine, and also wore twine decorated with feathers around their arms, necks and headbands.

It was dark by the time we'd walked the couple of hours to their village. We'd been expecting huts or treehouses, but this tribe lived in a cave, or a series of caves, under a rocky cliff, still high in the mountains. We were relieved to sit down.

There were mostly older men and young boys back at the village. It looked as if the more able-bodied members of the tribe were with us on the recovery mission. There didn't appear to be any women around, which seemed rather strange to me. The men who'd remained were busy preparing food over a fire. After indicating where they wanted us to sit, the tribal leaders and then we were served food consisting of birds, sago palm, and grubs of the sago beetle, all heated by fire or ash. We were so grateful to have been found and hungry enough to eat anything we were given.

By the light of the fire, I could make out the mouth of the largest cave. Serving the same role as a long house, the inner entrance seemed to be decorated with wooden objects carved variously in the shape of crocodiles, birds, and faces. Looking closer revealed that some of the faces were, in fact, preserved skulls.

After the meal, we were led to a smaller cave nearby. Two young men appeared to be assigned guard duty at the mouth of the cave. Making rough beds with our packs and blankets, we helped Arthur to settle. The cave was dark. But we were out of the weather and with full stomachs, which made it much easier for us to get some sleep. The outside fire had been extinguished with its remains pushed inside the tribesmen's main cave.

As I went to sleep, I thought about this strange remote village. Something was wrong here, and I couldn't quite work out what.

LIZA

Trapped

We woke at dawn to the clattering sound of a helicopter close by. Our instinct was to run outside and wave at the chopper to try and catch their attention. But the tribesmen guarding the entrance to our cave barred our way. Desperate to get out to see the helicopter, Franz tried talking to them, pleading with them to let us get past. They brandished their machetes and clubs, blocking our way. Franz was shouting now. Obviously unimpressed, the tribesmen grew silent, shaking their heads, determined to keep us imprisoned.

"What the hell are they saying?" I asked.

Franz looked bewildered, "They say that no one knows they are here. No one will know they are here." We looked at each other as the implications of this sank in.

"What?" said Ken.

We listened in horror as the chopper moved further and further away, until we couldn't hear it anymore.

"Have we still got that EPIRB?" said Dirk.

We went through our bags, but nobody could locate the device. Had we left it at the crash site, lost it on the 'rescue' trip, or had the tribesman taken it from our luggage? Things had taken a decided turn for the worse.

Arthur pieced it together first. "If they don't want anyone to know that they are here, they aren't going to let us leave, in case we tell others about them. So will they keep us here forever, or will they just kill us to shut us up?"

"Why are they so secretive? What have they got to hide?" asked Franz.

"And where are the women and children of their tribe?" I asked. "They don't seem to live at this site. Is it a secret men's place or something?"

"They wouldn't tell me anything," said Franz. "They just clammed up and wouldn't answer my questions."

"I've got a really bad feeling about this," said Ken. "What do we know about these people? Why would they have a secret village? Why are they hiding in these caves?"

Dirk had been quietly thinking, and now he piped up, "Does anyone have a torch, or charge on their phones?"

The remaining phones could be solar-charged, so could act like rechargeable torches. We had two cigarette lighters, but not many ciggies.

Dirk continued, "If they won't let us out of this cave, maybe a couple of us should explore what's further in."

We waited for an opportunity, and it didn't take long. After being let out for our morning meal we were led back to the cave, but this time only one guard was left with us. He promptly fell asleep, so the two able-bodied of us, Ken and Dirk, headed further into the cave to explore.

They heard the water before they saw it trickling down from the ceiling of the cave a few 'rooms' in. The men had been travelling slightly uphill, and this chamber was tilted downwards, with water pooled to one side of the floor. From there it must have been draining away deeper into the cave system.

"Great!" said Dirk. "We have plumbing!"

They stopped for a drink – the water was cold and fresh.

Further in again there was a bigger surprise waiting for them.

"Look! There's light!" Ken said, lowering his phone and striding quickly towards the next cavern.

A hole in the left wall let in the sunlight, fully illuminating the chamber and partially lighting the one they'd just left. Both men rushed to look out of the opening but were disappointed when they realised that it opened out to a cliff that dropped steeply away and rose just as steeply above their heads. There'd be no escaping through this hole. They turned to examine the rest of the cavern.

In the corner was what appeared to be a body, old and dried out, lying on a bed of hides and paperbark, under an old blanket. Next to this was a disused fireplace – just a circle of rocks, with a billycan resting on it. And there was a pile of papers made from paperbark with writing. The writing looked like it had been made with black soot from the fire. The man, who was obviously long dead, was dressed in ragged clothes and lying as if asleep. Long greyish hair was still attached to the skull.

"Jesus Christ," whispered Ken. "Who was this poor bastard?"

Dirk walked closer, crouched, and lifted the blanket from the body. The corpse had been tall and skinny. The skin still clung to his thin arms.

"Poor rich bastard, you mean," said Dirk, indicating the gold watch still on the wrist of the dead man. "He's got a Rolex."

"If we can read those papers, I'll bet we can find out who he was," said Ken, walking towards the pile. The papers were stacked and held down with stone paperweights. Ken gathered them up, wrapping them in his windproof jacket.

"Let's get back and tell the others. We can read these there."

They decided to leave the poor dead guy with his nice watch, but they did take his billycan to fill with water on their return trip. When Ken and Dirk returned to the mouth of the cave, they told us of their discovery. Ken unwrapped the old, flaky papers.

"I've got some specimen bags in my medical bag that could protect these pages," I said.

Arthur read them out, and as he finished I put each piece of bark into a snap-lock bag. The pages were numbered. This is what was written:

> It is my sincerest hope that someone will one day read these words, and send them back to my parents. I am Michael Clarke Rockefeller, and my parents are Nelson and Mary Rockefeller of New York city. It is now 1975, though I am not sure of the exact date, as I have lost track of the days and the months during my travels and illnesses. I have not spoken to another white man since 1961. I came to West Netherlands New Guinea, first in 1960, to study the Dani people for the Peabody Museum. I was fascinated by this place, and returned the following year to study the Asmat people. I was on a boat with my fellow researcher, Rene Wassing, when we capsized.
>
> Our boat had been caught in unseasonal winds and monstrous waves, and we were blown off course and out to sea. We couldn't right the vessel. As I was a strong swimmer, I decided to swim for the shore, and try to get back to the village of Otsjanep and get help.

When I finally got ashore, I didn't recognise the land or any of the people. The tribesmen seemed hostile, although they took me to their longhouse and gave me food and a blanket. When I had recovered from the long swim, I thought they would take me back to the missionary's village, but I was mistaken.

A team of young tribesmen walked me through the jungle, up through the foothills, and into the mountains. We stopped at various villages along the way. At first, the Asmat people there were more civilised, covering themselves. There was an absence of the skull collections that the priests had banned.

As we travelled further inland, the people were just wearing their belts and gourds, decorated with brightly coloured feathers. The longhouses had skulls on display, at first just inside, but the farther we travelled, the more skulls I saw – decorating doorways, even worn on head-dresses. I prayed in earnest that I would not become one of those skulls. But these skulls were mostly of warriors, from rival villages. The Asmat used to conduct regular raids on their neighbours, killing men to eat, and stealing wives and children.

The missionaries had told me that this practice had been wiped out. When we got to the mountain village, I learned of my fate. I was to be traded for five young women – wives for the warriors who were escorting me on my journey. The women, children and pigs lived separately in this village, in a collection of huts huddled under the high cliffs of the mountain range.

They tended gardens along the banks of a stream and kept some pigs in the huts with themselves. A few men guarded the women and children, and the rest lived separately.

When I arrived, a boy was dispatched to bring the tribal leaders, who would negotiate the trade. When the men arrived, the negotiations started. It was brutal. Young girls were separated from their mothers, kicking and screaming, and herded into a hut, where they were guarded. The coastal tribesmen inspected the girls and argued with each other about who deserved which one. There was a big feast that night, with singing and dancing. Both parties seemed to think that this was a successful day's trade.

The next day, the chiefs led me to the mouth of a cave hidden by branches. Carrying flaming torches, they led me up and up through a warren of caves, small and large. Water collected in some of the caverns, and we had to wade through deep water in one of the caves, frightening the boys in our party who could barely swim and who couldn't touch the bottom.

Later, we emerged on the other side of the mountain, higher up than the chief's camp. Only men were allowed to make the journey there. And only certain men – men of this tribe who'd been initiated into manhood. Because I wasn't one of them, I wasn't allowed to live in the large communal cavern.

Mtengwe was the chief's name, and he told me that he could not let me live with them, but that I could be their neighbour, and live in the cave next door. I could eat with them outside, but I could not enter their long-house cave, or they would have to kill me. So I found myself both a guest and a prisoner.

Over the years, I was called on to teach some of the young men to speak pidgin English, and even a little English. These men do not trust the missionaries. They have the skull of a missionary in their skull collection. They do not trust the traders, or the medics or even the tribes who live closest to them. Once venereal disease came to the tribe. The man who was infected was killed, and now his skull hangs in the collection, too. His wives were both killed; because they were only women, they were thrown alive off a cliff in front of the rest of the tribe.

This is the mountain tribe's way of dealing with problems. I fear that there is no escaping from these people or this place. I pray to God that one day I might be rescued. My father would have the wealth to send a rescue party. I do so miss my dear twin Mary, and wonder every day about her life and what has become of her. Also, my fondest regards go to my brothers Rodman and Steven, and my older sister Ann. I hope you have all found love and happiness in your lives. I always wanted adventure, and I certainly found it, though living out my life in a humid cave was not quite the life I had planned.

Your loving brother,

Michael

Arthur looked up at us as he finished reading.

"Christ," was all that Ken had to say.

Franz replied, "I'd heard of this Michael Rockefeller. But everyone thought he had died back in the sixties."

"The poor bastard," said Arthur, who with his broken leg was in a scarily similar predicament.

"That also explains why there are no women here," I added.

"But we can't hang around here until we die in this cave like poor old Michael. We've got to come up with some sort of a plan," said Dirk.

"There's water in our cave, just a small stream. We brought back the dead man's billy full of it," added Ken.

"Is it far up the cave to the water? Can we help Arthur up there to clean up that leg? We could wash all the blood out of Franz's hair as well," I asked.

"It's probably only fifty or sixty metres, and we can support him to walk there," said Ken.

We helped Arthur and Franz to the water, where they washed their wounds, taking care to pour the dirty water away from the clean. Franz's short buzzcut hair was a great style for healing wounds – the old scabs washed away without his hair adhering to it. We were out of phone range, but the phones still came in handy as torches.

"So our cave is a dead end, but the tribesmen's cave next door leads out of here?" asked Arthur, as he looked around the cave with the water in it.

"Ken and I have been looking around the walls and the window hole, but we can't find a connection to the main cave," said Dirk.

Ken added, "We'll have to come in here at dawn when the hunting party heads out and see if any of their torchlight is visible through any cracks."

"If you did find a crack, we could work at it to enlarge it. This rock is similar to the limestone that we cut through at the mine," said Arthur.

After that, things got worse. Two men came into our cave, grabbed me, and dragged me away.

"Where are you taking her?" asked Franz in pidgin.

"She will be the new wife of the chief," said one villager.

"Do you mean Mtengwe?" asked Franz, meaning the younger chief.

"No, Swando, son of Mtengwe, father of Semu," said one of them, as they dragged me away. Other tribesmen stopped the guys from following me, threatening them with machetes and confining them to their cave.

They dragged me past the longhouse cave, to another small cave with a fire just inside the entrance, throwing me in. They sat guarding the entrance, facing the outside. When my eyes adjusted to the light, I could see the older chief, Swando, sitting on a bed of animal skins looking at me. He looked about forty, of average height, but muscular. He wore the customary boars' tooth through his nose, and a headband decorated with feathers – brightly coloured parrot feathers and plumage from a fluffy bird of paradise. He offered me some food from a wooden plate. Hungry, I ate the food, which seemed to please him. He asked my name – 'you' and 'me' are common to pidgin and English – and seemed happy to have something to call me.

"Mi Swando, mi Luluai," said Swando.

I guessed that meant he was the chief.

"Me Liza, me doctor," I said.

"Ah, dokta! Dokta Liza," said Swando.

Swando pointed to the feathers on his headband.

"Kumul bilong Luluai," said Swando, miming a bird.

"Kumul must be bird of paradise" I said, recognising the feathers. This was the national bird featured on the PNG flag. They probably ate it.

That was as far as our conversation went.

I knew what would happen next. I also knew that I had no choice in the matter. I was on the pill, but I only had about five months' supply with me. But, I figured, we wouldn't still be here by then.

Swando already had two other wives, so he at least knew what he was doing. He didn't hurt, but he was pretty rough compared to what I was used to. As I lay awake afterwards, I thought that if I was to be kept separate from them in this cave I would miss talking to the other guys more than anything else. I felt terrible about the whole thing, and had a bit of a cry. I was also dying for a cigarette.

Meanwhile, my mind was racing.

We needed a plan of escape. I had my medical supplies, but did I have enough sedatives to knock out the whole tribe for a day, giving us a head start to get away? Could we wait until Arthur's leg healed properly, or should we try and leave now and risk travelling slower while it was still broken? Which way should we go? The locals walk on trails. We could follow their trails. We could walk south until we found a mission, or west towards the mine.

I wondered how much scotch we had left. We could put the sedatives in that. They wouldn't be able to taste drugs if it was mixed with scotch.

MIKE

She's not dead

Meanwhile, in Cairns, I was getting pissed off. I was on the phone to Liza's mining company boss, Jim Sinclair, who'd recruited Liza. He'd flown down to Cairns to interview her. I'd met him that day and thought he seemed alright.

"So, you've found the chopper, and two bodies, but not Liza's? And now you've called off the search?" I asked Jim.

"The others must have been lost in the thick jungle, it's very mountainous."

"Look, Jim, it's just not good enough. What if it was your wife lost up there?"

"Mike, we are very sorry, and we are working on insurance payouts right now."

"I don't want a dammed payout. I want my wife back. Are you sending out another search party any time soon?"

"We've been waiting for the monsoon to pass before sending out another search party. We can't afford to lose another chopper. We're working at capacity, and now we're one chopper and one pilot down."

"You didn't answer my question. I'm taking time off work, I'm coming up there, and I'm organising my own search party with or without your help, Jim, because you sound like you don't give a flying fuck."

"Look, we do care, we've lost a doctor, a pilot and five experienced mining engineers on this chopper. We're doing everything we can."

It didn't sound like it to me.

"I'm organising my own search party. Send me the co-ordinates of the helicopter wreck. Actually, send them to Liza's email, I've got access to that. I'll fund my own search party and I'll find Liza. My lawyers can talk to your lawyers about the costs."

My next phone call was to my friend Steve. Steve had been a friend since our days at Queensland Uni. We used to get together for role-playing games. Now Steve was a private investigator.

"Steve, I need your help. Liza's been involved in a helicopter crash in Papua. The chopper's been found along with two male bodies, but she and the others are missing. The mining company did one pathetic search, spotted the two dead men, and gave up."

"Jesus Christ, Mike. I read about that crash. Four Aussies on board"

"That's the one. I'm not convinced the mining company has tried hard enough, so I want to organise a search party, and you have to come with me," I was pleading to Steve now.

"Of course. Anything to help. I can make myself available. How soon do you want to go?" asked Steve.

"There are just a couple of logistical problems. I want to take some personal protection. I will need a piece. And I'm not sure that we can carry one of those on a plane," I said.

"You're right, Mike. If we're packing, we'd better go by boat instead. Know anyone with a boat?" asked Steve.

"My boss at the hospital has a boat. He goes out on fishing cruises," I said, thinking of David Stone.

"Call him. Beg, borrow, or even better get him to come with us. If he can drive it, and is used to taking it out, he could be helpful. What kind of protection have you got?"

"Er, actually, I don't have any protection, but I thought that you being a private investigator would either have a gun or know where I could get one from."

"Right. I do have some. If Liza and her workmates have been kidnapped by the Raskols, they will want to trade them for more protection. How many are missing?"

"Her boss said he lost a pilot and six workers. If two were dead, that means five could still be alive."

"Right then, I'll buy five nice presents to trade for them, that should make a fair deal. And a piece each for us and one for the captain of the boat," said Steve.

"His name's David. Right, if you text me your bank details, I'll make a deposit to pay for those 'presents'. Do we need anything else?"

"Do you know anyone who speaks pidgin English who could come with us?"

"Yeah, maybe. There are some staff at the hospital from PNG who I talk to. I'm going there next, so I'll have a quiet word."

"Very quiet. We have to keep this very quiet. Talk in person whenever you can, rather than on the phone," warned Steve.

"Will do. Is your office still down near the market?" I asked.

"Yes. Drop by soon. Let's try to get this happening as soon as possible."

I sped down to the hospital and went straight to the boss's office. David Stone was at his desk and waved me past his receptionist.

"Mike, what's happening with Liza?" David asked.

"Those mining company bastards have just written them off. One shitty aerial search, two male bodies sighted, and that's it. Now the prick is talking about payouts. I'm organising my own search party. David, I need your boat."

"Whoa. I understand. You can borrow the boat. Have you got someone tough to go with you?" asked David.

"I'm taking my PI friend Steve. He's army trained, he's smart and quick. He reckons the Raskols will trade hostages for guns."

"Yeah, things are still pretty wild up there in Papua. You need to get her out quick," said David.

"David, who do we have who's trustworthy, speaks pidgin, and can come with us?"

"You know we've got about ten cleaning staff from PNG. Why don't you try one of them? In the circumstances, the least I can do is organise some paid leave," said David.

"Right, I'll go and see if I can persuade one of them to come with me," I said.

"When you said 'we', did you mean you want me to come too? I can drive the boat, and stay with it while you go inland," David said.

"David, that would be great. Thanks so much. How soon can you get the boat ready?"

"I'll get straight onto it."

Down at the cleaners' office, I wasn't sure what to do. It was day shift, and most of the Papuans worked nights. I read the whiteboard to see who was on duty. The only Papuan name I could see was Jenella. Luckily, she worked on a general ward, not in Emergency or anywhere she would be missed. I made my way up to her ward, and recognised the Papuan girl, in her twenties. I remembered she was studying something, but it wasn't nursing.

"Jenella, it's me, Doctor Mike." I wasn't wearing my coat or badge.

"Not working today, Doctor Mike?" asked Jenella.

"Jenella, my wife has gone missing up in Papua."

"Oh, Jesus!" said Jenella.

"The chopper she was in crashed and when they found it, she was nowhere nearby. I need to go and find her. But to do that I really need someone who can speak pidgin to come with me. I know it's a big ask, but are you doing anything important in the next week?" I asked.

"Not really. But I'm not sure I've got much leave owing," said Jenella.

"Doctor David said he will get you some paid leave if you can come up to Papua with us and act as our interpreter," I said.

"Really?" asked Jenella sceptically.

"Yes, really," I urged. "I'm so worried that the Raskols might have found her. I'm taking a friend to help as well, and we're sailing up on Doctor Stone's boat," I said.

After a moment's hesitation while she considered the proposal, Jenella said, "OK, if my manager can cover my shifts for me, I can go. I'm sure my flatmate will be happy to feed my dog."

"Do you think they would feed my dog too? But please don't say too much about why you're going," I said.

"No, of course. I'll say I'm going for a funeral. They happen suddenly. If it were a wedding, I'd have been talking about it for ages. I'll make it an old uncle. We've got to go to these things. Big shame if we don't," she explained.

"Yeah, that's a good story. Here, put your number into my phone, and do what you have to do to get ready," I said.

"OK, and I'll ask my flatmate about your dog," said Jenella. She was on board.

LIZA

Planning the escape

Back at the village, we watched and planned. I managed to speak to the guys at mealtimes. Luckily, the tribesmen didn't understand English.

Over the next few days we studied them, learned their names, their routines.

We noticed that the hunting parties usually went out at dawn, about five or six men, different men and boys each time, unless it was raining, then they left once the rain had cleared. The hunting parties must have hunted until they found enough for the day, as they came back anytime between 10 am and 2 pm, carrying different animals, birds, grubs and vegetable matter. Once the hunting party returned home, the fire was lit, usually just outside the mouth of the big cave, but if it was raining, it was just inside. The fire would be quickly extinguished, or pushed inside in case of rain, or helicopters. Different men would cook, but usually it was Semu, Swando's son, who was in charge of the cooking.

If they caught something big, like a benetii – a cassowary – they would chop it into bits with machetes before cooking it.

Franz gave the tribesmen lessons in Tok Pisin and Asmat, picking up a bit of vocabulary and a few of their names in the process, while I treated a few of the men for tropical sores, cuts and scratches. They'd seen me checking Franz and Arthur's wounds and changing dressings. Franz's head injury was much better, all scabbed up, so I removed the stitches. Arthur's leg was getting stronger every day.

Arthur volunteered to stay behind when we escaped, so he wouldn't slow us down. But the men decided that we'd all be leaving together, as soon as Arthur could walk at a reasonable rate. Dirk, a bit of a fitness nut, gave Arthur a regime of strengthening exercises for his legs to do every day.

Dirk was always doing pushups and squats, and he encouraged us all to work out so we'd be fit for the escape. It was all we talked about. We had a purpose and we had hope. There was no more feeling sorry for ourselves. Instead, we watched, learned, waited and prepared.

I was getting used to being Swando's wife, but I was adamant that there'd need to be a few changes. It was his dirtiness that I disliked the most, so I insisted he washed. I carried water to our bit of cave, at first in a wooden bowl, then I was given a bucket. I washed myself in front of him, in a bit of a sexy way, making out that it was foreplay. Then I would wash him, or at least the parts of him which were most dirty, and that I had to touch. He seemed to like this. I think it was rather novel for him and like any man, he loved the attention. This made things more bearable. There was a red ash, or soap tree, not far from the cave entrance. The crushed leaves of this tree made a kind of soap, which I could use to wash my greasy hair. I didn't want to get dreadlocks like all the tribesmen. The tree also attracted the pretty green-banded blue butterflies, which I would think about as a distraction whenever I did anything unpleasant.

I'd washed a lot of dishes to help pay my way through medical school, and the restaurant where I worked had lemon trees just outside the kitchen. I tried to think about my studies when I was washing dishes, but I often found myself gazing at the black and white butterflies that the citrus trees attracted.

I looked forward to talking with the other survivors during our afternoon meal and my daily rationed cigarette. We could wander the hills outside the cave to find a toilet spot, we all knew there was no way down except for through the cave. Dirk walked to the extremes of the upper hills, and did rock climbing on the cliffs that hemmed us in. He couldn't find a way out, which must have been why the tribesmen let us roam up there.

Then one day, the hunting party returned early accompanied by some other men. These men were Papuans, but they wore T-shirts and shorts, and carried backpacks and sports bags. There was a lot of fast talking. The new arrivals went into the main cave to talk to Swando and Semu in private. They must have been honoured guests, because a welpig, or wild pig, was killed for dinner the night they arrived. The women must have kept pigs in their half of the village, below the cave.

That evening at dinner, we listened as they talked of swapping, trading and selling, all the while sizing us up. Franz confirmed that the tribesmen were planning to sell us, but to whom and for what, he couldn't say.

The visitors spent most of their time talking about the Indonesians. They reported how many Indonesians there were in Papua now, and which villages were currently being surrounded by the Indonesian Army. They described the army forcing the Papuans to leave their villages with only what they could take on foot. When the old people and children had been carried from their homes, the military burned down the longhouse, and all the other houses. Then they started building roads and western-style houses for their own 'transmigrants'.

Some of the villagers fled to other villages, or to the larger towns. Others were attempting the trek to PNG. These visitors were here trying to recruit the younger tribesmen to join them, but they also needed food, money and weapons. Their leader was called Konia. He spoke passionately, often saying "Papua Merdeka" – Free Papua.

We talked among ourselves as we sat around the fire smoking a couple of rationed cigarettes.

"Right, I'm beginning to see what we might be traded for," said Franz.

"They want to swap us for guns to use against the Indonesians, don't they?" said Dirk.

"Can't say that I blame them. But who are they going to trade us with?" I asked.

"The Raskols are armed, but I heard they mostly carry machetes, not guns," said Ken.

"Surely the Indonesian Army wouldn't trade with them," said Dirk, who was thinking about his place in Bali.

"I wonder if the PNG army would trade them weapons?" asked Franz, whose own base was in Port Moresby. "A lot of the civilians in PNG are armed. They defend themselves against the Raskols there, who are more like thieves than freedom fighters."

"There would be a lot more arms available across the border. I wonder if the Indo transmigrants are armed?" asked Ken.

"But who would want to buy us?" asked Arthur.

"Would Freeport Mine buy us back?" I wondered.

"The Australian government would never trade with kidnappers," said Ken.

"This is probably the tribesmen's problem – they're trying to work out who to sell us to," said Franz.

"Liza is probably more sellable than us, but is Swando going to give her up?" said Dirk.

"Would they sell us off one at a time?" asked Ken.

"I guess we are most valuable to our families. But unless they knew we were here, and could be bought with guns, we are in deep shit," said Dirk, and he was right.

The mission

Dave, Steve, Jenella and I made good time, despite the monsoon rains sweeping across the ocean in the afternoons. The cruiser had big twin motors, recently serviced and powerful, and tanks of extra fuel for when we ran out. We made great speed through the day, went a bit slower through the rain, and travelled all night as well.

Dave had stocked up with food and a couple of cartons of energy drinks, so he was happy to take the helm all night; he told us he'd sleep when we got there.

It was about 2,800 km from Cairns to Amamapare on the Papuan coast; we managed it in two days, thanks to Captain Dave.

Once we arrived, Dave stayed with the boat, while Steve, Jenella and I caught a lift into Timika about 30 km to the north, where Jenella helped us get a second-hand four-wheel drive for a good price. She haggled for fresh fruit for our packs, and located a shop to buy a water tank for the jeep, which we filled before heading off. The supplies shop also sold us some topographic maps of the national park, with the tracks pencilled in. The storekeeper wished us good luck for our journey, and hoped God would go with us. I didn't ask which God he meant.

We continued our journey north on the roads towards the Grasberg mine. The co-ordinates of the crashed chopper were to the northeast, in the highlands of Lorentz National Park. We knew that we could only drive so far before we'd have to abandon the jeep and walk.

Once we crossed into the national park, the trail deteriorated. We were soon driving through thick jungle, on tracks following the valleys and creeks. When we came to a small village we decided to stop. Night was approaching fast, as it does in the tropics.

Jenella asked the locals where we were and if we could camp the night. They told us their village was called Mopozap and that our party were welcome. They also said that the road was navigable for just another 20 km to the north and after that we'd have to walk. Jenella thanked the village spokesman, and asked if we could perhaps hire a couple of men as guides to get us nearer to Ilaga. The man said he'd ask around.

We camped by the track with our portable stove, dehydrated food, coffee and beef jerky to eat.

As we ate, the man returned with two young men. These fellows, he said, would be our guides, and proceeded to negotiate a price. They'd accept rupiah (Indonesian money), kina (PNG money) or US dollars (universal currency). The deal was done. They left saying they'd return at dawn ready to leave.

We zipped ourselves into our sleeping bags complete with hoods and a mosquito net covering the face openings. We burned mosquito coils, too, but these wouldn't last all night.

Rudol and Nollen arrived just before dawn, carrying their own supplies in dilly bags on their backs hung from headbands around their foreheads. We jumped into the jeep, and drove the last section of road, with Rudol giving directions. The road ended at a wide stream that was obviously too deep to ford across in the car, so we parked and unloaded the backpacks.

Steve and I put on huge backpacks and gave another large one to Jenella.

"Why is it so heavy?"

"You're carrying the stove and some food and water," I said.

"Well why are yours so big?" said Jenella.

"We're carrying the trading goods, and more food and water. We've all got a sleeping bag, but no clothes, I'm afraid," said Steve.

"As long as I've got some insect repellent, I'll be alright" said Jenella.

We strapped on the packs and set off.

A narrow suspension bridge made of cables, ropes and vines spanned the stream. We crossed in single file, following Rudol's lead as he found and cleared the track ahead with his machete.

After a couple of hours, we stopped to rest. We boiled up some water for tea and soup, which we shared with the Papuans, who seemed surprised. They liked the tea and the biltong.

Nollen asked, "Where are you from, Jenella?"

Jenella explained, "My family are from Daru, but I went to Port Moresby for High School. After that, I moved to Cairns to study law at James Cook Uni – I work at the hospital to pay my way."

"We both finished school with the missionaries. Are you married to Mike or Steve?" commented Rudol.

Jenella laughed. "I'm not married and I don't have a boipren. I'm too young."

"How old are you?" asked Nollen.

"It's none of your business," said Jenella, shutting them both up.

Jenella was pretty with her long hair tied back in plaits, but with a fringe of shorter curls gathered around her face. Slim and fit, she was usually very quiet.

Rudol and Nollen were both in their late teens, with hair cut short. Rudol, a little older than Nollen, acted as leader.

After our break, we packed up and kept walking in a northerly direction.

After a couple more hours, we took another break. Rudol left us to go and tell some locals that we were nearby; when he returned he told us they didn't want any visitors to their huts.

As we sat eating the men turned their questions to Steve and me.

"Are you fellows here for the mine?" asked Rudol.

"My wife was a doctor at the mine, but she has gone missing," I said.

"We are sorry to hear," said Rudol.

"There was a helicopter crash. We are trying to find it," I said, translated by Jenella.

"I will ask at the next huts we go past," said Rudol.

Rudol and Nollen talked among themselves.

"If we find her, do you have anything to trade for her?" asked Rudol.

Steve opened his pack and took out a handgun. The men gasped, then nodded their heads.

"We will find her. You will get her back. You are smart men," said Rudol.

We walked for another few hours. The tracks were steeper now. We were gaining altitude, but as we climbed the mountains became shrouded in mist and clouds – we couldn't see very far. When we arrived at the next village Rudol talked for a while with some of the men, returning to us with some news.

"These people will let us camp near their huts tonight and will show us which way to go in the morning."

He led us to a flattish spot in the village garden, among the banana trees and taro. We rolled out our sleeping bags and set up the stove to make our afternoon meal. First, some children crept through the garden, to watch what we were doing. Next, some women came close, but sat back, watching. By the time we were eating and drinking, about fifteen highlanders in grass skirts and possum skins were watching our party. Jenella offered them some chocolate, but they wouldn't take it. Then she gestured to some ripe bananas on a tree, and to the chocolate. A man nodded his head, and a woman picked the bananas, offering them to Jenella, who gave her the chocolate block in return. These villagers would not accept gifts, but a trade was acceptable.

The tribe went back to their huts, to make their own evening meal.

Rudol and Nollen made a small fire surrounded by stones to keep us warm overnight.

In the morning, with Jenella listening and writing down the instructions, the villagers gave Rudol and Nollen a list of directions. It sounded like there was at least another day of walking to do, most of it up hill. They asked if we had ropes – Steve nodded and patted his backpack. We set off, worried about how hard this walk was going to get.

The Ples Tambu

B ack at the caves, a lot of discussions had been going on, with Swando, Semu and the newcomers talking and shouting at each other for a few days now. At least I'd prepared us all for a hard hike. But what would become of Liza?

Konia said, "Let us take them all away to be traded."

Swando said, "Let me keep Liza, you can take the others."

"Arthur can't walk properly yet and will slow down any walking that Konia wants to do," Franz pointed out to them.

Konia decided, "We will take these three men on the first walk and come back for the cripple later."

So myself, Franz and Ken were told to be ready to travel first thing in the morning. Konia and his men left their brightly coloured T-shirts at the caves – along with the bulk of the bags they'd arrived with – instead dressing in camouflage shirts and khaki shorts, or, for some of them, just the shorts. They made Ken, Franz and me change into our plainest clothes, and smeared us with dirt. They didn't want the party to be seen; we had to blend into the jungle. A couple of the Asmat men came with us. They, too, blended with the jungle in their penis gourds and belts.

At first light, the newcomers led us down through the caves and out past the women's village. We set off towards the east, towards PNG. The mountain range that we were on stretched from west to east, like a spine across the island, transversing the two countries. The tracks followed the ridges, but not as high up as the great emergent peaks. The walking was hard; Arthur would never have made it. The Papuans pushed us to walk as fast and as far as we could between breaks and didn't camp near any other villages along the way.

DOCTOR DAVE

A better use of my time

Meanwhile in Timika, I'd caught up on some much-needed sleep, and then came up with a strategy of my own. I'd planned to guard the boat myself, but soon decided to pay a local man to do this job. I wouldn't waste skilled labour at the hospital, and likewise I wasn't going to waste my time here. I paid for a ride into to the Mozes Kilangin Airport in Timika, located a charter service and started negotiations to hire a helicopter and pilot. If there were choppers for the miners, there had to be choppers for tourists too.

I booked a chopper for the next day. It was being flown back down from Jayapura later that day and would be ready in the morning. It was expensive, but another doctor's life was worth it.

I returned to Amamapare, looking forward to tomorrow's flight. Walking towards the boat, I noticed two soldiers from the Indonesian Army, guarding the jetty. As I boarded, I could hear an Indonesian customs official inside the boat questioning the Papuan guy I'd paid to guard it.

"I'm Doctor Dave Stone, this is my boat, Officer."

"I am Wayan Chan, Customs Officer with Border Patrol. Do you have a visa, Doctor Stone?"

"Nice to meet you, Mister Chan. I came to Indonesia for a medical emergency. Let me show you my passport. Can I apply for a visa here?"

"Doctor Stone, let me see your passport?"

The official followed me into the cabin. I unlocked a cabinet, found my passport and handed it to Wayan Chan. Chan examined the passport.

"I see that you have visited Indonesia before this. Why did you not get a visa this time?" asked Wayan.

"This time I came at extremely short notice, for a medical emergency. I will pay for a visa now, no worries," I said.

"What is this emergency? Did you bring other people on the boat?"

"Yes, I brought another doctor, a nurse and a guide to help find the patient," I said.

"Do you have their passports?"

"Yes, they're in this cabinet," I said.

I retrieved the other three passports, and showed them to Chan.

"This woman is from New Guinea. Why did you bring her?"

"Nurse Jenella speaks the local language, and will help us to find the patient," I said.

"Who is this patient?" asked Chan.

"The other doctor's wife. She's lost in the national park and needs urgent help."

"So the others are in the national park?" Wayan asked.

"Yes. They went to find her. I can pay for visas for them as well," I offered.

"Very well. Do you have any contraband items aboard this boat Doctor?" asked Chan.

"No. Only medical supplies, food and fishing supplies. I usually just take this boat fishing," I said.

"Very well. You must come back to my boat, where I can issue you with visas. Do you have rupiah?" asked Wayan.

"I have American dollars, is that acceptable?" I asked. No one wanted our Australian dollars.

"Yes. This way, if you please," said Chan.

I followed Wayan to the Customs boat moored on the next jetty. Fortunately, it seemed to be just a formality, paying for the visas for we three Australians and the New Guinean. I was glad I had emptied the boat of all but the essentials before the trip, mindful that I might be bringing five extra people back. The boat didn't look like it was stacked with contraband, and my passport said I was a doctor, my ID confirmed I worked for an Australian government hospital. I smiled when I thought about how I didn't look like a gun and drug runner, though, when you think about it ...

MIKE

Three men rescued

Steve, Jenella and I made good progress. Rudol noticed that Jenella was the slowest walker, so he swapped his dilly bag for her backpack, allowing her to speed up considerably. The bridges over the ravines were getting more rudimentary. The first one we crossed had a narrow floor and handrails made of ropes. Later the bridges were just one thick rope to walk on, lashed to handrail ropes at the sides, while the last bridge we crossed was simply two ropes, one for feet, and one for hands, which we negotiated by walking across sideways. The higher we climbed, the more stunted the vegetation became. We filled our water bottles from the clear streams as we crossed. The heat became more bearable at this elevation, and by night time we actually felt quite cold.

That night our camp was near a small village, the home of just one family. We had to camp nearby as there was no other level land on the mountainside we'd just climbed. Rudol talked to the father.

"He said that the next village was a 'ples tambu', a forbidden place," translated Jenella.

"What does that mean for us?" I asked.

"He said that this Ples Tambu was very traditional. The women and children live in the first part of the village. Strange men cannot go there. The men and older boys live in another part of the village, a secret place, and none of us are allowed to go there."

We all turned to look at Jenella.

"I think that means that you are the only one of us who can visit this village, Jenella," I said.

"Oh shit. What will I say?" said Jenella.

"We'll keep a close eye on you, and we'll have a couple of guns at the ready. If anything happens, we'll come in and bring you back. We've already lost Liza, we're not losing you too. No way," I said.

"And you will probably have to dress in the traditional way too," added Steve.

"Oh, great," said Jenella, not looking convinced.

Rudol and Nollen quickly helped Janella gather materials for her outfit, making a belt out of vines and a skirt out of leaves. Rudol let her carry his dilly bag. It was very basic.

As we settled down for the night, Jenella insisted that neither I nor Steve would take any photos of her in her outfit the following day.

She was interrupted by a call coming through on the satellite phone; it was Dave.

"Oh, thank God these things work," he said.

"I'm rather grateful as well," I replied.

"Look, I've managed to hire a chopper. It's on its way down to Timika now. Tomorrow I'm going to fly over you guys, and look for this chopper wreck," Dave said.

"That's great Dave. You probably won't be able to land any-where around here, though."

"That's OK, we'll look around, and see what we can see," said Dave.

"Who's minding the boat?" I asked.

"Oh, I paid a local guy to keep an eye on it. It'll be safe. I've got the keys to the engines, so it's not going anywhere," said Dave.

"OK, if we see you overhead, we'll wave. We are close to a village that forbids men to enter. Only Jenella can visit. We'll keep an eye on her, and we'll keep you in the loop if we find anyone or hear of any clues."

"Are you close to the co-ordinates now?"

"Yes, if this phone's sat nav is working right. But it is extremely mountainous, and it's taking us a long time to travel short distances."

We all slept better knowing that Dave had found another approach, and that the phone worked.

In the morning, we made our ascent to the Ples Tambu. This was where we needed the ropes. A steep hard and rocky slope that was crumbling at the base meant one man had to ascend first with the rope tied around his waist. Nollen, a natural climber, volunteered, scrambling up in bare feet. He secured the rope to a tree and steadied it as the next climber ascended. The three large packs went up on the rope the same way, making it easier for us to scramble over the steeper parts. There appeared to be only one way to go up the track, which was barely discernible by now.

When we'd all scaled the slope, Nollen and Rudol stopped and squatted behind some rocks. Beyond this peak was a high valley, between two rows of mountains. At the far end of the valley was a village with some stunted banana trees, and a small group of huts, built up against the shelter of the high cliffs of the next mountains. So this was the women's village. The trees were sparse between where we stood and the village. This would be as far as us men could go.

"I guess it's time for me to get into my outfit," said Jenella, as she started taking off her shoes and clothes. Jenella had not worn much as a child in Daru, but did at least have shorts, T-shirts and sarongs. She had moved to the city for high school and had worn shoes ever since. We could see she was embarrassed at being topless and naked under a grass skirt, so we diplomatically averted our eyes as she got dressed. Steve busied himself with getting his rifle loaded and set up. He also made sure that the two handguns were loaded and in working order.

"Right, I'm ready to go now. I'll walk over, ask some questions, then walk right back here," said Jenella with a look of grim determination.

"If they try anything, we'll come right after you, with our guns. We'll watch you the whole time," Steve reassured her.

Jenella stood up and walked straight towards the village. She was scared but tried to give the impression she was calm, smiling at the surprised women.

"Hello, I'm Jenella, from Daru. I've come looking for my friends. Liza and four men were on a helicopter from the mine, and it crashed. I am looking for them so I can take them home. Have you seen them?" she said in pidgin.

The women looked at each other, then back at Jenella.

"They were here. But not a woman, we don't think. Three or four strange looking men, they were here," said one of them.

"Were here? Where did they go?" Jenella asked.

"Raskols came. The ones who say 'Papua Merdeka'. They took the men, they went that way," said the tribeswoman.

The woman pointed towards the east of the plateau, where the trail must drop away again. Jenella had approached from the south.

"How long ago did they leave?" asked Jenella.

"Only yesterday. They are only one day ahead of you," the woman said.

"Thank you so much. I'm going to walk that way with my friends who are men. They won't come to your village. We'll walk directly to that track."

"Go quickly, Jenella. You can catch up with them. Take your men friends and go quickly."

Jenella ran back to us. She quickly dressed, telling us what she'd found out. Time was short; we departed hurriedly, heading towards the eastern track as fast as we could travel.

Before leaving, I noted the co-ordinates of the village. It was the first place that had confirmed the strangers were here. As soon as I could, I would ring Dave and ask him to fly over this place.

I was worried that the woman had said "three or four strange looking men" and "no woman". Was Liza dressed as a man? Were these the only survivors? For now, we had no choice but to follow the eastern track.

I called Dave on the satellite phone, relaying to him the news and the co-ordinates of the village.

"I've just seen the crash site. The chopper came down between some very steep mountains. We flew as close as we could, and I was able to see the remains of one man in the chopper. We are currently circling the peaks around that site. We will proceed to the co-ordinates of your village after we locate the second body which had been reported."

Only five or ten minutes after the call, we heard the chopper approach overhead. We stopped to wave.

Dave called back, "We saw the second guy, or what was left of him, on a peak high above the crash site. If the others hopped out when he did, they are up among the peaks too."

"Can you go ahead of us and see if you can see the group that we are following? We think they are Papuan freedom fighters, from what they said at the village," I said.

"I'll try, but they might hear us coming and hide from us. If I find them, I'll call straight away. Otherwise, I'll take another flight tomorrow to check on you. I might be able to find a landing spot," Dave said.

We continued on our trek.

Rudol and Nollen were getting excited. They kept pointing out signs that another group had passed this way recently. There was freshly cut vegetation, places where they had tied ropes or vines, even spots where they had gone to the toilet. If we walked all day and all night, we could catch up with this group.

At a meal break, I decided it was time to break out the caffeine pills. I handed them around to everyone.

"These are safe, we use them at the hospital when we have to work a double shift. If we have to walk two days' journey in one day, these will keep us going," I told the others.

I also had dressings for people's blisters and mosquito bites, and said I had painkillers if anyone needed them. Steve had packed lights on headbands, and let the first, third and fifth walkers wear them, so each person could see the way when it got dark.

We walked through the long night. Fortunately, the worst descents were in the first part of the walk, with the slopes getting gentler as we followed the ridge along the mountain range.

We were travelling slowly, but at least we were moving. In the early hours, Rudol smelt a fire.

"Paia," said Rudol, pointing towards it.

We could see it, off in the distance. Steve stopped the party and unpacked the packs. Taking out two handguns, he gave one to me. Rudol and Nollen wanted one each as well.

"Do you know how to use one?" Steve asked Rudol.

"Can we teach them in a short time?" I wondered.

"I think it would be best to only show them two guns, so they don't think we've got a whole lot of them," said Steve, unsure about giving guns to our Papuan friends.

"I agree, two should be enough," I said.

"And we want to be quick," said Steve.

We turned off our head torches and walked quietly down to the camp site. We came across nine Papuans, and three expats. The group were chatting around the fire and didn't hear our approach.

"We're here to make a trade," said Steve.

"We won't shoot, we want to make a deal," I added.

The Raskols jumped up as a group, but quickly froze when they saw the guns pointed at them.

Ken was wide awake, "You guys are Aussies?"

"Are you blokes from the helicopter crash?" I asked. Steve kept his eye and gun on the Raskols.

"Yes. We thought we were dead meat. I'm Ken."

"Where's Liza?" I asked.

"She's back in the cave," said Ken.

"At that village where there are only women?" asked Steve.

"The women live in huts. The men live in a cave above the village, but the entrance is hidden. We left Liza and Arthur there, he has a broken leg," said Ken. "We didn't have any choice in the matter. These men took us to trade us for guns."

"We have guns. We'll trade three guns for you three men," Steve made the gestures towards the guns, and the men, while Jenella translated.

"But we want Liza as well, and the other guy too," I added.

"I'm Ken, this is Dirk, and Franz. The mountain tribe found us and led us to their cave. But when the rescue chopper came looking for us, they wouldn't let us out of the cave," said Ken.

"I had a head injury, and Liza dressed it for me. Arthur has a broken leg, and she made him a splint. Arthur couldn't make the walk out," added Franz.

"What about Liza?" I asked.

"The chief, Swando, wants to keep Liza as his wife," said Ken.

"Well that's too bad because she's already my wife," I said. "We have to go and find the others."

"If we do the trade now, these men will probably walk straight back to the Ples Tambu, and they could take Liza and Arthur. We walked all day and all night to catch up to you guys, and we need some rest," said Steve.

"We could rest for a bit, and make the whole crew walk back to the cave with us," I said.

"We could give them the guns, but not the bullets, until we've got Liza and Arthur as well," said Steve, thinking fast.

"Now we're thinking straight. A combined party with weapons might persuade the chief to hand over his new wife," I said. "I'm going to call Dave right now and fill him in. There was a flattish area in the women's village where he could land in that chopper."

"This is sounding more like a plan," said Steve.

"OK, this is how it's going to be," I said. "We will give you these three rifles now, in return for these three men. We will all walk back to the Ples Tambu together. You will help us make a trade for the other two hostages. If you can do that, we will give you two more guns for those two people."

Steve waited while this was translated into pidgin, and the Raskols nodded their heads.

"Then we will give you ammunition for all five guns. We will meet our friend in the helicopter, and he will take out any injured or as many as can fit. We can split up then, some walk back to our jeep, you guys can go you own way."

There was more translation, and a bit of argument. Steve and I waited for the response. The highlanders in their tribal gear appeared to disagree with the Raskols, arguing in their language.

"The bullets bit is OK, but they don't want you landing near the Ples Tambu. It must remain a secret, no pilot must know about it. It is their most secret place. These men will show you another place where the chopper can land, an hour's walk away. They say it is a flat place, on the plateau, and not too far away. They will guarantee your safety to get there," translated Jenella.

"Alright, I understand they need to keep a place secret. We'll trade for Liza and Arthur there, then walk to the flat place, and meet Dave's chopper," I agreed.

Steve and I handed over the guns. There was much shaking of hands, and examination of guns.

"These guys are happy, they thought they would have to walk all the way into PNG to do a trade, and they were worried about getting ripped off, and ambushed," said Jenella.

A meal was prepared, and more caffeine pills swallowed. Doctor Dave was called. He was delighted we'd achieved at least a 60 per cent success rate!

The next morning, the combined group started walking back the way we'd come, with the three head Raskols carrying their rifles over their shoulders, military style.

LIZA

Escaping the cave

Meanwhile, back at the cave, I was getting desperate. At the afternoon meal, I talked to Arthur.

"Arthur, how is your walking going?"

"I'm quite strong now. It still hurts a bit to put all my weight on it," Arthur said.

"Could you walk if I gave you painkillers?" I asked.

"Yes. I think I'd prefer to get away before I turn into long pork!"

"Arthur, I think it could be time to break out the scotch."

Arthur had put the sedative drugs into the scotch bottle that was hidden in his cave. It mixed well and it looked like scotch. He returned to the cave to retrieve the bottle, bringing it out to the tribesmen sitting around the fire. "It's my birthday! Let's all celebrate!" he exclaimed.

He pretended to have a swig on the bottle, then handed it to Swando. Swando had a big swig and then handed it to Semu. And so, the bottle went around the fire, and all the men drank, with Arthur and me pretending to drink as well. They ate, then slowly the men started to nod off.

We waited until they were all asleep, then went back into the caves to retrieve our bags. We crept into the cave Arthur had shared with the others, then to the larger cave where the Asmat men slept. We started towards the back, lit by a mobile phone. The first room was full of carvings, skulls and drums. The next 'room' held the bags belonging to the Raskols. Arthur had a quick look; curiosity had got the better of him.

"What's in there, guns?" I asked.

"No, gold. Heaps of it," Arthur replied.

"Well, hopefully it will fund their liberation campaign," I said.

We left it there and hurried off. We couldn't weigh ourselves down with anything non-essential. Not that we would steal their gold, either. These people were poor, and this was all they had. The Europeans, and now the Indonesians, had already stolen their land, and now they were trying to kill them off. We weren't here to rob them.

We came to a cavern with the water, like the one we'd found in our cave, and had to first wade, then swim across. I put my phone in a waterproof pouch. We'd left most of our belongings behind, only carrying some warm clothes, medicine and dressings, all in plastic bags. The bags floated, as we made our way across the water to the next bit of the cave, then down, down towards its other entrance. We were surprised to find no one on guard there.

The 'tambu' or taboo must be so strong that the women never seemed to even attempt to enter the cave. The sun was setting towards the west. We decided to head towards it and hopefully towards the mine. A woman saw us and tried to stop us. She was pointing towards the east, repeatedly saying something emphatic in Asmat.

We could only work out that the others must have gone that way. We didn't fancy becoming captives again, so we pointed to the west and said "Freeport" and "Grasberg" a few times, then took off. The woman gave us a hand of bananas as we left. PNG, we thought, was a lot further away than the mine. The mine was our best bet for survival. The track led down for a bit, then followed ridges of a steep range, up and down, and around the larger peaks. The clouds blew away, and the night air became still. The moon was almost full, lighting our way quite well. We walked until we could no longer go on.

Exhausted, we found a sheltered overhang and set up camp for the rest of the night. We ate the bananas, drank water, and went to sleep. I had rebound Arthur's leg so that the splint was only on the outside, not on the inside as well. The inside bit hampered his walking, rubbing against his other leg. He still favoured his stronger leg, but he could limp pretty quickly. At dawn, we rose again, I gave Arthur some painkillers, and we kept walking. Arthur found a straight tree branch and used it as a walking stick on his bad side. With his strong arm, he could take part of his weight on the stick and take a load off his leg.

We walked all day, and as night fell once more, we smelled a campfire nearby. We decided to head down the wooded slope towards it. We came to a tiny clearing, inhabited only by an old couple and two children. With a little Tok Pisin, I asked if we could sleep here for the night, and they agreed. The family ate a simple dinner of sweet potato, which they shared with us. I showed them the red cross on my backpack and opened it to show them my medical supplies. I'd noticed that both the adults had tropical sores on their legs, which I offered to treat. First the woman agreed, and I carefully cleaned and dressed her wounds. After the old man had seen the process, he agreed to also being treated. He had a huge sore behind one knee, and I used the spray on skin to seal the wound after I had cleaned it. I left them some bandages, for when these ones were soiled. They seemed happy to have had a home visit from a flying, or at least walking, doctor.

As we lay down to rest, Arthur asked, "Liza, wasn't there another Liza Fraser, who I learned about in history at school?"

"That was Eliza Fraser. Her husband was Captain James Fraser, and they survived the wreck of the *Stirling Castle* on the island that became known as Fraser Island. He later died, and the Aborigines looked after her until another shipwreck survivor led her down the coast to Moreton Bay. Unfortunately, her claims of mistreatment by the tribe led to them being massacred."

"And your parents named you after her?"

"No, I was born Liza Connors, I married Mike Fraser – it's my married name," I said.

"Right. I grew up in north Queensland, and we learned a lot of stories like that at school. There was a really sad story about a couple with a baby, and a Chinese cook. The man left his wife on an island, but it was an Aboriginal sacred place. When Aborigines returned, they demanded the newcomers leave. The husband had taken the boat, so the wife, cook and baby set sail in a big cooking pot. They all died. Her diary was found with their bodies," said Arthur.

"That was Captain Robert Watson, who left his family on Lizard Island, near Cooktown. Mike and I went there for our honeymoon," I said.

"You must miss him," Arthur said.

"Hell yeah," I said. "Mike and I've been together since our fourth year of med school. Mike had dated a couple of the hottest girls in our year, but things didn't work out. And I was always busy working and studying, so I didn't go out with anyone. Then

I had to do a group assessment and we ended up in the same one. We got on really well. He asked me out."

"Where was your first date?" said Arthur.

"It was just a weekend lunch. I worked six nights of the week and studied five days. I hardly had a spare minute. I remember Mike gave up his rock-climbing sessions to spend time with me, so I knew he liked me. His parents didn't think much of me because my mum wasn't rich, but we got married anyway – just after graduation."

"So what made you study medicine in the first place?" asked Arthur.

"I was a premmie baby, in hospital for ages, and then a sick kid, in and out of the children's hospital. I loved the doctors and nurses, because they gave me loads of attention and made me well again, and I wanted to be like them. When I was in fifth year at med school, my mum got motor neurone disease. I studied it and realised she would die, and soon. I did what I could for mum, but she was in hospital, then a hospice. She only lasted three months from diagnosis to death," I said.

"I'm so sorry to hear that, Liza. But it has made you into a tough woman – a survivor," said Arthur.

"In the kids' hospital, I saw quite a few of my friends die. I wanted to live, and to live my life to the full. I didn't care how hard I had to work to make my dreams a reality," I said.

"I grew up in a small town near Townsville. There, the only career options seemed to be the army, fishing on trawlers, or seasonal work on farms. I wanted to make money, and I saw the miners coming into town, flashing the cash, so I studied engineering. I fancied an Aboriginal girl called Ngaire, who I met at uni. But I never asked her out, because I was worried about what my parents would think. I don't know where she is now," said Arthur.

"You lost contact with her?" I asked.

"Yeah, I have looked for her on social media. But I think she might have changed her name. Her brother was trying to find their tribal name, so they didn't have to keep using their 'English master's' name. They shared their surname with a local politician who was a racist National Party idiot. Even her parents wanted to change names," said Arthur.

"It must be hard, living between two cultures," I said.

"Ngaire and the Aborigines I met were all nice people," said Arthur. "In Townsville, their families had been rounded up and sent to Palm Island reserve, but people were gradually making their way back to the cities and country."

"Yeah, I studied with a Murri guy called Greg. Aboriginal students didn't need quite the same entrance marks as white kids, and some of the med students were shitty about that. Very few young doctors wanted to work in the regions, but the Aboriginal doctors wanted to help out their hometowns. My friend Greg told me he felt stuck between Mount Isa and Brisbane, lost and at home," I said.

"I know how they feel. I feel like a tourist in England, and Papua, and now in Australia too," admitted Arthur.

"I feel the same way. I thought I'd learned something about this country, but really, it's all a matter of opinion."

MIKE

Following Liza

The rescue party was making good speed back. As we walked, Ken questioned the Raskols about their cause. Since Jenella had arrived, these normally quiet men were being much more vocal about their lives.

"So, you want to get your land back from the Indonesians?" Ken asked.

Konia replied, "We hate them, more than we hated the Dutch. The Dutch at least left our villages alone and gave us work on their farms. The Indonesians just bring in their own workers. They drive us away and even kill us," said Konia.

Konia asked Jenella, "You live in Cairns, but you came from Port Moresby, do you have family there?"

"My mum only lived in Moresby while my brothers and I went to school. When my youngest brother finished, they all moved back to Daru."

"What does your dad do, Jenella?" asked Konia.

"He used to just run the farm, but he got into fixing his own tractor, then other people's tractors. Now he has a shed where he fixes farm machines and cars, but he still runs the farm too. Where are you from, Konia?" asked Jenella.

"Oh, I come from Modowi, in West Papua. Things are very bad there now. The Indonesians came and took away all our farms. They burned our houses, they killed my dad and my uncle," said Konia, looking down.

"God, that's terrible," replied Jenella.

"Yeah, my mum took us up into the hills to find a new place to live. We set up a new hut and started a new garden. But then the Indonesians army came again. It's like they were following us. My brother Kupsy and I saw the local men fighting the Indonesians, so we ran off to join them," said Konia.

"Do you know where your brother is now?" Jenella asked.

"In our Organasi Papua Merdeka, or OPM, we are many small bands. We meet up and then disperse. It is the safest way. If we were in the same band, we might both be killed. I will see my brother again. We will take these guns back to another place, where they are needed," said Konia.

Nollen spoke up then. "I would like to join your movement. Our family is safe in the national park, but we hear lots of stories of families like yours, being shot and having their land stolen. I would like to fight back against those Indonesians who come here and steal our land, cut down our forests."

There was a general murmur of agreement among the highlanders.

Konia replied, "Most of our young men at the Ples Tambu also want to join up with us. For now, we use their village as a place to keep supplies, and to retreat to if anyone needs to disappear. But when the fighting comes this way, and it will, you men will be welcome to join the fight."

As Jenella and Franz translated for the rest, the expats were surprised that most of these local men felt real hatred for the Indonesians, to the point that they would willingly join the fight against them, unpaid, and with great risk of being jailed or shot.

That night we camped close to a village, ready to start again at first light.

I called Dave again, and arranged a rendezvous point on a plateau part of the way to the Ples Tambu.

We arrived at the spot just in time to hear the clatter of the chopper as it approached. Dave had found the meeting point. The chopper was a four-seater and could only take two passengers back. Dirk, super fit and enjoying the hike, volunteered to stay with the walkers, while Franz and Ken, who were looking forward to warm showers and civilisation, elected to fly out. They took turns on the satellite phone contacting their families, who had all been notified that they were dead. With that they were happily loaded aboard. Rudol and Nollen took the opportunity to have a good look inside the chopper, as they'd never seen one up close before. The mountain men were not so keen to look, and the freedom fighters only gave it a cursory glance.

As the rest of us returned to the Ples Tambu, Konia talked to Jenella, asking her if she could help their cause in any way.

"I've thought about that, and I think the best way to help you will take some time," Jenella replied.

"What do you mean?" asked Konia.

"I have been living in Cairns so I can study law. I work as a hospital cleaner to pay my way, so I can only study part time. It's going to take me a couple of years to finish my degree. But when I am a lawyer, I can come back here and represent your fighters when they are in prison or charged with criminal offences. I can't fight with guns, and I don't want to, but I could fight legal battles," Jenella said.

"That would be very good, Jenella. You're a smart lady." Konia smiled at Jenella. He was obviously quite taken with her.

When we got to the women's village, there was a lot of excited talking. Jenella tried to work out what was being said, as the men all talked, and the women pointed in all directions.

Then chief Swando appeared and checked out the new foreigners and the guns on the shoulders of the freedom fighters.

"Have you bought me more hostages?" asked Swando.

"No, these men traded us guns for the other three hostages. Now they want the woman and the other man. They will trade us guns for them too," replied Konia.

"It is too late, they've escaped," said Swando.

"What? How?" Jenella translated.

"They gave us alcohol so we fell asleep, then they ran away," said Swando, looking annoyed.

Dirk said, "Right, they enacted our plan while some of the men were away – less to drug and less to follow them."

I was frantic. "Which way did they go?"

When Jenella translated this, the village women pointed towards the west.

"To the mine."

Steve and I decided to follow them immediately.

"No, wait!" said Konia.

"This had better be quick," I said.

"I will buy the other two guns off you," said Konia.

"With what?" asked Steve.

"With gold. Wait here. I'll get back really quickly," Konia said, as he raced off towards the secret entrance of the cave.

As good as his word, Konia made the journey into the cave and back in record time carrying a heavy bag. He opened it to reveal gold nuggets and bags of gold dust. None of it had been pressed into bars yet, because it had never made it to a smelter.

"This nugget is worth a thousand US dollars. I'll give you two this size for those two guns" said Konia.

"No," I said, emphatically. "I'm not selling you guns – they were to trade for Liza."

Steve jumped in. "Now, let's not be too hasty, Mike. If we find Liza, we won't need to buy her. If we trade a big heavy gun for a marble-sized nugget, we will travel a whole lot faster with lighter backpacks." Then he spoke to Konia, "How about two guns for three of those nuggets, mate?"

"It's a deal," agreed Konia, searching the bag for another two similar sized nuggets.

The deal was done quickly. And Konia was delighted that one gun was a semi-automatic.

"If you don't find Liza, and we do, we will take good care of her and bring her back to this place. Good luck my friends," said Konia. Then he added, "If any of you can bring more guns back to this Tabu Place, we will buy them from you with gold. If I am not here, my brother Kupsy might be here, or you can talk to Semu, the younger chief. You are our friends now. Papua Merdeka!"

With that he departed and headed back towards the cave with his men and their booty.

"I don't believe we just did that," I said to Steve, as we started along the western trail.

"Look, if we do meet the Indonesians, it will look much better if we just have one handgun each, rather than a couple of big rifles as well. We're still protected, with lighter bags, and we will find Liza and Arthur. We know they came this way," said Steve.

We walked on with renewed hope, a smaller crew, and all of us fit for fast walking. Dirk was happy that the Aussies had brought muesli bars, chocolate and coffee, and we all scoffed down caffeine pills to help keep us going. I called Dave on the satellite phone, filling him in on the news. He decided that he and the pilot could do another flight to the west of the Ples Tambu to look for Liza and Arthur – about a two-day walk away. He promised to call us if he sighted anything.

As we walked, we talked about our discoveries.

Dirk said, "The men of Swando's tribe have been living in that cave for ages. They bring their fire inside, so choppers flying past can't see the entrance. There is a reservoir of water in the cave, which has to be swum across. They've got carvings and preserved heads, and they still hunt with machetes and spears. They hunt every day and live on what they find. But I never realised they had gold."

"That was a huge bag of gold," said Steve.

"They could buy a pile of guns with that much," said Jenella.

"I think that their problem would be where to get the guns from, rather than what they would buy them with," I said.

"Franz told us that his parents used to teach for the missionaries that came here. My parents were Dutch colonists – farmers and traders," said Dirk.

"Are they still here, Dirk?" I asked.

"No, most of the Dutch left when the Indonesians seized the country in 1966. Dad and Mum lost everything they couldn't take with them. They had a boat, but they lost their huge plantation and their big house full of beautiful furniture. They took some rugs, money, jewellery but they lost all the big stuff. They were used to being rich, having a houseful of servants. They hated losing everything, going back to being average people, having to work and look after themselves. They moved to Darwin at first, but they hated it, so then they packed up again and went back to Amsterdam," said Dirk.

"Is that why you came here to work, Dirk?" asked Jenella.

"Mum and Dad talked about how beautiful the country was, the exotic birds and animals. They had photo albums of their plantation, pictures of them at a big Sing Sing, with tribesmen from all over the country. After I studied engineering, I saw that work here was well paid, and that there were still a lot of Dutch people in Indonesia, so I applied for the job and got it," said Dirk.

"Liza and I studied in Brisbane. My parents were quite well off and supported me through uni, but Liza had to pay her own way, clocking up a massive student debt in the process. When we graduated, we both got internships at Cairns Hospital, but as interns, our wages weren't huge. So when Liza saw the job advertised for a doctor at the Freeport Mine, which was only a few hours flying time out of Cairns, she applied. Her wage is more than double mine, and it's allowed her to start repaying her student loan. But neither of us dreamt that anything like this could happen. I thought the mining company would keep her safe. Those arseholes don't care about their workers. One aerial search, and they've written them off. Now they are talking about payouts, recruiting new staff, and buying a new chopper," I said, feeling angry.

"Ken had been with the mine for twenty years. He reckons they lose about one chopper a year. I wonder if any other survivors made it out alive," said Dirk.

"Makes you wonder, doesn't it?" I replied.

We had just finished a meal break and started walking again when the satellite phone rang.

"Dave here, I've just seen two locals along that western track with bandages on their legs. There isn't a clinic for miles, so I'm guessing that a doctor has paid them a house call."

"Oh, that's fantastic Dave. You're on the right track. I'll text you our current co-ordinates as well," I said.

We walked on with renewed hope.

"Hopefully, you can make some procedural changes when you go back to the mine, Dirk," I said.

"I'm not going back to the mine, Mike. Freeport Grasberg can rot in hell for all I care," said Dirk.

"That's the spirit, Dirk!" said Steve.

"I think I'll get a lawyer to sue their pants off," added Dirk, all fired up now.

DAVE

Rescuing Liza

The pilot spotted them first. He was used to scanning the deep forest. He spun the chopper around so he could see the survivors in front of us and started looking for a place to land. As the chopper came into land, Arthur and Liza, who'd been waving bright shirts at the chopper, walked towards where it was lowering down. In just a few minutes, they found the landing spot.

I hopped out to greet them.

"Liza! Thank God you're alright! And you must be Arthur!" I said.

"Dave! Did you come with Mike? Where is he?" said Liza.

"He is on foot, not far from here. Hop in, and we will go and meet them." I gestured towards the chopper.

We helped Arthur climb in; his leg had swollen beneath the bandages.

"Thank you so much for coming. We thought we'd been left for dead," Arthur said.

"Freeport Mine left you for dead, but Mike mounted his own rescue mission," I replied.

As the chopper fired up it became too noisy to talk.

Very soon we located the rescue party. Once we found a landing spot, Liza and Arthur jumped out to greet Mike, Steve, Jenella, Dirk and their guides. Mike hugged Liza, digging into his pocket to hand her a packet of cigarettes. He must really love her, to think about bringing her cigarettes when he doesn't even smoke.

Arthur insisted that Mike take his seat in the chopper to take Liza back to town. He would jump on the next trip in the morning. But I'd seen his leg. I insisted he take my seat in the chopper. If these poor buggers had been out here for weeks, I was sure I could handle one night in the jungle.

I watched them take off. Mike was running his fingers through Liza's long dark hair. Usually curly, it had become matted almost to the point of being dreadlocks.

"He is worried about her Gras Bilong Het," said Jenella.

"Grass belong to head? You mean her hair?" I said.

Jenella was teaching me Tok Pisin.

Steve, Jenella, Rudol and Nollen, Dirk and I walked a little further, then set up camp for the night.

Steve was so pleased that they'd managed to find all the survivors. Jenella was also happy but was starting to feel queasy from the food or the water. She had a bad case of the trots.

"I think I've got pekpek wara, where my poo is water. It's not as bad as pekpek blut, when there is blood," said Jenella.

"So pekpek wara is diarrhoea, and pekpek blut must be dysentery. I think I'm learning Tok Pisin," I said.

"Well done, Dokta Dave," said Jenella.

"I have some Imodium in my bag. Take one now, and another in a couple of hours," I said, and gave her a dose. We doctors are always prepared.

"Thanks Doctor Dave, and thanks for splashing out on the chopper too," said Jenella.

"After you'd all gone, and I'd managed to grab some sleep, I thought about how else I could help. I paid a local to mind the boat, so I could make myself useful," I said.

Dirk said, "If you like, I can stay with the ground party, and give you my place on tomorrow's chopper. I like hiking, I've already hiked in the Mamberamo mountains, and I'd hoped to hike here in the Lorentz National Park as well."

"Thanks, Dirk," I said. "I don't really like roughing it. But I know that some people love it."

Steve said "That's why I joined the army after school. I loved camping when I was in the Boy Scouts. I loved climbing trees and cliffs and any kind of adventure sports."

Steve had considered just leaving the jeep for Rudol and Nollen, but he'd spent a couple of grand on it, and wasn't sure if the local men knew how to drive. So tomorrow, the chopper could pick up Jenella and me. Steve and Dirk could drop the guides back at their village and meet us in Timika.

We changed our course, hiking south, down from the steep mountains and back into the forested hills. We washed ourselves in a cold mountain stream – perfect after a day of walking and sweating. Rope bridges once more straddled the watercourses that were too deep to wade across. We still had dehydrated food and tea in our packs, along with our sleeping bags.

Fortunately, Rudol and Nollen had a good idea as to where we were.

The villagers we met were either friendly or just wanted to keep to themselves. Some had grown wary of any foreigners, which was hardly surprising. We camped near a village and phoned in our location to the others.

I was glad to be back in that chopper the next morning. The forest was beautiful, but the insects were huge, and everywhere. Giant ants, huge leafhoppers and moths, biting flies and mosquitos. One night was enough roughing it for me.

LIZA

The gun runners' plan

At the guest house in Timika there was much celebration, with plenty of beer and whisky and junk food, and the joy of mobile phones working again. It's always great to tell your family and friends that you're not really dead, that you survived!

At dinner, we discussed our plans.

Ken and I were returning to the mine, but we both wanted to make changes to our work, safety and travel procedures. Arthur was thinking of returning to work, but only after he'd taken some sick leave to allow his leg to mend properly.

Dirk and Franz both planned to leave the company and mining and were hoping to get a payout from the company after being abandoned in the jungle.

I decided to return to Australia with Mike in the boat; we offered Arthur a ride as well. The others could take a chopper back up to the mine and would have some great stories to tell their workmates.

Dirk and Franz tried to talk Arthur out of returning to work. They would collect their personal belongings from the small flats where they lived at the mine site and move on from there.

I still had Michael Rockefeller's letter in my medical bag – the dead man we'd found in the cave. I decided to scan it as soon as I got home and see if I could track down any relatives of his and send it to them. Hopefully his sister was still alive; if not, maybe there were some nieces or nephews.

After dinner, I did a quick internet search, and found that Mary Rockefeller Morgan had written a book in 2012 about losing her twin, so she might still be alive. I decided to try contacting her publishing company.

Later, Dirk, Franz, Arthur, Steve, Mike and I moved on to a bar, while Dave, Jenella and Ken headed back to the guest house.

"Do you guys know what I'm thinking?" said Dirk.

"You're thinking about that bag of gold that Konia showed us?" asked Steve.

"No, I was thinking about how powerless Swando and the tribesmen really are. When they held us captive, they seemed powerful, but really, they are powerless, and desperate," said Dirk.

"I agree. Konia and his freedom fighters are fighting the good fight, but against the power of the Indonesian Army, they haven't got a hope," said Arthur.

"I want to help them. I want to offer medical services to those remote villages. Those people have nothing," I said.

"I think we could help them in other ways too. The freedom fighters can't fight without weapons, and we could help by supplying them," said Dirk.

"I'm not sure that is the right way to help them," said Mike.

"It is what Konia most wanted. He asked us to wait while he fetched the gold to buy those last two guns," noted Dirk.

"That bag of gold that Konia grabbed, he could fund a revolution with that. He had kilos of the stuff," observed Steve.

"I'd prefer to help improve the Papuan's healthcare system. I took an oath to help people heal, not hurt each other," I said. "But I can see your point."

"The Indonesians have been killing the Papuans for the last fifty years. They won't stop for any reason. And they force the locals to convert to Islam. As a Christian, I oppose violence, but I can see what Dirk means about helping them however we can," said Franz.

"But where are we going to buy what they want? And how are we going to get it here?" asked Arthur, thinking of the practicalities.

"Look at how Mike and Steve came in. They asked Doctor Dave to borrow his boat, and they carried seven of those things up into the national park, in a jeep, then on foot," observed Dirk.

"So we'll need a boat," said Arthur.

"If we all get a payout from Freeport, we could probably buy a boat. Or if we've been saving our wages," said Dirk.

"This would be a dangerous and illegal business," warned Franz.

"You'd need some sort of a cover business," said Steve. "I have clients who do illegal things, grow cannabis, deal drugs, but the smart ones have a cover business to launder the money. A café, or an art gallery, a place where they can conduct their business, where people can come and go, so it looks like a regular business."

"Where did you buy your bargaining chips, Steve?" asked Arthur, always the practical one.

"I bought those things in Cairns. But you could probably buy them in Port Moresby, or Bangkok, or Manila," Steve said.

"They might be a lot cheaper in Bangkok or Manila," commented Dirk.

"And we could be 'operating fishing cruises' in those areas," suggested Franz. "I've always wanted to run fishing cruises."

"Bali would be a great place to run fishing cruises from," said Dirk. "I've got a place in Bali, and it's crawling with tourists all year round. The rent is cheap, the food is cheap. Stocking up the boat would be cheap there too."

"We could run fishing cruises and help the Papuans out between trips. It could be done," said Franz.

"We could always get Rudol and Nollen to 'be our guides' and help us to carry packs up to the Ples Tambu," said Arthur.

"Yes, those boys were keen to be a part of the action," said Dirk.

"And five can carry more things than three can," added Franz.

"If you look at this map of the national park, you can see that we cut out half the distance from the coast to the mountains by driving into Timika and Akimuga, then hiking up to the highlands," said Dirk.

"OK, so it sounds like we have a plan. Have you guys got any money saved, or do we need the mining company payouts to get ourselves set up with the boat and the first load?" Arthur asked the other two.

"I've got a bit put away" said Dirk.

"Yeah, me too. There's not much to spend it on when you're up here," said Franz.

"Where is going to be the cheapest place to buy a boat?" asked Arthur.

"Port Moresby could be a good place to buy a boat, or the Philippines," said Steve, looking amused by the three men's plans.

"Right, let's look into these things, and meet again tomorrow at lunch time. What time are you heading off, Arthur?"

"Not sure we've set a time yet. I think Dave wanted to buy some fresh food before we head off."

"Cool. Now let's just check we've all got each other's phone numbers, and email is probably a good idea too."

"I can't say that I agree with your plans, but I know your intentions are good. I wish you luck, but warn you that what you are thinking of doing will be very dangerous," I said to them.

"I agree with Liza. I wish you all the best, but I'm going to pretend that I never heard this conversation," said Mike, as he took my hand and led me back to the guest house.

Back at the guest house, Mike didn't want to let me out of his sight. I was in the shower.

"Can I borrow your razor, Mike?"

"Sure, darling."

"I haven't been this hairy since, well, ever."

"I'm just so relieved we managed to find you. That idiot Jim Sinclair was trying to convince me you were dead, and was talking about giving me a payout," said Mike, sounding mad.

"Oh, I've got a few well-chosen words for Mr Sinclair and his superiors when I get back. I'm going to make some changes at Freeport Grasberg mine. Some huge changes," I said.

"Good for you, Liza, and I'll do whatever I can to help," Mike said.

"Darling, you have helped so much already. You organised your own search party. You rescued me. And the other guys. You're my hero."

"I would never give up on you. I didn't care what it cost. I would have done anything to get you back," Mike said.

"You've got me now, Mike, and we'll always be together," I reassured him.

"As we were walking, Konia told us that the Indonesians had taken their village, burned their huts, and killed his father and uncle. His mum took the kids up into the hills to start again, and the Indonesians stole their land and burnt their hut again. They are committing genocide, right under our noses," I said.

"It's just like how the Australian settlers stole the land from the Aborigines," said Mike.

"But that stopped last century. This is happening right now. As we speak. Look, I'm grateful that you traded the guns. I don't even mind that the boys are planning to run guns. How else are these poor bastards going to fight back?" I asked. My brain was hurting and I needed a cigarette.

"There aren't even any journalists in Papua who can tell the world what's happening," said Mike.

"Maybe I should start writing a blog? I could write it as an anonymous aid worker in West Papua. I could tell people what's really going on here, but I'd have to disguise my identity so I don't lose my job or wind up in some Indonesian jail," I said.

"Good idea. The world needs to know. I wonder if any of the aid agencies run clinics up here. I wonder if they need any more doctors?" asked Mike.

"No, Mike, you've got to stay in Cairns. I'd go crazy if I couldn't get out of this place every ten days," I said.

"There must be something I can do to help the cause."

"We'll think of something. But in the meantime, just hold me."

WIRA

Kopassus office and Colonel Yuda

"Wira, take this phone call, you useless shit," said Colonel Yuda.

"Kopassus, Corporal Wira here, how can I help you?" I said to the phone.

"Hello, it's Wayan Chan here, from South Papuan Border Control."

"Hello Wayan, do you have something to report?" I asked.

"Corporal Wira, I have to report some suspicious activity at the port of Amamapare. An Australian boat docked on the night of the twenty-third, and the occupants immediately left for Timika.

"I searched the boat and found nothing illegal. But I left a guard there, and when the skipper returned, he didn't have a current visa in his passport," said Wayan.

"What was the skipper's name, and nationality?" I asked.

"A Doctor David Stone, from Cairns, Australia. I checked and he works at Cairns Regional Hospital. He had been to Indonesia before, but his previous visa had expired, and he hadn't applied for a current visa," Wayan reported.

"What was his reason for travelling without a visa?" I asked.

"He said he was attending a medical emergency. His passengers included another doctor, Mike Fraser, whose wife was the subject of the medical mission. But he also transported a Mr Steve Stanson, who is a registered private investigator, also from Cairns, and a New Guinean national, Miss Jenella Daruna," said Wayan.

"You're right, that is suspicious. What action did you take?"

"I demanded he pay for visas for himself and his passengers straight away. I reported it to my superiors. I kept his boat under surveillance, and I ran criminal history checks on the four passengers, which all came back negative," said Wayan.

"Why are you reporting this to us at Kopassus?" I asked.

"When Doctor Stone returned, he brought back an extra two passengers. One was Doctor Liza Fraser, who had a working visa for Freeport Mine, and no injury. The other was Arthur Neilson, also on a Freeport work visa, who had a broken leg," said Wayan.

"So why do you think this is suspicious?"

"Neilson was flagged in my search for having a conviction for possession of cannabis in Cairns in 1999," said Wayan, sounding a bit excited.

"Is that it?" I asked. This guy was an idiot.

"Those doctors were harbouring a criminal on their boat," shouted Wayan.

"A criminal with a legal working visa to our country? A miner who smoked cannabis twenty years ago? When did they leave the port?" I asked the idiot.

"They left on the thirtieth, heading for Cairns, Australia," answered Wayan.

"So what do you want us at the Secret Service to do about it? Chase three doctors and a patient across international waters?

Have you ever heard the term 'Diplomatic Incident'?" I asked the idiot.

"Just doing my job, sir," said Wayan, as he hung up.

"Colonel Yuda, you are right about that Wayan Chan. He is a time-waster and a fool. Still, I'd better call our man at the Freeport Mine and see why they couldn't deal with this accident themselves. Have they reported a medical emergency requiring evacuation to you?" I asked.

"Freeport did report a helicopter crash recently. But they said there were no survivors. Make yourself useful and look into the matter for me, Wira. This sounds like sloppy management at that mine again. That sort of thing annoys me. Foreigners dying in our jurisdiction always looks bad, but surviving and having to be rescued by other foreigners looks worse," said Colonel Yuda.

Plans into action

Ken, Franz and I were heading back to the mine, but we needed to organise a few things first. Franz and I were leaving our jobs and seeking a decent payout, so we were looking for a lawyer in Timika who could represent us during negotiations.

Alexander Mulder kept a neat office in the main street of Timika.

"How can I help you gentlemen?" asked Alexander.

"We both work for Freeport Mine, and were recently flying out on leave. The helicopter crashed, we survived and sought shelter from the rain in a cave. Freeport sent one chopper to look for us, but we couldn't get out of the cave in time to attract their attention. They left us there in the jungle, in the Lorentz National Park," I said.

"Bloody hell!" said Alexander. "That sounds a bit negligent. How did you get out of there?"

"Luckily, one of the mine's doctors, Liza Fraser, was on board with us. Her husband mounted a rescue mission from Australia using a jeep and a private chopper, and brought us out on foot," answered Franz.

"So the mining company left you there to die?" asked Alexander.

"We'd still be there now without the doctor's private rescue mission. We want to sue their pants off. Will you represent us?" I asked.

"Well, it sounds like you have a pretty good case against them. They are also likely to want to keep this incident very quiet. I'd say that they will cough up quite a bit of hush money to stop you fellows selling your story to the media. Imagine what your story would do for their share prices, let alone recruitment?" Alexander said, as he smiled.

"Our friend Arthur Neilson was also on board. He suffered a broken leg and has returned to Cairns with the doctors who rescued us. He wants you to represent him as well. We have his contact details," said Franz.

"I will also need the contact details for Liza and her husband, to verify and witness your account. I can build a strong case with this material, and I'd say we could land a substantial out-of-court settlement for all three of you gentlemen. Will the doctor's husband be approaching the mine for reimbursement of his rescue costs?" asked Alexander.

"Doctor Mike Fraser will definitely be doing that. His party rented a chopper and brought in a private investigator and a translator, so it's got to add up. Lucky for us, they had the money to cover it," I said.

We shook hands on our agreement.

Ken, Franz, the lawyer and I hired a chopper to take us up to the mine. Negotiations went well. Very well. I would be paid hush money, on top of the severance pay and super that the company was obliged to pay me.

Franz and I cleared out our rooms in the low-rise flats we'd called home for some years. We prepared to fly to our home bases; Ken was given some stress leave.

The other mine workers couldn't believe it when the three of us walked into the canteen. Franz and I couldn't say anything, but Ken hadn't signed a non-disclosure agreement. As he filled up his tray, other men gathered around him saying things like "We thought you were dead," and "How on earth did you get out of the jungle, and back here?"

Ken might have been told not to talk to the media, but he was certainly going to talk to his mates. Everyone on shift break gathered around his table listening to his story. He didn't give away too much information about the Ples Tambu, as he knew how important that was to the Free West Papua movement. But he did tell how the highlanders fed and housed us, and helped the rescuers.

Franz and I stood behind him and smiled.

"These two can't say anything. They are leaving and had to sign a non-disclosure agreement. But you can ask me, and I'll tell you," said Ken.

"What did they feed you?" asked one man.

"We got pork on a special day, but other days we ate birds, possums, sago grubs, yams. It's all good when you're hungry," said Ken.

"Who else was on board?" asked another man.

"Sadly, John the pilot and that young American, Robert, were killed. Doctor Liza survived, and was able to fix up Arthur's broken leg. Franz here had his head split open, and she fixed that too. She's coming back after her down time. I don't know about Arthur, I think he's still deciding," said Ken.

A local man who worked as a cleaner asked, "Which village were you at? Who was the chief?"

"We were in Swando's village. I think the nearest big village was called Ilaga," said Ken, carefully.

Most of the mine workers met very few locals, and very few of them ventured into the national parks, or away from the towns. As fly-in fly-out workers, they had very little contact with the Papuans, and little understanding of them. They'd been told that the Raskols had hacked up a chopper load of mine workers, and consequently they feared all locals. Ken's story of being sheltered and fed by villagers changed many of their minds.

Port Moresby

The first thing I did when I returned to Port Moresby was have dinner at the yacht club, and pay my membership fees. After a big seafood dinner, I hung around the bar asking other members if they knew of any boats for sale. Apparently there were a few. Malcolm, a merry older gentleman, arranged to meet me the next day and show me around the harbour to see boats that were on the market.

The next day I met Malcolm and inspected a range of boats from yachts to cruisers of various sizes. I took notes on the power, speed and price of each boat, and any work they needed to ensure they were seaworthy.

"An American boat," Malcolm said. "A retired American couple crossed the Pacific in it. The husband was keen to keep travelling to Australia, then across the Indian Ocean. But the wife had jack of it. She had complained about the cold in Alaska, hated the 'rude Chinese and Japanese', and by the time they'd narrowly avoided pirates in the Philippines she'd started to talk about going home. The boat is only two years old and needs very little work done."

"This boat looks perfect for our fishing charter business. It's got heaps of deck space, a sound engine and modern equipment, and the price is right," I said. "I'll have to ring my business partners and inform them, but I'd say it's a deal."

At the bar, I got out my phone.

"Hi Dirk, it's me, Franz," I said.

"Hello Franz," said Dirk. "Been busy?"

"Mate, I've found an excellent boat. It's 50 feet, sleeps eight but can be sailed easily by two men, harder but possible for one man. It's only a couple of years old, but some older Americans need to sell it," I said.

"What do they want for it, Franz?" asked Dirk.

"A hundred and twenty thousand US dollars," I said.

"Let's buy it. I can put half that amount in your account. Arthur can pay us each twenty grand when he gets back. Have you got enough?" asked Dirk.

"Yeah mate, with your half, no worries," I said.

Though I'd worked as an engineer for some years, not knowing where I'd settle, I hadn't bought a house and only kept a cheap car in Port Moresby. The boat was the biggest thing I'd ever bought.

Cairns

I decided to get my leg X-rayed. Although it felt stronger all the time, I just wanted to be sure that the bones were set straight. It still felt weird, and I could only walk properly for a bit, then I wanted to limp and favour the good leg.

Dave, Mike and Liza had all looked at my leg. When we returned, Dave organised an X-ray for me. I usually operated heavy machinery, and if I couldn't stand all day and lift heavy things, I'd have to get into a different line of work. Maybe it was a good time to take up gun running?

I plugged in the phone to charge and was surprised to get a call from Dirk almost immediately.

"Franz has bought a boat in Port Moresby. I'm flying over there tomorrow to help him pick it up."

"Cool, Dirk. That was quick!" I said.

"Then we'll head on a shopping trip to the Philippines, but we can meet you in Bali next week if you're up for it," said Dirk.

"I should be OK. I've just had my leg X-rayed. The tibia had broken but it is mending, and the fibula has some small fractures. But they're both straight. The radiologist was pleased with how it is healing."

"That's great, Arthur. Liza's bush medicine did the trick, eh?" said Dirk.

"I'd have been dead without her help. I wonder if those tribesmen would have eaten me?" I joked.

"I wouldn't put it past them," said Dirk. "Those skulls hanging in their cave – I bet they ate them."

I returned to my share-house, stocked up on groceries, and spent the next week sorting out my things to sell, give away or throw away.

DIRK

Shopping in Manila

I met up again with Franz in Port Moresby where we visited a fishing shop and got a great deal on ten fishing lines, some nets, and a couple of spear-fishing set-ups. We bought lockable trunks for the fishing gear, and life jackets and wetsuits as well. If we were going to be running fishing cruises, we needed all the gear, and we needed to know how to use it. We attached fishing rod holders to the rails around the side and back deck. We bought detailed maps of the Indonesian islands, and books about fish species and fishing.

While Franz and Malcolm got the boat ready, I had a crack at designing a website, putting up contact details in Bali, as well as a map and the price for a three-day fishing trip that we could comfortably run around Bali, Lombok and West Nusa Tenggara. We decided to limit the range of the fishing cruises – most tourists were on a strict timeline, so a three-day cruise was probably the longest people would go for.

I liked messing around on the computer. I found stock photos of the islands, and people holding up huge fish. I downloaded some maps and pencilled in some fishing trip routes. I also called the Denpasar Port Authority to book a mooring for the boat. We only wanted a cheap one – it didn't need to be close to all the action and the big inter-island ferries. Taxies were cheap on Bali, and tourists could come to us. Anyway, even the quietest moorings would still be close to the international airport, and the hotels of Kuta Beach.

Next day we set sail for Manilla, with fridges full of food, a satellite phone, and stacks of fishing gear. It would take four or five days each way, and it was still monsoon season, so we might have to wait out storms if we encountered any. Getting the boat out of harbour at the Royal Papua Yacht Club was the hardest bit; once we were in the open ocean, it was reasonably plain sailing.

About four days later, we sailed into Manila. We were greeted by two-way radio message, informed where to moor, and told to check in to the Customs office. There we paid for our three-day visas and the Manila Yacht Club membership bond, then hit the city for a hot meal and a couple of beers.

We taxied to Hidalgo Street, in the Quiapo district, where people went to purchase electronic equipment and cameras. I'd found the name of a shop but had to ask around a few times before we found it. It was down a side alley with virtually no signage. The front room was full of binoculars and telescopes. Franz looked at some binoculars, while I asked quietly if they sold guns. The sales assistant checked us both out then ushered us through a door into the next room. This room was like an Aladdin's cave of guns. There were counters full of handguns, and racks of rifles of all different shapes and sizes. Franz and I looked at each other and smiled. We could get whatever we wanted here.

If there were going to be the three expats and two villag-ers making the return hike, we could only buy as many guns as

ARTHUR

Guns for gold

Next morning, Dirk, Franz and I set off on our trip to Timika. We sailed east along the island chain, passing Lombok, West Nusa Tenggara, Komodo, then past East Nusa Tenggara, or Flores as it is still known. From there we passed many smaller islands to the south and then sailed to the north of Timor and Timor Leste, two countries on the one island.

Timor was an island like Papua, which the Indonesians had invaded. The Indonesians have proved to be rampant colonists like the British. We took note of anywhere that looked quiet and clean and good for fishing. We crossed the Arafura Sea to West Papua through open water, with our navigational instruments setting the course; luckily it was smooth sailing through the night to reach Amamapare. We docked in the small hours. At first light I went to find the border official in order to show him our passports and the boat's papers. Wayan Chan noted our Indonesian visas and pocketed a small bribe for his trouble.

After we'd rested, we set off in the jeep. At Timika we purchased some fresh fruit and veggies. Just out of Timika we gave the jeep a spray paint, and then headed into the national park.

We drove in to Mopozap, parked and went in search of Rudol and Nollen. The Papuans were surprised to see us again but were happy to act as our guides. Our party of five left the jeep at the mighty river, and set off on foot, all carrying backpacks. At the end of the day, we set up camp, made a meal, and slept soundly. Franz and I hadn't seen the lowland jungle with its the great watercourses before, and Dirk only recognised bits and pieces.

Rudol and Nollen took us the same way they had taken Steve, Mike and Jenella on the first journey. When we stopped for meal breaks, they asked about the others, especially Jenella. The walking proved to be hard on my leg, so I bandaged it more firmly, which gave it some support and stopped it from swelling.

On the morning of the third day, we reached the Ples Tambu. The five of us approached together, waiting for the tribesmen to appear. We knew that each morning the hunters would go out and return later. They would be able to summon Swando or Konia for us if they were still here. The women showed us a place where we could wait but didn't stay with us. When the hunters returned, they ordered us to wait some more, while they went to get Swando.

Chief Swando arrived with some other men.

His son Semu made the introductions, saying, "This is Kupsy, Konia's brother."

Kupsy spoke a little English. He explained, "Konia has taken his men to the Paniai Lakes. My men and I have come to Ples Tambu, on our way to New Guinea. Konia said a 'waitman' might come back, and told me what to do if you did."

I said, "We brought you some guns to help in your fight against the Indonesians."

"Thank you, brother Arthur. Free Papua. Papua Merdeka!" said Kupsy.

Swando led us into the lower mouth of the cave, but no further. The transaction was to occur here, away from the eyes of the women. Kupsy walked further into the cave and returned with a bag of gold. Dirk, Franz and I unloaded the guns and ammo, and laid them out for Kupsy to inspect. Kupsy seemed pleased and began to bargain. He reached into his bag and produced small electronic scales, so he could accurately measure out an ounce of gold for each gun.

Dirk, Franz and I were happy with how straightforward the bargaining had been. Dirk had made sure that Kupsy and his men knew which ammo went with the rifles and which went with the handguns. To keep it simple, all the rifles were the same model and so were all the handguns. He then showed them how to load the firearms and use the safety switch.

"My friends, these guns are very good, the men are happy with them. But Konia asked me for something," said Kupsy.

"Is it a different kind of gun they want?" I asked.

"Yes, but it might be too difficult to bring in, specially to carry in through the forest. We want a big gun that will bring down a chopper. Do you think this is possible?" asked Kupsy.

"So you'd be wanting either a machine gun, or some sort of rocket or grenade launcher?" asked Dirk.

"Up in Paniai, the Indonesians are mowing us down from their choppers. They have burned down the forests all around Lake Paniai, leaving very little ground cover, and they shoot us from the air. They've been shooting old men, teenage boys, even toddlers," said Kupsy.

"And I guess rifles aren't much use against armed choppers," observed Franz.

"That's right. And with the forest burned down, the topsoil has all run into the lake, so the gardens are not so fertile, and the lake floods. Malnutrition is everywhere around the lakes now," said Kupsy.

"We'll see what we can do. These kinds of guns are bigger, but they probably break down into pieces that we can carry," said Dirk, who knew more about guns than I did.

"Our Ekagi brothers and sisters from the lakes would be so grateful to you. Already, you are bringing us hope, and weapons for the young men who flock to our cause. We will take our land back from the Yelopela Indonesian imperialists, and we don't care how many of us have to die to do it," said Kupsy.

"Have you lost many men?" I asked.

"We've lost about a hundred people in the last few years – men, women and children. Benny Wenda estimated that the Indonesians have killed 500,000 Papuans in the last fifty years. We don't shoot the settlers, only the men in uniform," said Kupsy.

"I always wondered why there were a lot of army men surrounding the mine when I worked there. Now I know why," I said.

"Yes, it might be a long time before we are strong enough to attack the mine again. In 1977, the OPM attacked the mine, and the pipeline that carries the slurry containing the ore to Amamapare. The army attacked us and killed eight hundred men and women.

"For now, we just try to protect the villages. They have already taken most of West Papua, and our people live like starving beggars there. We must fight to protect each village as they try to steal it from us. Paniai is the battleground now," said Kupsy.

"I know how you feel. The Indonesians stole my family's plantation in the 1960s. Though I suppose the Dutch settlers had already stolen it from your people," said Dirk.

"So you are a son of Dutch settlers, Dirk? Welcome to our Organasi Papua Merdeka," said Kupsy.

"My parents were teachers for the missionaries in Otsjanep. The Indonesians made them leave the mission because they wanted the children to be taught Indonesian, not Dutch. Only the priests and nuns were allowed to stay," said Franz.

"Yes, the Dutch thought that if they left, we would get independence, but the Indonesians invaded straight away. They knew since the 1930s that there was a mountain of ore here, that is what 'Ertsberg' means. The Indonesians offered a special deal to the Americans to set up the mine, our country became just a pawn in their game. The Americans mine the gold, keep most of the money, but pay tax to the Indonesians. In 2010, they made four billion dollars in profit, out of six billion in revenue. They hunt us like animals. But we are men, smart men. We will fight to take our country back. We don't care how long it takes. We will fight to the last man," said Kupsy.

"We wish you well in your fight for freedom. Free Papua!"

"Papua Merdeka!" I said.

The trade had gone well, and Swando invited us to stay for a meal before we headed off. We ate in the women's village. Before we left, Kupsy bade us farewell, and said that if he or Konia were not here when they returned, then Semu could bargain on their behalf. Semu had been watching how Kupsy used the scales and counted the guns. Then we started down the mountain again. We could still get in a few hours of walking before dark.

Walking downhill and with lighter packs, we made better time on our return walk. Rudol and Nollen asked us to show them how our handguns worked, so we showed them how to load, unload and clean the Berettas we carried, but we didn't fire them in the forest. Later, as we crossed a deafening, thundering river, Dirk took out his gun, saying to Rudol, "Fire it here if you like."

"Oh, thank you, Mr Dirk," said Rudol eagerly.

Dirk showed them both how to brace their arms as the gun kicked back. Excited, Rudol and Nollen both fired a shot, aiming at some rocks on the other side of the river. We made sure we cleaned the gun afterwards and then continued our trek to Mopozap. There we left the guides, and drove on to Timika, Amamapare, and the boat.

We'd noticed how well fenced the pipeline was, and how there were guards all over the dock where the pipeline filled the container ships. Now we knew why.

In Timika, where we once again had phone reception, Dirk was surprised to have received a few enquiries about fishing cruises. After some discussion, we decided to plan our first fishing cruise for the day after Christmas, which would be after we'd done our next buying trip to Manila. It would be a good idea to break up gun-running trips with legitimate fishing trips. We might meet some nice female tourists, and we might even catch some fish.

Dirk returned the phone calls from the enquiries, giving them the date and price. We calculated the fee by estimating the food and fuel costs, and factoring in a profit as well. I updated the website with the next cruise date.

And the we set sail for Manila once more.

LIZA

Plans for expansion

As I suspected, there was no flying doctor service in Papua similar to the service our remote communities in Australia had. Perhaps this was to be my mission – to provide medical assistance to the most remote Papuans, who lived too far from hospitals or clinics, and were too impoverished to travel. But communications were going to be a problem. If the highlanders had no electricity and no phones, how would they call the flying doctor when they needed it? Solar panels could provide the power to charge up satellite phones, but these things cost money to set up and required some training to use. If I was going to implement this sort of a system, I would need financial backer, or to maybe set up a not-for-profit organisation.

In Cairns, Mike and I had some quality time together. We walked the dog on the beach, drove to Port Douglas and took Dave's boat to Fitzroy Island. Mike really wanted me to quit my job, but I knew that I couldn't afford to. I'd have to hold the job for six years just to pay off my student loans, and more if we wanted to buy a house together instead of renting. I'd only been there for three years, so I was committed to at least another three.

I started looking into different ways of offering medical aid to the highlanders, and counting down the days until I had to return to work. Travelling by jeep could only reach so far into the national park; the mountains were too steep for roads. To get anywhere remote, I would have to travel by helicopter. But the locals were scared because the Indonesians shot them from helicopters. It was going to be difficult to gain the trust of the local people.

Then I thought about Konia. He was literate and travelled on foot between the most remote villages. People like him could be useful in calling out for medical aid when it was needed. Perhaps it was men like Konia who needed to be trained to use satellite phones and perform some simple medical techniques. If he could call my base when serious medical attention was needed, I could fly out to meet patients for surgery or childbirth assistance, or whatever was needed.

This whole experience had opened my eyes to the way the highlanders really lived, what they valued, and what they needed.

Mike said, "Don't you already help out at a few of the local clinics?"

"Yes, but they're established clinics. There's one for the mine workers, Timika's town hospital, and then there's the Tiom Clinic, which was set up by missionaries. It's next to their church," I said.

"So if it's already part of your job to look after the locals, why don't you see if you can expand the services and get the mining company to pay," said Mike.

"That's a great idea, Mike. If we are already doing it, it must be part of the company's charter. They've obviously got a huge budget. They make massive profits and pay us all well. What if one condition of my staying there is that they pay to set up communication stations in a bunch of surrounding villages. It's only going to mean a solar panel, a satellite phone, and someone local who's trained to use them," I said.

"You really want to help those tribespeople, don't you? Even after they held you hostage?" said Mike.

"They are good people, Mike. They rescued and fed us. They are just desperate, and don't know how they can change things," I said.

I'd sent an email to Mary Rockefeller Morgan, and she had responded quickly. In the end our correspondence went back and forth.

I scanned the letter from her brother and added a couple of photos of his remains and his watch, which we had carefully secured to bring out with us. She'd been very excited, giving me her address so I could send her the original letter, which I was happy to do. Mary was convinced by the photographs that this was her brother, and in particular by the watch. She asked me about his resting place, and if it would be possible to repatriate his remains. I thought hard about my response to this one. I told Mary that he was resting in a taboo place, accessible only to the tribesmen who were initiated and where not even the tribes-women were allowed to enter. Mary Morgan was not convinced by this argument. She countered that I'd obviously been there, and wasn't I a woman? I explained that my fellow crash survivors and I had been taken prisoner by the tribe, and that two of us escaped after the other men had been sold off. I said that I respected the tribesmen for keeping us alive, just as they'd kept her brother Michael alive, but that they would stop at nothing to keep their village a secret and sacred place.

Mary Morgan wrote back that her father had sent search parties looking for him, and had offered a $1 million reward for his return, back in the 1960s. I wrote back that money didn't mean much to the highlanders, but the secrecy of their village meant everything to them. When Mrs Morgan wrote back to me again, I thought I would mention that I was shocked by the poverty in which the highlanders lived, and was currently fund-raising to create a flying medical service that could reach the more remote villages.

It was then that Mary Morgan told me how much money her uncle Godfrey had made out of Freeport Mine, so at least they had made something out of the place. I guess I will never think like the one per cent of wealthy capitalists do.

When I returned, I also had to speak to Jim Sinclair and the mine managers. I had received an email from Ken, who gave me his version of events between the crash and the rescue, and I intended to make my story fit with Ken's.

On the flight back, I viewed Papua in a different light. I wasn't just flying over jungle, I was flying over hundreds if not thousands of indigenous Papuan people, who continue to live their lives with very low impact on the jungle. It wasn't empty, as I thought before – certainly not a *terra nullius*. The church has been protecting them, and I would protect them too, with money from the mining company. The Papuans I'd seen in Timika were only a fraction of the local population who lived uncounted in the great forests.

It was hard switching from the plane to the chopper, even though the pilot, Grant, shook my hand.

"Ms Fraser, we're so happy that you decided to remain with us at Freeport," said Jim Sinclair.

Jim Sinclair was sitting in the boardroom with senior members of the mine's executive management team. Sinclair introduced himself as the head of Human Resources; there was also the Operations Manager, a man from Project Assurance and Compliance, and a man whose job was titled Corporate Social Responsibility.

"I'm happy to remain here, but I would like to make some changes." I said.

"After we spoke to Mr Ken Knight, we changed our policy on the safety supplies in our helicopters, adding a number of satellite phones, EPIRBs and food supplies into each vehicle," said Sinclair.

"That's great. I was actually thinking about adding to the medical help that we supply to the local people in our vicinity. The tribe who took us in had no contact with medical services, to the point where they killed villagers who contracted sexually transmitted diseases, to prevent the spread and because they had no treatment. I treated people with tropical sores that have festered for many years, and heard that many women still die in childbirth, and children die of malnutrition," I said.

"This doesn't sound good," said Sinclair.

"Our mine is making a lot of money out of this country, and the local people are not really benefitting from our being here very much at all. I would like to suggest that we train some local villagers in the use and maintenance of satellite phones and solar panels to power them, and that we increase our local medical services to five more sites around the area. I usually work seven days for the miners, then three for the locals, and I would like to increase my time and physical availability to the local people who need medical help," I said.

"That sounds reasonable. We receive excellent feedback from the hospital in Timika and the Tiom Clinic, and this is one way in which our company can contribute to the local people," said the Corporate Social Responsibility Manager.

"I'd like to meet with the helicopter pilots to map out where it is feasible for them to land, and where we can find and train local leaders to contact us. I would like a budget to supply the locals with communication devices and solar panels to power them. We must have staff fluent in Tok Pisin and Asmat who can help to train local people to be able to contact me for medical help. If my schedule could be more flexible, it would free me up to attend emergencies, like childbirth or accidents, and I could still maintain the health services to our own workforce," I said.

"We can certainly organise for you to meet with the pilots, and we also have a couple of translators on staff. We employ quite a number of local men and women here. Our finance director can organise to fund your extra medical services. All of your requests can be met," said Sinclair.

"When we went down, we did not expect to be rescued by the locals. Our men were frightened of being cut up by Raskols. But what occurred was the opposite. They took us to their village, they shared their sparse food with us, and gave us a place to sleep. These people have nothing, yet they were prepared to share what little they had with us. We are living up here in first-world conditions, and they are living a couple of days walk away in third-world conditions, in abject poverty. Considering that the mine has been here for more than forty years, we've done very little to improve the lives of the indigenous people," I said.

Jim Sinclair sat back in his chair: "Freeport Mine is primarily here to make a profit for its shareholders, but we have budgeted some funds for community development. We could argue that the taxes we pay go into helping the local community, but we've found little evidence of that. We need educated locals to fill jobs here at the mine. When we first set up, they were mainly illiterate. Some funds have been spent on education for local children and adults, to get them to the minimum standard to be employable. And likewise, this is why we started the local clinics – to keep our workers healthy. We support any initiative to extend our clinics in the local area. The Community Development Officer here can help you to plan and budget your project. We can easily sell this project to our executive in the US. It will be featured as a 'feel good' item in the shareholders' annual report."

Apart from the last bit, Jim Sinclair was showing a surprising and deeper side to himself.

"Thank you. I'll look forward to meeting the Community Development Officer. This is a real way to repay the Papuan people for keeping myself and my co-workers alive. I know that some of the locals don't want much contact with us, and some won't take gifts from us but are willing to trade. I hope that we can find local people willing to work with us to improve the health of their communities," I said.

"Our history here has not been altogether positive," said Jim. "In 2013 a tunnel collapsed killing seventeen miners and injuring many more. Our doctors at the time did what they could for the men, but really, it was the mine engineer's fault for not taking into account the drainage needed to cope with the monsoon rains. But in my mind, the worst tragedy we had was in 2002, when three of our teachers were shot. We believe Kopassus was responsible. We were disgusted, because our company had helped the army and police force to the tune of twenty million dollars in the five years before those shootings occurred."

"Since then, we've increased our private security, and stopped donating to the local law enforcement, simply because they can't be trusted. I want you to understand that our position here is very precarious. We may need to send security with you when you first establish field offices. Many of the locals practice pay-back justice. They might still want to pay us back for the massacre that took place after the 1977 attack on the pipeline. The army and Kopassus went ballistic after that one, and slaughtered whole villages, hundreds of people."

"So you thought that they would do payback killings to any helicopter survivors?" I asked.

"They've done it before. Your group were lucky they chose to keep you alive," said Jim.

I knew what it was that kept us alive. It was Franz being able to talk to them. Straightaway, they talked to us and treated us like humans. Franz's language skills, and Swando's ability to see the value in human lives – that is what kept us alive.

I left the meeting with a much deeper understanding of how the mine management operated. I also came to understand how the locals had come to work at the mine, and how the gold was getting out of the mine site to the Ples Tambu. I knew that security was pretty strict at the site, with all miners and engineers having to pass through metal detectors on their way out of the mine. But there were all of these other workers around the site who weren't at the rockface, but who were down there making food, cleaning, maintaining vehicles, but who obviously had made friendships or arrangements with those who were there. There must be a number of workers here who felt an affinity with the poverty-stricken locals and were helping out in their own way by smuggling out gold dust and nuggets to fund the freedom fighters.

All that gold in the cave had to have come from somewhere.

WAYAN

Customs office

Right, what am I going to do now? The Australian criminal has been back and brought two associates with him. I can't call Kopassus again, they practically laughed at me last time I called. I'll have to just call the army office in Timika and hope somebody from there will listen.

After a couple of calls, I finally got through to Army Intelligence.

"This is Major Honan here. Who am I talking to?" said Honan.

"My name is Wayan Chan, Customs Officer for Amamapare Port and the South Papua Coast. I want to report some suspicious activity," I said.

"What is this activity?" Honan said.

"In November, an Australian boat came into port with two doctors – Dr Stone and Dr Fraser – a private investigator and a New Guinean translator. They didn't have visas, so I made sure they paid. They went into the national park, and came back with Doctor Fraser's wife, who is another doctor, and a miner from the Freeport Mine who had a broken leg. His name was Arthur Neilson, and he has a criminal record for cannabis use in Australia. Now this Neilson has returned on a different boat, with two other mine workers, Franz Seevink and Dirk Feldmuller. They stayed for six days, then left again. If they were working at the mine, they would either stay for ten days or fourteen days. I thought their visit was suspicious," I said.

"Did you search these boats? Did you call the police to take their dogs through these boats?" asked Hunan.

"I searched both boats. I didn't find drugs or weapons. I called the Timika police, but they said they were too busy to attend," I said.

"Please write down your report, and send it to Major Hunan, Army Intelligence, Timika Barracks. Thank you, Mister Chan," Hunan said.

"Thank you, Major Hunan," I said.

Someone would listen to me.

ARTHUR

Manila again

There were eight bunks on the boat, and we decided that we could take eight tourists. We blokes could sleep on cushions on the deck, and still be comfortable and out of the weather.

During the sail to Manila we slept in shifts to make sure there was always someone awake to check for other boats and pirates. Having worked at the mine for years, we were used to shift-work and long shifts. Sailing around was a breeze, even if hiking in the forest was more like hard work. I unwrapped my leg – the scar was healing nicely, the swelling was going down, and it was looking good.

When we got to Manila, Franz volunteered to stay with the boat, and let Dirk and me do the shopping.

When we entered the binocular shop the sales assistant recognised Dirk from his last trip. We were immediately admitted to the back room where I was stunned to see the hoard of weapons on display. This time we'd brought our own bags stuffed inside one backpack.

The shopkeeper, Han, treated Dirk like an old friend, pouring us both a beer. We talked guns and told him how pleased we'd been with our last load. We told him about our target practice near the river – Han had a good laugh at that. Then we got down to business.

"How many rifles today, Dirk?" said Han.

"Actually, we were thinking about a machine gun," said Dirk.

"Well, we do have some of those in stock."

"I am looking for one with anti-aircraft capabilities," said Dirk.

"Oh, we have some military grade automatic weapons, also grenade and missile launchers," said Han.

"Right, and we need something that can be broken down and carried on foot," said Dirk.

"Come with me, I have just the thing," said Han, taking us to a work bench.

Han showed us how to take the gun apart and re-assemble it, then we practised doing it ourselves a couple of times. The M60 weighed about ten kilos. The ammunition rounds for this weapon were also pretty heavy – about two kilos each, with 100 bullets per round. So we figured that two men could carry an M60 and ten rounds each, and the other three could carry four rifles each. So this time, we bought two machine guns with ten rounds each and twelve rifles.

The M60 machine gun was too long to carry assembled in a backpack. We learned how to take apart the bipod assembly, barrel assembly, buffer, trigger assembly, feed tray cover and feed hanger using just a cleaning rod and a small hammer. The gun came with a manual, but the lesson in disassembly helped us to feel the various tensions that held the gun together. Broken down, it didn't even look much like a gun, except for the trigger assembly, which resembled a handgun. This bigger gun had a bigger price tag as well.

Han worked out the total in American dollars.

"We know you like the US dollars, but we have gold if you would prefer," I mentioned.

Han's eyes lit up. "Show me this gold, then?"

Dirk unwrapped the nuggets. Han was pleased.

"Ah, I like nuggets because they are pure gold, twenty-four carat. Today's market price is US$1217 per ounce. I have scales, just under here."

He pulled out a set of scales. Dirk handed over the pouch of nuggets, which Han handled lovingly, rolling them around in his hand.

"This stuff appreciates in value more than pesos or US dollars," Han said. "Takes up a lot less space, too."

On the way out, I looked at the cameras. I had lost mine in the chopper crash.

"Wait, I should buy a camera to replace the one I lost," I said.

Han picked up a good digital camera with a decent lens and put it in my hands.

"You are good customers. This is on the house. It's a pleasure doing business with you, gentlemen," said Han.

Han drove us and our bags of goodies back down to the dock in his Mercedes four-wheel drive. He helped us to unload, admired our boat, then bid us goodbye.

We sailed away, pleased that we could buy the guns and spend the gold in one trip. We cracked some beers and set sail for Bali.

LIZA

New clinics

I did my first couple of days at the mine's clinic, then had a meeting with Janette, the Community Development Officer. Janette was a middle-aged lady who'd worked as a teacher, then in Foreign Aid. She told me that she'd set up the local school, with children being taught during the day and adults in the evenings. She'd also been instrumental in co-operating with the Timika Hospital and setting up the Tiom Clinic.

I told Janette about my experience in the Ples Tambu and the smaller villages along the way.

"Do you have any contacts who might be useful for setting up the communication posts?" Janette asked.

"My husband hired two guides from the Mopozap village – Rudol and Nollen. They're intelligent young guys. They said they'd finished school, so they can probably read. Their village is near the end of the four-wheel drive road into the Lorentz National Park," I said.

"They sound like the kind of people we want to train. When you next fly up to Tiom, ask patients if they know people from their villages who can read if at all possible," said Janette.

"I did notice that a lot of the villages don't have names," I said.

"Yes, that is one problem we face. Another is that these people are unused to locating themselves on maps," said Janette. "Some people call a village by the name of their chief."

"So the Ples Tambu might be 'Swando's village'?" I asked.

"Yes, the only trouble then is that when the old chief dies the village gets a new name," said Janette.

"Right, perhaps we need one of the bilingual workers to accompany me to Tiom. From there they can walk out to visit other villages. That way they can locate them on a map, and find a useful name for the place," I said.

"Yes, a local man or woman would be accepted by the high-landers and could map some sites for us. It's a pity they'll have to travel by foot, but I suppose that is the only way to get to some of these remote places," said Janette.

"If we give them a satellite phone, and a solar charger, they should be able to call us from wherever they end up," I said.

"I'll start asking around our local staff to find a field worker or two. We should also try to get to the areas north and north-west of here, even though there is unrest towards the Paniai Lakes," said Janette.

"If there's unrest, there'll also be injuries requiring medical assistance," I said.

"We just don't want to get shot or hacked up by machetes ourselves," said Janette.

"But if we have the red cross on our chopper, and our clothes?" I asked.

"Between you and me, I've heard that the Indonesians have shot at the locals from helicopters marked with a red cross," said Janette.

"That's terrible" I replied, truly shocked.

"That is how it is here. We're in the middle of a frontier war. The Indonesians treat the Papuans like forest animals they can shoot without recrimination," said Janette.

"If we want to help these people, we can't go all the way to Paniai, but we can stop somewhere along the way. Somewhere like Wandai or Enarotali," I said.

"That sounds good. If we could set up communication stations in villages in all directions from the mine, we would really be helping the highlanders," Janette said. "I'll talk to the pilots too. They've got a good handle on how many people are where, and where they can land."

"OK, I'll do my Timika trip today. See if you can find a field officer who can come with me to Tiom tomorrow," I said.

"Right, and I'll start looking into the sources for satellite phones, solar panels, and start writing up a budget too," said Janette.

I'd made a good ally in Janette. We would get this done together.

I was in bed asleep when I heard a banging on my door, and my phone ringing too. I got up and stumbled to open it, flicking on the light switch at the same time.

"Doctor Fraser, I'm Adinda, I'm here to drive you into the mine. There's an emergency. You'll need to bring your medical kit," said Adinda.

"What has happened? What will I need?" I asked.

"There has been a collapse in one of the mine shafts. A man is trapped by his legs. You may need to amputate," said Adinda.

"Right. I'll need to grab my kit from the clinic now," I said.

"Here, put on this jacket. You'll need it in the mine. I've got a hard hat for you too," said Adinda.

I collected a medical kit, including tourniquets and the bone saw. I really hoped I wouldn't have to use it. Adinda and his crew quickly packed me and my gear into an enormous truck, then headed out to the mine, yellow emergency lights flashing as we went. It was dark and very cold, and the access road was steep. We drove up to the portal to the underground tunnels and were waved straight through.

It's something else down there. The driver zoomed through the network of tunnels, lit only at intersections or parking areas, but dark for kilometres in between. The driver was on his two-way, chatting away in Indonesian, making sure he was driving to the right place, and that no trucks or excavators were in our way. The roads are straight, tunnelled in a grid or comb pattern, layer below layer.

When we got to the emergency area, a floodlight had been set up. There was a lot of dust in the air. Some workers were attempting to hose the dust down, while others dug frantically with shovels instead of using their usual tractors.

"Doctor Fraser, this way please," said Adinda, as he led me through the dust to the edge of the cave-in.

A pile of rocks covering the front half of an excavator machine and filling half the height of the tunnel lay ahead of me. I could see a worker lying on his side with both legs trapped under the rubble. The tunnel we'd driven down was only about four metres high, but where the man lay the excavators had drilled and collapsed the ceiling of the mineshaft to about ten metres. This section had fallen down before the equipment operators had managed to get out of its way.

I rushed over to the man. He was conscious.

"I am Doctor Liza Fraser. I am going to check you out while the men keep working around you. What's your name?"

"I am Manusama. I can hardly feel my legs. I have breathed in a lot of dust."

"You'll be alright," I reassured him, although I was not actually sure that he would be.

I gave him some pethidine straight away. With both of his legs possibly broken, he was bound to be in a lot of pain, even if he was in shock at the moment. I put an oxygen mask on his face, so he could breathe the pure gas into his dusty lungs.

His vital signs were not too bad, considering. The miners continued digging around him, hosing down the dust, the cold water spraying over us both and running across the flat floor of the tunnel. I asked Adinda to fetch some towels or blankets; we needed to keep Manusama warm and dry.

Adinda brought me what I needed.

The miners slowly revealed an enormous rock pinning Manusama's legs to the floor, with smaller boulders both above and below it.

"They cannot use explosives this close to the man," said Adinda. "They can use the back-hoe, that small digger, now they can see what they need to move."

As the workers lifted each rock from Manusama's legs, I cut his trousers and examined and dressed his wounds, bandaging his foot and lower leg up to the knee. It would definitely need X-raying.

The other leg wasn't looking good at all. His foot was jammed underneath an enormous bolder, his shin broken in numerous places.

Adinda looked at me and said, "That is as much of it as the workers can safely remove. To shift that rock will risk the ceiling collapsing on us all."

"Well, I'll have to decide between amputating at the ankle or the knee," I said, gritting my teeth. This is never a pleasant decision to have to make. Manusama could learn to walk again with an artificial foot or lower leg. His tibia and fibula both looked like they had been broken through. I thought that I would amputate at his ankle now, and if his shin bones were that bad, he could always have a knee amputation later on, in a surgery.

"Let's get most of him on a stretcher," I said to Adinda and his team.

We lifted him and wedged the stretcher in underneath him, with his better leg bent up.

"Manusama, I am afraid I'm going to have to amputate your foot. I'm going to give you painkillers that will send you to sleep. We'll carry you out of here to the clinic. We'll look after you. You will be alright," I reassured him.

"OK," he said, eyelids drooping as the drugs quickly took effect.

Even with the tourniquet in place, a lot of blood gushed out as I sawed through his skin, muscles and bones. It sprayed on my face. Adinda wiped my glasses so I could keep on sawing and get it done in one go. It was like sawing a thick branch, I kept telling myself.

When I finished the operation, his leg recoiled automatically, and Adinda and another man had to hold it down so I could stitch the larger arteries and veins, then dress the wound so I could finish the job up at the clinic in surgical conditions.

They strapped Manusama to the stretcher, then loaded him into the emergency truck.

I sat with him in the rear of the truck during the drive out of the tunnels and back to the clinic.

This had been my first time down into the labyrinth since my orientation a few years ago. It reminded me that the underground mine was as big as the open-cut one above it – just hidden. The tunnels were complex – they even had a canteen and admin rooms down there, so that miners didn't have to resurface for breaks, and admin were on hand to oversee the work. A manager had seen the accident via the internal surveillance camera and had sent for me as soon as it happened.

Manusama was alright, he recovered well, and the company's health insurance would provide a prosthesis and therapy for him.

ARTHUR

Bali fishing trip

Although it was raining again, we were happy to set sail to Bali. We rolled down the clear vinyl sides of the top deck to make the boat as weatherproof as possible. Dirk drove, while in the galley Franz cooked a fish and veggie stew.

Dirk said, "I've been thinking about how the Indonesian military organise their operations. In places like the Paniai Lakes, they obviously do whatever they please – burning the forest, shooting from choppers, shooting at peaceful protesters. But they'd have to operate differently in the national park. The missionaries still run the mission schools throughout the park, and aid groups have their offices in the towns like Timika."

I said, "As it's in a national park, they're probably limited to jeep and foot patrols in the Asmats' land, and being as it's under the eyes of churches and aid agencies. If this is the case, they'd be limited by how many men they could fit in a jeep, just like we are."

Dirk said, "My Beretta takes a clip of ten bullets, and I'm a pretty good marksman. I'm not sure if you or Franz can shoot well, but I think that we could probably take care of a jeep load of men if we had the element of surprise, camouflage, and three handguns."

"Let's hope it doesn't come to that," I said.

"Do you guys know how to shoot well?" Dirk asked a bit louder, so Franz could hear.

"I've gone to a rifle range with my mates a few times. I'm OK," said Franz.

"I can fire a gun, but have never done it much. I could do with some practice," I admitted.

"Right then, when we find a quiet spot, we'll have a little shooting practice. Just using tins on rocks. It's an important skill to have," said Dirk.

Back in Bali, we caught up with emails and phone calls. We stocked up on foodstuffs for the fishing trip, along with beer, wine, premixed drinks and soft drinks. The boat had a big fridge and freezer, and we filled them both up. We also bought bait, worms, small fish, chunks of meat, and labelled each separately before stowing them in the freezer. The boat was ready, now we needed to make ourselves look ready.

The camouflage gear and hi-vis mining suits weren't going to cut it for a fishing cruise, so we hit the shops in Denpasar and bought loud Hawaiian shirts and baggy coloured shorts. We bought plastic wine glasses and cocktail glasses, ice cube trays and cocktail umbrellas. We bought woven straw hats at the street markets, and baseball caps and cheap sunglasses. Now we were ready.

The morning of the cruise, the tourists found the boat, some early, some late, some with too much luggage.

Franz had anticipated this, saying, "Listen up, each person has to limit their gear to one small bag. We've arranged a lock-up room here at the dock for suitcases, backpacks and surfboards."

Without the excess bags, the tourists fitted into their cabins and sorted out who slept where.

The tourists were all either Australian or American, young to middle-aged, mostly single. They chatted on deck as the boat cruised the southern coast of Bali, and across to Lombok. The first stop was the Gili Islands, just off Lombok, with a great view of the volcano, Mount Rinjani. The Gilis are fringed by reef, harbouring heaps of fish, and white sandy beaches. After a couple of hours fishing, some of the tourists were bored, so Franz suggested putting on snorkel masks and fins and swimming to the beach. Half of the group decided to jump in, while the serious fishers stayed on board with the lines.

We swam to shore easily, and a couple of the women sunbathed while two guys kept snorkelling. Later, we came ashore to collect everyone. I rounded up our people and headed back to the boat in our inflatable. We'd caught quite a few fish, so it was fresh grilled fish for dinner, with salad and bread rolls. We washed it down with beer and wine. Everyone was happy.

Dirk decided to sail through the evening, to our next spot, to give them something to look at, and so we could have a couple of fishing sessions the next day.

We sailed across the north of Lombok, and east to West Nusa Tenggara. Another volcanic island, West Nusa has a string of volcanic peaks and a large bay hidden behind the small island of Pulau Moyo. Dirk headed into the bay, a large body of water with several rivers feeding into it. This was supposed to be the best kind of place for fishing, as long as it wasn't polluted. We moored for the night in a sheltered spot, and everyone slept soundly.

The next day, fishing started early, and was going well. So well, that I suggested "Right everyone, from now on, we are throwing the small fish back, as well as the ones that are too large to fit on the stove without being chopped up."

"Why?" they all asked.

"We've only got one fridge and one freezer. We'll keep the plate-sized fish for us to eat. The big ones don't cook on the inside, and the outside gets burned. I'll take your photos with the big fish, then they go back in the water," I said.

The fishermen were fine with this idea; we took photographs of the largest fish before we released them. I didn't like scaling and gutting big fish, but the plate-sized ones were fine. The tourists were happy to eat fish they'd caught and cooked themselves, and some were even happy to help scale and gut them.

We sailed around the bay and tried different spots. There are numerous small islands in the bay, and the fish teemed around these. It made good snorkelling too, though much rockier than the coast of Lombok. The river mouths did not prove to be good fishing spots, so we probably wouldn't try there again. Some of the Indonesians still used the rivers as dumping grounds, and the water was coming out littered with plastic rubbish. After dinner, we sailed around to the north shore of the island, and moored in a sheltered bay off Sape, across the strait from Komodo Island. There was much excitement about the giant lizards, which we saw sunning themselves on rocks.

In the morning, we sailed west along the south of West Nusa Tenggara, and stopped near a beach between rocky headlands, so that the snorkellers could swim to a beach again while the fishers fished. Everything was going smoothly. The snorkellers saw rays and sharks, but nothing large, and nothing that followed us. The fishermen caught red and silver mullet, mackerel, bluefin tuna, yellowtail kingfish, tailor, red snapper and sand whiting, and were very pleased with themselves.

The final night of the cruise was spent moored on the south coast of Lombok, in a bay near the Sunut peninsula. The south coast of this island is rocky and jagged, with occasional beaches, but lots of quiet coastline with little traffic. The final day was spent peacefully cruising from one headland to the next, snorkelling around reefs, and watching sea turtles. Even the older tourists hopped in for a swim on that day, donning wetsuits for protection against the rocks and stingers. All the fish caught were thrown back; the freezer and fridge were still quite full, despite the space made by all the drinks that had been consumed. I checked our supplies, and was happy and relieved that they'd lasted, although the fresh milk was gone and we were drinking powdered milk in our coffees now.

The tourists were happy to be dropped off back at Denpasar. Bali seemed so busy now, compared to the quieter islands next door and down the chain.

ARTHUR

A second gun run

During the long days of sailing, Franz had devised his own version of target practice. At the Denpasar port, he had acquired some large polystyrene fishing floats, and drawn concentric circles on them. He let these out on ropes behind the boat at various distances, bobbing along in our wake. Franz and I practised firing our handguns towards the floats. Out in the open ocean, we weren't disturbing anyone, and our skill and confidence with the small weapons improved. Dirk was pleased that we were practising our marksmanship, and he even had an occasional shot himself.

Once more we docked at Amamapare, drove to Timika for petrol and fruit, then headed straight to Mopozap. Rudol and Nollen were waiting for us, ready to set off again. This time my leg was just about fully healed because I was feeling much better as I walked. I noticed more of the wildlife around me – butterflies, insects, frogs, and the fabulous birds. I stopped briefly to photograph the wildlife. Soon, Nollen noticed this, and started to point out birds and monkeys to me. I managed to snap some good photos of the wildlife, and some of features like the rope bridges, waterfalls and flowering trees.

During the walk, we talked.

"I thought we were gun runners. But really, we are freedom fighters," said Franz.

"I'm not a freedom fighter, I run fishing cruises," said Dirk.

"We are freedom fighters, though we have only shot a gun once. We carry the guns to the fighters, so we are part of the movement," said Rudol.

"I hope these guns can help you to protect your land. I hate the Indonesians as much as you guys," said Dirk.

"If the Indonesian Army catch us with a lot of weapons, they'll throw us into jail, maybe kill us," said Rudol.

"Then we'd better make sure they never catch us. I hope I don't have to use my own gun. But I will if I have to," said Dirk.

We walked on in silence, each man thinking his own thoughts. I took more photos on the walk, getting close to some of the different birds of paradise. I recognised the feathers from the ones that Swando and Semu wore. I'd wanted to photograph the men but realised their privacy was important.

The wildlife here was something else, there were butterflies as big as birds, and giant moths too. The villagers would eat the moths, and other insects and grubs as well. There were brightly coloured fungi, some of which Rudol warned me not to touch. I even got a shot of a wild pig, as it raced through the undergrowth. Also snakes and lizards – there was stuff everywhere in the dense forest.

When we reached the Ples Tambu, Swando came down with the men, Konia bringing up the rear and looking pale. Konia had his left arm bandaged up, and he looked sweaty. When Franz spoke to him, he said he'd been injured and his friend had tried removing the bullet with a knife. We spoke to each other about what we could do. We had contact numbers for Liza and Ken at the mine and offered to call or text them. Konia refused to be met by helicopter anywhere near the Ples Tambu.

"What about Ilaga? Could you walk there in an hour?" I asked.

"Liza was talking about setting up another clinic in Ilaga, like the one in Tiom," Dirk said.

"Or if not a clinic, at least a communication and pick-up spot. It's a known village, with a missionary," added Franz.

"I could walk to Ilaga," said Konia.

"OK, so today, we teach you how to use the gun. Then, you will walk to Ilaga, and meet Liza and her helicopter," said Dirk.

We couldn't reach Liza, so we sent her a text. But I did get onto Ken, who was sleeping off a night shift.

"Arthur, what are you doing back here?" said Ken.

"Ken, I've come back to do a photo story for a magazine. But listen, the highlander Konia, he has an injury. We think it was a bullet wound, which his friend has tried to cut out with a knife – it looks infected. He said he'll walk to Ilaga. That's a known village about an hour's walk from the Ples Tambu. If Liza could meet him there, it will probably save his life," I said.

"Right. I'll ring Liza too. I'm not sure if she is at the clinic here or on her rounds today. Either way, the comms office will be able to contact her. I'll call right away," said Ken.

"Great," I replied.

"I thought you were in Bali?" asked Ken.

"Yeah, we've been running fishing cruises from there. It's going well. But I had some time off between trips and thought I'd come back here to get some photos."

"Mate, I'd love a good fishing cruise. I'll look you up on the internet for when I next get some time off," said Ken.

"Cool. It's Fish Lombok dot com – check the website," I said.

"Will do, Arthur. Take care," said Ken.

"Thanks buddy," I said, feeling bad about lying to my friend.

Dirk and I sat in the lower cave with the freedom fighters and went through assembling and breaking down the gun. It was a complicated process, and then there was the language barrier. But we kept repeating the process over and again until they got it. We passed the instruction book around, and each man had a turn at each step of the assembly. It was tricky, and we decided to number each piece in the order that we needed it.

Then came the bargaining. Dirk had paid a lot for the machine guns. He apologised, "I'm sorry, but this big gun cost a lot more than the rifle. It was $20,000. I couldn't get the price lower than that."

Konia replied, "To be honest, I did not think that you would be able to get such a gun. I know they're expensive. Our men in New Guinea said that they didn't know where or how they could get one, only rifles."

"Our man in the Philippines knew that we would not even know how to use it. He sat us down, poured us a beer, and gave us a lesson like we are giving to you now," said Dirk.

"We have the gold. We can pay the price you ask. They will be our only machine guns."

"We brought some other rifles, and ammo, of course," I said.

"Thank you, my friends. We will have to take these to a special place where we can hide them. We will train up other men to use them too," said Konia.

The deal was done, with some larger nuggets this time. Dirk, Franz, Rudol, Nollen and I headed back on our walk. Konia planned to walk with just one man to Ilaga, leaving the rest here with the guns until he returned.

Back at Mopozap, we told Rudol and Nollen, "We might be a little longer this time, as we have to do a fishing trip."

Rudol said, "We will be here, it is no problem."

These young men obviously liked the excitement of the walk up to the mountains; it was a break in their routine of hunting and working in the gardens. Neither of these men had wives yet – they said they were "still looking". Perhaps they were saving money for a bride price, or perhaps there were no young women of marriageable age in their village yet.

Dirk, Franz and I were happy to have met these knowledgeable, useful and quiet men who were now an integral part in our new business.

Back at our boat in Amamapare we were surprised to see the military waiting there with Wayan Chan. Wayan greeted us, but said that he was sorry, they would have to search our boat.

After a short argument, we unlocked the boat and the soldiers made their way through it. They found the fishing gear, and the food supplies, and that was all there was, really. Then they demanded to search our packs. In them, they found more food supplies, sleeping bags, and three locked cases. After demanding the keys, they unlocked three handguns.

"Why are you carrying these?" asked Wayan.

"We are licensed to carry these guns. Our employer recommended that we carry one," said Dirk.

"What are you going to do with them?"

"Defend ourselves against any thieves or Raskols if they attack us," said Dirk.

"Have you used these guns?"

"No. Look, they are clean, unfired. They haven't been out of their cases," I said.

"Where did you get them?" asked Wayan.

"Well, I live in New Guinea, and every expat who lives there carries one," said Franz.

"I got mine in Australia. Freeport recommended that employees carry one for personal protection," I added.

"I was in the army in the Netherlands, and I brought mine with me from there," said Dirk. Our guns were all second-hand and looked different from each other.

"What do you do for a living?"

"We were working at the mine, but now we run fishing trips all around the islands," said Dirk.

"Are you going to bring tourists to Papua?" asked Wayan.

"We were thinking about it, but if we get harassed by the army, we definitely won't," I said.

"You will find it difficult to get tourist visas for Papua. You should stick to New Guinea or the other islands of Indonesia," said Wayan, in a menacing way.

"We thought the Indonesian visa would cover this island as well," said Dirk.

"No, you will need special visas for Papua, and they are difficult to obtain," said Wayan.

"It's a pity, because the fishing is very good along this coastline. But if you don't want our money, we'll happily spend it in other places," I said.

"You three are free to go. But your working visas expire at the end of June. You might find it hard to get new visas if you are no longer at the mine. And don't think about bringing tourists here if they haven't got a special visa," said Wayan.

"Alright, we get the picture. Goodbye," said Dirk.

Wayan Chan and the army men left the boat, and we fired up the engines and sailed off.

LIZA

Konia injured

I got Ken's message over the two-way radio on the chopper. We were on our way to Tiom, so we could visit Ilaga on the way back.

What the hell was Arthur doing back here? It was a bloody long way to come to take photos. But then again, magazines like *National Geographic* paid top dollar for very remote locations and unusual animals and landscapes. I was glad he was doing fishing cruises from Bali. I decided to look them up on the internet when I got back to the mine. I wondered if Arthur, Dirk and Franz had gone ahead with their other plan. Was Arthur really just taking photos?

It was Konia who was injured. I liked this young man, and the explanation about the fight for independence he'd given us. I hoped we'd find him, and someone who lived permanently in Ilaga who could work with us.

The Tiom Clinic kept me busy for a few hours. I checked and weighed the children and babies and gave them their immunisations. They were a bit malnourished, but not starving. I'd bought a box of muesli bars to give to their mums to dole out daily. I also brought seaweed paper. Seaweed paper had plenty of vitamins and minerals and was yummy to eat. It was easy to explain what it was and I could eat it with them, to show it wasn't poisonous. I'd given out blankets at this clinic in the past, and some had come back cut up as clothes. I was glad they were being put to good use, no matter how they were used. There were a couple of pregnant women to check and the usual list of tropical sores.

The pilot knew where Ilaga was, though he hadn't stopped there before. While I was seeing my patients, Max the pilot used his two-way to find a phone number for the missionary in Ilaga. This young Brother, Johannes, ran a one-room school in the village, and had a satellite phone. Max rang him to ask about any landing site he might use. Johannes said that there was a small field at the bottom of the village, which they used for sports. It had a stream running through the middle of it, but a chopper could land on either side of it. Johannes would meet us there.

So we flew to the village of Ilaga, and found the small field where we had room to land next to a shallow creek. It looked as though the creek would expand to fill the field when very heavy rain occurred. This might explain why it was not used as a garden. Johannes met us there. He was a thirty-ish Dutchman in a cassock, with messy blond hair and bare feet. He guided Max and I up through the village, past his schoolroom to a hut near the longhouse at the top.

Konia was already there lying on a grass mat, not looking great.

"Konia, it's me, Doctor Liza. I heard you needed help," I said.

"Doctor Liza! I never thought I'd see you again. I thought Mike would take you to Australia for sure," said Konia.

"Mike is there, but I came back to work. Now what happened to you? Let me see your arm," I said.

I took the rag bandage off Konia's arm, and saw the infected knife wound.

"Oh, Doctor Liza, it was such a stupid accident. The boys were shooting tins for target practice. These were in front of a rock wall. I think a bullet bounced back at me off the wall, and it was just shallow in my shoulder. Then my friend tried to cut the bullet out, but it had broken up. He got a bit, but there was lots of blood," said Konia.

"Now you are infected. I will need to clean your wound and sew it up."

Turning to Johannes, "Do you have a big desk at the schoolhouse?" I asked.

"Yes, Doctor, or we can put desks together to make a big table," said Johannes.

"I need to get him off the ground, so I can disinfect the wound properly. Can you men help to move him to the schoolhouse?" I asked.

Max and Johannes helped Konia to the schoolhouse, while I carried the medical supplies there. Johannes arranged the schoolroom into a makeshift doctor's surgery and brought me buckets of boiled water.

I injected Konia with antibiotics and a local anaesthetic. I disinfected the table, my instruments and myself, washed Konia's arm and torso with the hot water, then wiped him with disinfectant. I waited for the anaesthetic to work and disinfected myself again.

I reopened the wound, wiping away the liquids and solids that had accumulated there. The bullet seemed to have missed major arteries and veins, but there was considerable bleeding. I followed the bullet hole and found fragments around his bone. Using a scalpel, I dug out a few fragments, and cut away infected areas of muscle. When I was happy that I'd found all the fragments, I sewed back the cut muscle, then the skin and dressed the wound. I looked up at his face to tell him that it was finished, but he'd passed out. When I checked Konia's vital signs, he was OK. His temperature was already going back down towards normal.

I sat with him until he woke up, then told him how to care for the wound, change the dressing every day and apply disinfectant cream. I left him a pile of bandages, tape and tubes of cream, and made sure that Johannes watched when I taped the bandage around his shoulder.

"Johannes, I am trying to extend the mine's medical service to the surrounding areas. We have a small clinic in Tiom, and I visit the hospital in Timika too. But I have been wanting to train up locals to use and maintain a satellite phone and solar panel to charge it up, then call us at Grasberg when there is a medical emergency. If you could do that for us here, and if you could recommend any other adult who can read and write in another village, that would be great," I said.

"I would be honoured to be a medical contact for you here, and I will ask around at some of the other villages that I visit. There is actually a very pregnant lady in this village at the moment. I wonder if word has got around to her?" said Johannes.

They looked outside the school, and there was a small woman with a huge stomach waiting on the ground, with a couple of other women. She stood up, helped by one of the others.

"Idesah, please meet Doctor Liza," said Johannes.

"Hello Idesah. You look like your baby is due very soon," I said.

"Still another month, Doctor Liza," said Idesah.

"Do you mind if I touch you?" I asked.

I ran my hands over Idesah's belly.

"I think it could be twin babies. Are they moving around a lot?" I asked.

"Always kicking, Doctor Liza, even at night," said Idesah.

"They are pushing each other out of the way. Johannes, you must ring me or my colleague as soon as Idesah has any pain or bleeding. I will come, even if it is at night. Twins are always a little bit trickier than one baby. Myself or the other doctor, Fred, will come for the birth," I said.

"Liza, we should start heading back before it gets dark here," said Max.

"Yes, navigation is harder in the darkness of the mountains. If we do need to come back at night, you might have to light small fires down on that field, so we can see where to land," I said.

"Thank you for sewing me up, Doctor Liza," said Konia.

"Goodbye, and keep changing those dressings, Konia."

KONIA

Going to Paniai

When I was up to walking again, I rejoined my men at the Ples Tambu. Taking the machine guns to our people at the Paniai Lakes would be our most important mission so far. We couldn't lose these guns at any cost, so we planned the trip using the utmost stealth, walking the final stretches of the journey by night in order to minimise being seen by the Indonesian police or military. It was a route we took quite regularly, so we had a series of villages where we could stop and get rest along the way. We carried food for ourselves and for trading, as well as some spare machetes.

Some kids called us the 'naif men' or 'machete men'. To others we were 'Raskols' or 'OPM', but many did not give us a name, or take much notice of our comings and goings.

The path to Paniai went past the mine, to the farthest northwest corner of the national park. Then we followed the ridges down through settled Papua towards the three big lakes. There weren't really roads up here, but there were tracks that a tractor or a four-wheel drive could follow. The villagers in the province of Papua wore more clothes than those in the national park and their gardens were a little more like farms, with bigger patches so they could grow more food to trade with neighbours. There was still plenty of forest along the ridges between the villages, but larger and larger valley areas were being felled and cleared.

Once we passed Bibida, my men and I walked through the night. It was dawn when we saw the headwaters of Paniai Timur, the river that feeds the lake.

Outside of the village, there was a Haus Tambaran – a spirit house, a taboo place – a burial cave filled with the bones and skulls of the village ancestors. My men and I took our packs into the back of the small cave where we'd previously dug a hole and installed a hinged lid over it. We stashed our weapons in the hole, then covered it over with bones and dirt, then we quietly emerged from the cave. We crept into the long house and went to sleep near the other single men of the village.

We made our way around the Lake to Kebo, where there was a big group of freedom fighters. They greeted our news about the new guns with much excitement. There was a place among the cliffs on this side of the lake where the men could practise shooting; as our groups were always on the move, more men needed to learn to operate the machine guns. We needed a group who knew how to operate them close to where the guns were at all times. There also needed to be a way to transport the big guns without the Indonesian military or police discovering them. The Kigani men told me that they'd hidden rifles under a dead man in a coffin before, and told anyone who asked that he had to be taken back to his village for burial. Next time anyone dies in Paniai Timur, they would have to be buried at Kebo, and they would carry his or her coffin by canoe or by hand to our place among the cliffs.

I heard news of the famine all around the lakes; the Indonesians were taking more than their share of fish and crops, leaving the Kigani to go hungry. Since the army had burned the forest, each time it rained the run-off carried away topsoil into the lake, making the fields less fertile, and muddying the fishing waters as well. When the forest was still standing it never flooded, but now it had become a common event. The forest acted like a giant sponge, holding the land together. But the Indonesians hated the way it provided cover for us, so they burned it for kilometres around.

I'd wanted to walk around the biggest lake, but my friends told me the army was camped between the big lake and the two smaller lakes. Because I couldn't safely pass south of the lake, I would have to retrace my steps.

ARTHUR

PNG and Solomons

Franz suggested that we sail for Port Moresby, he had his apartment there, and didn't want to return to Bali if the Indonesian Army were going to hassle us. Dirk wanted to go to the bank so he could sort out our finances. So we sailed east towards PNG, along the southern border of the Lorentz National Park. Seven or eight large rivers flowed into the ocean there, the clear waters full of fish, crocodiles and sharks. The jungles reached the beaches, which were dotted with tribal villages and small mission buildings with crosses on their roofs. It looked idyllic and would make for terrific fishing cruises.

After the national park, we passed the southern coastal towns of Indonesian Papua. Here the forests were cleared, with farming and industry jostling for positions right along the coastline. The rivers ran brown and were littered with flotsam that floated out into the ocean. Clear felling meant that the topsoil washed into the rivers and out to sea, and the brown waves washed onto brown beaches and mudflats.

When the sat-nav system suggested we leave the coastline to skirt the Kimaam Peninsula, also known as Yos Sudarso Island, we happily sailed out to sea for the short cut. The degraded coastline was not so scenic compared to the national park. Fishing tourists wouldn't particularly like to see this. It would be like doing a fishing trip around Java, with polluted rivers one after another, the rubbish of hundreds of millions of people emptying into the ocean.

While we were sailing, I downloaded my photos onto the laptop.

I grouped the photos in folders, according to types of animals or plants. I also had a 'landscapes' folder. In one folder, I arranged the physical landmarks which marked out our walk from Mopozap to the Ples Tambu. Most of it looked much the same; thick jungle, then thinner land cover as we rose up the mountains. But I was marking out in my mind the river crossings, the climbs, the valleys and the mountain peaks that we passed along the way. If we ever had to make the trip without our guides, we would need something besides the elevation map to follow.

I had the map next to my laptop, trying to mark the points where the photos were taken. It was harder work than it sounded. I was pretty sure that I'd got the Ples Tambu in the right place, and the crash site, but the points along the walk were educated guesswork. I didn't write anything on the map, just made dots. If anyone ever questioned me I would say I was taking photographs for *National Geographic*, and these were the locations where I took photographs of wildlife.

Of course, this argument would fall apart if I had a backpack full of big guns.

During our meal, Franz checked out my photos.

"Oh, Arthur, they are just like my parent's photos, but theirs were in black and white. You've really captured the colours of these creatures, they're terrific," said Franz.

"Thanks, Franz, now check out this folder and tell me what you think," I asked.

Franz looked at the Landscapes folder, flicking from one shot to the next.

"These are more boring, except for the waterfalls," Franz said.

"But can you see what I've done with them, the order they're in?" I asked.

"OK, there are jungle ones first, then the mountains," said Franz.

Dirk came over to look over his shoulder. "You're showing the landmarks along the way of our walk? And, yes, they do look boring, like second-rate photos. Well done," said Dirk, who'd worked it out.

"I'd like to know that we could get there without our guides in case anything ever happened to them, or us," I said.

"Yes. We've been lost up there before. Better to have some idea of where we are going," said Franz.

We returned to the coastline at the Wasur National Park, right on the border between Papua and New Guinea. We sailed across the border as evening was falling, watching the lights and campfires of the coastal villages as we passed.

Franz said, "Daru, where Jenella's family live, is just along here somewhere."

"That woman has come a long way, to be studying law in Cairns," I said.

"Jenella wants to help the cause, in her own way," said Dirk.

"Isn't it different now we're trading with them, as compared to being their prisoner?" I asked

"It's opened our eyes to what's really going on in that country," said Franz.

"I used to think the Indonesians were alright, just very business-like. But now I think they're a bunch of thieving, murdering bastards," said Dirk.

"They're no different to the English or the Dutch colonising other countries," I said.

"But that happened in the past, before the United Nations and Amnesty International and Human Rights and stuff," said Franz.

"It looks like the Indonesians have the answer to all that – no journalists, no tourists, no legal services, just kill the poor bastards and steal their land," I said.

"Yes, it's screwed, isn't it?" commented Dirk.

We sailed across the great southern bay to Port Moresby, docking at the Royal Papua Yacht Club. We had dinner there, then headed to Franz's flat in an expat compound, surrounded by high brick walls with razor wire on top. It had a swimming pool surrounded by frangipani trees, lush lawn and tropical flowers. Franz's unit had two bedrooms, an open-plan living area, a big tv, a small stereo and a big collection of CDs.

"Yeah, we could do with some music on the boat," said Dirk, as he flipped through the CDs.

"That will all fit on the boat. Are there many tourists in Port Moresby?" I asked.

"No, not like there are in Bali. The city is a bit dirty. There are nice beaches, but they are a way out of town. And PNG has the reputation of being dangerous. I think that keeps the tourists away more than anything," said Franz.

"Is it dangerous?" I asked.

"Well, when I go out to dinner with my friends in this city, all the men put their man-bags down on the table, and they all go 'clunk'!" said Franz.

"So there are thieves here?" asked Dirk.

"Maybe if there was more of a social safety net, it wouldn't be so bad," said Franz.

"No wonder the Papuans walk all the way here to buy guns," said Dirk.

"There are probably heaps of Papuan refugees too. But they all pretend to be New Guineans so they don't get deported," said Franz.

Next day, Franz and I went shopping for food supplies.

At the markets, Franz met a woman called Kate whom he knew from church.

"So Franz, are you back from the mine again?" asked Kate.

"Actually, I've finished up at the mine, and now I'm running fishing cruises with my friend Arthur here, and another mate," said Franz.

"Wow!" said Kate. "I've always wanted to go on a fishing cruise."

"We might be able to run a cruise up to New Ireland, Bougainville, and the Solomons this coming weekend," said Franz.

This was news to me.

Kate said, "I'll ask around at our youth group and see if anyone else fancies going."

"The limit is eight passengers, so don't invite too many people," said Franz.

"Would we all have to fly to Bali to do the cruise, or is it possible to leave from Port Moresby? It would save us all an airfare?"

Franz said, "I'll ask Dirk to see what can be done."

We got back to Franz's place and told Dirk; he thought it was a great idea.

"Can we get it together by the weekend?" asked Franz.

"I don't see why not, and it will keep us out of Indonesian waters for a bit," I said.

"Getting searched by that Customs guy has worried you, hasn't it?" asked Dirk.

"I don't want to sound paranoid, but I think that after we pay off the boat, we should think about another way to help the Papuans rather than selling them guns," I said.

Preparations were quickly made for the cruise, which Dirk had started referring to as "the church picnic".

On the day we were due to depart, the passengers started arriving not long after dawn. As soon as they were all aboard, we set off.

It was a lovely morning's sailing around the Loani peninsula, then north towards New Britain, passing some pristine smaller islands before slowing down on the south coast. We sailed east along the coast until we found a sheltered bay that looked perfect for some fishing, with reefs and a beach in sight for possible swimming. Everyone cast their lines. They didn't have to wait. Before long, fish were being hooked all around. Something big was also breaking off some lines, so a couple of the men changed to rods with heavier line, bigger hooks and larger bait. Franz was worried that it might be a shark, but Dirk showed him the images on the sonar navigation computer. We were close to the continental drop-off, so the big fish could be a large, deep sea fish.

The marlin showed itself soon, its large top fin breaking the water as it fought to get away. It was so strong it pulled the boat along for a bit.

Arthur advised the passengers, "If you catch this fish, it is photos only, then we are throwing it back."

The marlin proved too heavy to pull into the boat, so Franz and Mark, the guy who caught it, jumped in the inflatable dinghy, got close to it for a photo, then cut if free. Everybody talked excitedly about the marlin as they gathered on deck for lunch. It was the size of a man – actually longer if you included its pointy nose. I would not have liked cutting it up – it would have bled all over the deck. It was much easier cooking the plate-sized fish that everyone had caught. And our guests were so pleased to be able to eat their own catch.

During lunch, Dirk took the boat up through the passage between New Britain and New Ireland.

On the sheltered south side of New Ireland, the sea was shallower. We anchored close to shore.

I scouted around the reef and found a safe passage to the shore, I didn't see any sharks, so returning to the boat I declared, "I reckon here is a safe spot for some snorkelling."

Five of the fishing party said they'd join me, so we paired off as dive buddies, and jumped in. The equatorial water was quite warm, and teeming with life – turtles, dolphins, fish of all shapes and sizes, including squid and cuttlefish. We reached the shore and rested on the white sand, discussing what we'd seen.

On the camera, I showed Kate and her friends the underwater photos I'd taken.

"You should share them on Facebook and tag everyone in the group," suggested Kate.

Kayla, her journalist friend, asked me a lot about my photos. She flicked back to the Lorentz National Park photos and she asked me about those.

"I worked at Freeport Gold Mine for a while and visited the Lorentz National Park with some local guys. We can talk about it later. We've got to swim back to the boat. Let's talk at dinner."

We swam back to the boat, careful not to touch and damage the colourful corals, which grew like mushrooms, fans and lace curtains.

The snorkellers came back on board, the lines were pulled in, and Dirk set sail while Franz and I made dinner. Dirk wanted to make the crossing to Bougainville while it was still light, and anchor for the night in a sheltered spot.

At dinner, I spoke to Kayla, and we got talking about Papua.

Kayla said, "I've been to the Paniai Lakes, I walked in across the border, dressed like a village woman."

I said, "You're brave!"

Kayla said, "No, I was on assignment. I couldn't get a visa, so I decided to walk in like a local."

"So the border is fairly open?" I asked.

"There are border posts where the roads meet, but there are many footpaths through the jungle that are not patrolled. Local people usually don't have passports or visas, and just walk across for hunting or trade," explained Kayla.

I asked Kayla, "Where did you cross the border into Papua?"

Kayla said, "I drove my car up to Kopiago in the highlands, then walked to Tabubil. I stayed with a local family overnight, offering to pay for food and board. From Tabubil, I paid a guide to take me to a border crossing that was away from any paths. He pointed me in the direction of the path to Oksibil and left me there. I had a small backpack with water, food and a sleeping bag, and my phone to use as a camera. I also had a diary so I could make notes. I kept walking until I saw refugees coming my way. Then knew I must be on the right path. I kept passing refugees all the way to Oksibil. They were mostly mothers with children. So many had the same story – the father had been killed or taken away by the Indonesian police or military. The mothers decided to leave before the military came back for their sons as well. Many of these women were carrying babies or toddlers, as well as billums full of everything they owned."

"What route did you take from there?" I asked.

Kayla said, "I walked the tracks between small villages in the mountains, all the way to Tiom. The Indonesian authorities there ignored me. I wore running shoes for the big hikes, but took them off in the villages, to blend in with the locals. I had heard about the devastation of the Paniai Lakes. I had grown up hearing about this place as a paradise, supporting a large population of villages surrounding the three lakes, famous for fishing, and hosting large singsings with people from all around the district. People still lived in the high treehouses in the swampy areas near the lakes, so as to be up above the insect life. Others lived in huts and longhouses, travelled in canoes, and kept gardens.

"But the population harboured many Free Papua activists, who the Indonesian Army chased into the jungle. So the army decided to burn the forest around the lakes, including the treehouses and huts. They burned people's gardens and longhouses full of carvings and ancestral relics. Many escaped with just the clothes on their backs. Some old people burned to death in their huts. Then the rains came and washed the burnt trees and the topsoil into the lakes, causing flooding and muddying the drinking water. The people tried to rebuild, but it was certainly no longer a lakeside paradise."

"What does Paniai look like now?" I asked.

"I walked around the lakes, meeting people and interviewing them, staying with families or in schoolhouses. The forest still came up to the lakes on the west side, but the east and south areas have been burnt flat. Roads have been cut right around the smallest lake at the south, Tigi Barat, and between the middle lake, Yatamo, and the larger Paniai Barat in the north. Roads now run up the east side, connecting Paniai Timur to the other lakes, and the Indonesian towns to the south.

"These roads are used by loggers, traders, police and military, who all take whatever they can, maintaining a reign of terror. In 2015, they shot five teenage children during a protest over the bashing of another twelve-year-old boy. The Lake People, the Ekari, hate the Indonesians, and the feeling is mutual," said Kayla.

"Enarotali is now a small town, with lots of western-style buildings. Even an airstrip, a mosque, and a Catholic Church. I walked back along the tracks I walked in on," she added.

"So you could see why the Free Papua activists were fighting there?" I asked.

"It was like watching colonialism in motion, like seeing the history of my own country happening right there, right now," said Kayla.

"Did you take photos?" I asked

"I didn't take many, but I interviewed a lot of people, and wrote articles for the *National Newspaper* and the *Guardian*," replied Kayla. "You should write an article for *National Geographic* about the Lorentz National Park. Hardly anyone has been there recently, journalists are just not allowed in. You've been there, and you've got some great photos. I can help you write an article to go with them, or at least proofread it for you."

"Thanks. I'll type something up, and show you in the morning," I said.

"You've got to let the photos guide you from one part of the story to the next. Make a file of the photos you'll include, and add the captions you want with them," Kayla said. "Weave these things into your story, or at least give them a mention."

"I checked Google Maps, and found that some of the villages we walked past do have names, even if they weren't really used. But place names will locate the article much better," I said.

Kayla said, "OK, so the first paragraph has to paint a picture of the exotic unique location. It has to mention why the place is so special, what it has that nowhere else has. But the most important bit is how you got to see it, your adventure as a writer, how it changed your life."

"Well, I got to see it because my helicopter from work crashed and we got rescued by highlanders, but I signed a confidentiality agreement with the mine to not talk about that shit," I said.

"Damn. Well, we'll have to embroider the truth a bit. Did you visit by boat? Did you go up these rivers?" asked Kayla.

"Well, we did return by boat, but we just docked at Amamapare, then drove up to Timika, and into the park near Mopozap. Then we walked back up to the highlands," I said.

"Why exactly did you go back? I thought you'd be glad to be out of there after being lost for a few weeks?" asked Kayla.

"Ah, the boys and I saw a business opportunity, so we went back to the highlands to trade. We hired these guys, Rudol and Nollen, to be our guides, and they walked us up the dirt tracks into the mountains." I said.

"That's a great photo of those two. They'll be your 'friendly locals' who helped you get to your destination, and showed you their way of life," said Kayla, framing the story.

"Yeah, we would never have made it out of there, or back in, if it wasn't for them," I said.

"There's something you're not telling me, isn't there?" asked Kayla.

"OK, this bit isn't going in the article, and you've got to promise you won't mention it to anyone, alright?" I asked.

"I promise," said Kayla.

"The highlanders who rescued us actually kept us prisoner. They locked us in a cave. Liza was forced into being the second wife of their chief, Swando. A rescue chopper flew by, but they didn't let us out of the cave to flag it down. We were planning to escape by drugging our bottle of scotch with sedatives, but I was too injured to walk fast, so we were waiting for a good length of time. Meanwhile, Liza's husband decided to mount his own rescue mission. He arrived from Australia with his boss Dave in Dave's boat, and with his friend Steve who is a private investigator. They hired Rudol and Nollen to take them to where the crash had occurred using the co-ordinates from the mining company. Meanwhile, before we were able to escape, Konia and the Free West Papua guys came and took Dirk, Franz and Ken with them to trade for guns. Luckily, Steve had brought a few extra guns, so when they finally caught up with them, they were able to trade the guns for those guys, Dirk, Franz and Ken. Then they came back to look for Liza and me, but by this time we'd drugged the booze and made a run for it. Fortunately for us, Dave had hired a chopper instead of waiting with the boat. He found Liza and me and got us out," I said.

"Jesus Christ. You're right, you can't print that. You said you had a broken leg?" asked Kayla.

"Yeah. Thank God we had Doctor Liza with us," I replied.

"Right. How about this," said Kayla. "You were on a hiking trip with your workmates. You fell down a mountain and broke your leg. Your guides took you to a clinic run by the missionaries, where you stayed alone while your mates returned to get help. Your friends came back up one of the navigable rivers on the boat, then hiked back to where you were. Their guides helped them find you again and helped you back to the boat. You saw all this amazing stuff while you were recovering, and on the journeys in and out," Kayla summed up.

"That sounds great. We don't have to mention the mine, the choppers or anything. And can we not mention the exact route that we took?" I asked. "Ilaga and Jila are too close to the Ples Tambu, so I don't want to mention them."

"There is another village in the park called Jita. I think that you went to Jita, not Jila. Your workmates run fishing cruises, they already had the boat. You were looking for the highland crayfish, even though they are at the lakes more than in the national park streams. No one's going to really know that. You had fishing gear in your backpacks, not guns," Kayla said.

"Uh, we didn't really carry guns," I said.

"Look, I'm not stupid," said Kayla. "I worked out what your 'trading opportunity' was. You didn't meet the Free West Papua guys. The Indonesians leave the locals in the park alone. There are too many missionaries keeping an eye on things in there. The Indonesians are busy raping the rest of the land. They leave the park alone. You stayed in the park. The locals helped you, fed you, showed you the wildlife," said Kayla.

"Yes, you're right. We can mention how degraded the other parts of the coast looked, the clear felling, the poor farming, the run-off, and we'll say that the clear rivers attracted us into the park, along with the pristine jungle," I said.

"Now we're cooking," said Kayla.

The next day, we sat and wrote the rest of the story, with a sly reference to our fishing cruise business. We consulted maps and rewrote the route I'd taken.

Kayla knew some great folk stories about the various animals, particularly the bird of paradise, and the crocodile, and they helped to fill in some colour to the story. She also knew the names of many trees and flowers, which gave the readers more things to identify in the photographs.

"Can we mention your friend Liza by name?" asked Kayla.

"I'll have to ring and ask if that's OK, and run the story by her," I said.

Later that morning I called Liza from our satellite phone.

She answered, saying, "Hi Arthur, I'm surprised to hear from you again!"

I said, "Did you find Konia in Ilaga?"

Liza said, "Konia's recovered from his injury. He had an infected bullet wound, but I managed to clean it up."

"I think I mentioned that I am writing a photo story for *National Geographic*, and I've changed some of the facts to fit with our confidentiality agreement," I told her.

Liza agreed. "Yes, I only told the Freeport people what they needed to know. I have been setting up medical communication stations in the villages, including a communication station in Ilaga."

"Which other villages in the national park will you visit?"

"I have set up stations in Beoga, Wangbe and Geselma too," Liza replied.

"Is it alright if I say that you were the doctor who fixed my leg at Ilaga?"

She laughed, "It's was fine with me. If you don't mention the mine, we shouldn't be contravening our gag orders."

Kayla showed me the photos that she had on her phone including one of herself with Benny Wenda and his family – the best-known freedom activists on the big island. Benny and his close family were exiled in England now, but travelled a lot for the independence cause.

Her other photos were mostly of people, with some landscapes to demonstrate the way the land was used, the building materials and the sizes of the villages.

That afternoon, we headed across to the New Georgia group of islands. Even from a distance, they looked like something from another planet. The steep volcanic islands rose like green jewels out of an azure sea. Wood and grass huts clung to the hills and the beaches. The Solomon Islanders were out fishing, too, and greeted us as we sailed past. We found a quiet spot just off Vonavona Island, dropped anchor, and fished and snorkelled the rest of the day away. We stayed there for the night, certain that if the next day was as good as this, it would be the best fishing trip yet.

The third day, we took the boat to Santa Isabel, then to Honiara for a lunch stop, and to pay for visas. After that, we sailed through the afternoon to return to Port Moresby, with everyone downing some drinks and relaxing. The group disembarked, after which we took the opportunity to check our emails from Franz's place. There were more booking requests from Bali.

At Honiara, I'd bought a newspaper, the *Solomon Star News*. It made me realise how little I knew about the country or its politics. The paper gave me an idea about the country, but it would be good to have Kayla's opinion as well.

In Paniai and Freeport

Mike had loved having me at home again, making my time off as special as he could. I'd floated the idea of asking the Cairns doctors to be on call in the case of any really bad emergencies, which Mike and Dave had both agreed to. They said they'd ask around among the other doctors in Cairns, as well.

Mike bought me some nicotine patches and gum for the times when I couldn't smoke. He wasn't hassling me to quit, just trying to help me with the withdrawal symptoms, because I could get a bit cranky when I went all day at the clinic without a ciggie.

In our office in Freeport Grasberg, the whiteboard now showed a map of the surrounding areas, with village names, field officer names and phone numbers. Janette had worked out a roster for visits, with mornings booked at the Freeport clinics, and afternoons travelling to the field offices, two and three at a time. There were Timika and Akimuga to the south, Ilaga, Tiom, Jila to the east, Desa Wanda, Beoga and Bandar Udara Sinak to the north, and Wandai, Enarotali in the Paniai Lakes area to the west. These were the villages with solar panels, satellite phones, and a field officer to use them. There were other villages marked in between as well, so they could learn the location names.

Janette wrote out a rough schedule of visits, based on field officers' reports. Today's run would be the western run to Wandai, Enarotali near the Paniai Lakes. Wandai was the first stop.

When we arrived, I was shocked to see the number of Indonesian military personnel walking around this poor village, carrying guns, and gun-toting police officers too. As we flew over Wandai, I was shocked to see that fire had obviously wiped out this village recently, and the locals had been rebuilding with whatever they could find. Very few trees were left. Burnt trunks were used in some structures, along with canvas, bamboo, grass thatching, whatever could be found. Everyone in this village looked to be suffering from malnutrition, except for the army and police. These were the worst conditions I'd seen. I took some photographs to document the poverty, and then dressed tropical sores and old burns that weren't healing or had become infected.

Enarotali was the last stop for the day, quite close to Lake Paniai. So close, in fact, that I noticed the effects of recent flooding on the walls of buildings, and the deep gutters that hadn't drained away properly, leaving large smelly puddles of mud and rotting vegetation by the sides of the tracks through the village. Here, the people had symptoms of malaria, fevers, sweating, loss of weight. I stayed until the end of the day. As I headed back to the chopper, I saw the fishermen returning to the village in their canoes, which were full of fish and crayfish. The children ran down to meet their fathers, and the women waited in small groups, talking. The military approach the boats, taking fish and crayfish from the fishermen. No money changed hands. They just helped themselves to the fruits of these men's labour.

Disgusted, the pilot and I flew back to Grasberg, shaking our heads in disbelief.

I was working at the Freeport clinic when Ken came in.

"Ken, I'm surprised to see you. You're usually so healthy," I said.

"I'm not really sick, but I could do with a doctor's certificate for a few days off," said Ken.

"Well, what shall I say is wrong? Migraines? Back ache? Some other difficult to prove illness?" I asked.

"Ah, you'd better say migraines, or I'll have to fake walking funny and having trouble standing up and sitting down," said Ken.

"Right. Migraine it is then. I'll write you a certificate. Now, what's really wrong?" I asked.

"Well, I don't know if you know, but I've been going along to Tok Pisin classes at the community centre, and I speak it pretty well now," said Ken.

"That's great, Ken," I said.

"So, I've been listening in on what the locals have been saying. They reckon that there's going to be a big protest close to here, up in one of the mountain villages. Some of them are taking leave from work to go to the protest. I haven't been able to work out where it is, but it's going to happen on Friday night."

"This Friday night?" I asked.

"As far as I can tell, yes," said Ken.

"Jesus Christ. I'm going to need backup," I said.

"Will you fly in to help the wounded?" asked Ken.

"That's my job. Luckily Doctor Carmichael will be on his way over," I said.

"So you're supposed to be knocking off?" Ken asked.

"Yeah, but I'll stick around to help. Maybe I can get Mike and Dave to fly over too," I said.

"Well, if you need a big bloke to help out, just call me," offered Ken.

"I might very well ring you. I might need a big bloke to help me pick up patients. Thanks for the heads up, Ken," I said.

"Oh, you'd be surprised if you heard the gossip I've been listening in to. I've learned all kinds of things. The bosses have got some great nicknames. They call me 'big dick', but I think they call all the tall guys that," laughed Ken.

"Oh, I wonder what they call me?" I asked.

"They call you 'Pretty doctor lady'. They talk about you a lot, because you've been treating their uncles and delivering their nieces and nephews," said Ken.

"Oh, that's sweet. I must learn more of the language too," I said.

"Classes are Monday evenings. I wish I'd started years ago. It's easy to learn and it helps with heaps of things," said Ken.

"Thanks Ken. I hope I won't need you, but I'll call if I do."

I called Mike and Dave. Mike booked his flight straight away. Dave had to find other doctors to cover for them both in Cairns, then he booked a flight too. I asked them to bring extra medical supplies with them, so they both brought the largest first aid kit they could carry, stuffed with supplies. Unlike the mining company, which ran charter flights for their workers, the doctors had to fly commercial airlines, which meant flying Cairns to Bali, then Bali to Timika. So that meant four and a half hours to Bali, then three and a half hours back to Timika, whereas a direct flight would only have taken one and a half hours.

KONIA
Planning for battle

At Paniai, both machine guns had made it to the training grounds now. More than twenty men had been trained to use them, with only a little bit of ammunition being sacrificed. The men could all assemble the guns, knew how to feed in the ammo, and how to aim and fire. We worked out the pairs they would work in, and who was going to feed and who was going to fire.

Kupsy and our men were now ready to use the M60s, but we had to plan the 'when' and the 'where'.

There was a military base at Enarotali, so that ruled the lakes out. It would be too easy for the soldiers to get reinforcements; they could drive on the roads or fly to the air strip. It had to be in a much less accessible place, but it still needed good ground cover, few roads, and at least one track, if not numerous tracks, for the men to escape along after the fight.

The helicopters would come, as they had come before, but now that we had something to shoot them with it would not be such a one-sided massacre. We sent scouts up into the highland villages north of the national park, to see where the people were prepared to protest, and see where we could dig the guns in.

The scouts came back with good news. The villagers in the highlands were all sick of the Indonesian Army marching into their schools, raising their flag and forcing the kids to salute it. They didn't like the officers telling their women and little girls to cover their heads. We weren't Muslims, so why should we dress up to please these people? Why should our little girls cover their heads when they want to run and climb trees? The people of Mulia, Sinak, Homeyo, Agadugume, Sugpa, Puncak and Bibibida had all said they would host a Free West Papua rally with a flag-raising ceremony. So now I could look at maps and see which of these places might be best to try out our new weapons.

A group of village leaders came down to Paniai Timur and had a big meeting in the local church. We were supposed to be talking about famine relief, but instead we quickly got down to the business of organising an independence rally. At first, all the villages wanted to host the rally. But when I explained that the army might very well show up with guns and helicopters, many changed their minds.

Kupsy suggested that small children and anyone vulnerable should perhaps stay at home and not attend the rally, or even leave the village entirely to 'visit relatives'. People really began to understand what might be in store.

Then an old man called Loodstar, from the village of Mulia, spoke up. Loodstar said, "I am old enough to remember the Dutch taking over our area, as well as the English. When they left, the Indonesians stepped in. I am sick of other people being in charge of our land."

The village leaders all made sounds of agreement.

Loodstar continued, "Every man and woman in our village feels the same way. We're sick of the Indonesian Army coming into our village, making us salute the Indonesian flag and sing the national anthem. It makes me sick."

We all shouted, "Yes!"

"Our village only has one road in, and it comes from Tiom. To get here to Paniai, I had to walk a difficult track to the west. The army would take a long time to walk from here to Mulia. They could get there faster from Tiom, north of the range and to the east, but that road passes some very narrow breaks in the mountains. We can cut down a big tree or start a landslide with boulders blocking the only road into our village. There are walking tracks to the north towards Sinak, and to the south, towards Agadugume, and the national park. We heard there is a safe place for fighters in the park with a track that leads there. We still have plenty of forest on our mountains, it is only the valleys that have been felled. Our village would be proud to have a 'Papua Merdeka rally'. We invite men and women from all the surrounding areas who want their voices to be heard and to make a difference."

When Loodstar sat down there was a general murmur of agreement. The fighters and the supporters would walk to Mulia by night. We would take what was needed in separate trips, in case anyone was intercepted. We would set up our guns and create the landslide or fell a tree to block the road.

Once preparations were made, we'd call the rally. People in the surrounding villages could care for any children, young mums or old people who didn't want to be there for the action. The meeting finished with a sense of achievement; a decision had been made by the group. Plans were drawn up and action was going to take place. We'd scare the hell out of those Indonesians and hopefully send some of them there as well.

WIRA

Kopassus

Colonel Yuda had asked me to check with our man at Freeport Mine about the recent helicopter crash.

Sergeant Rick at Freeport told me that there'd been a helicopter crash, and that two of the survivors, Doctor Liza Fraser and Ken Knight, had returned to work at the mine. He made no mention of Arthur Neilson or the other two.

Perhaps Wayan Chan was right to be suspicious.

A search on the internet revealed that the other three men ran a fishing cruise business out of Bali, which appeared to be above board.

I reported back to Colonel Yuda, who was his usual angry self. He didn't want to hear any reports, nor did he want to do any investigations himself. The only thing he wanted to do was shoot the Papuans.

He appeared to be keeping a tally of how many Papuans he, personally, or his Special Forces had killed. For him it was like trophy hunting.

Then Major Honan from Timika Barracks rang me.

"Kopassus. Wira speaking," I said.

"Honan from Timika here. I've had a couple of reports that I need to inform Colonel Yuda about," Honan said.

"Colonel Yuda is not taking calls right now. If you give me the information, I'll ensure that it passes to Colonel Yuda directly," I said.

"Right then, Wira. I'll keep it short," said Honan. "Wayan Chan of the border patrol has reported an Australian and two Dutch on working visas making suspect landings at Amamapare, while our source at Paniai reports that there is gun training going on there among the freedom fighters. We think they are preparing for some action, but we aren't sure where or when."

"I have taken down that information, and I will report it directly to Colonel Yuda. Thank you, Major Honan," I replied.

I wrote these things up in my weekly report. Colonel Yuda would be pleased, but only if I could give him more reports and evidence.

Yuda likes nothing better than hunting down Papuan men in the jungle, preferably from the safety of a helicopter. He's a blood-thirsty man, and he frightens me.

The battle at Mulia

In Mulia, the men were busy digging in. The village was in a steep valley, so the big guns were being dug in halfway up the mountainsides, angled so that all directions were covered. Stone walls with an iron roof were built around the gunner's positions. These were then topped with vegetation. Other gunning positions were built for the riflemen, lower down the slopes and closer to where the action would take place. Down the valley towards Tiom, a 'landslide' of logs and boulders was set up, stacked above the only road into the village. The tracks to the other villages were maintained, with stone steps set into muddy slopes, and lean-to shelters constructed at intervals, to shelter from rain or to keep out of sight.

Even the school kids were painting T-shirts and protest signs, though most of them would be evacuated on the day. Nollen was in charge of leading a group of kids to the next village and keeping them safe. Kupsy was supposed to be doing the same thing with some of the elders.

The day of the protest dawned, with protesters travelling through the night from other villages and towns all around. Some people drove, leaving their vehicles by the road on the way into town, well ahead of the landslide. Nollen left the village with his group of school kids via the northern track to Sinak, supposedly to visit that village's school and see the local waterfall. Kupsy attempted to take his group of elders on a similar walk, but some of them refused. They were supposed to go to Malagaineri for a card game at the little church there, but some old men preferred to remain in Mulia for the protest.

The protesters dressed in red, white and blue T-shirts with a white star on a field of red, and painted blue and white stripes on their faces, arms and chests. In defiance, some chose to wear their traditional clothing, which they'd previously been ordered by the Indonesians not to do, because it was deemed 'immodest'. There was singing, dancing, eating and drinking in the lead up to the official protest.

Local police arrived on the scene well before the flag-raising ceremony and were quickly using their phones and two-way radios to call for backup. When I saw this happening, I decided it was time to trigger the landslide.

A runner was sent to the men further up the mountain. They could see police and military vehicles coming along the road from Tiom when they triggered the landslide. Some boulders and logs didn't fall immediately and needed some pushing, but soon a huge pile of debris blocked the road causing all incoming vehicles to halt behind it. The men quickly retreated so by the time the police and military started climbing over the huge pile of logs and rocks they were long gone. Meanwhile, in the village, the local police were waiting for backup before they tried to control the protest.

The flag-raising ceremony was underway by the time dozens of armed police and army men came striding into the centre of Mulia. They shouted orders at the assembled crowd to take down the flag, remove their protest shirts and put down their signs. The crowd ignored them and, if anything, waved their placards more vigorously, shouting "Papua Merdeka! Free Papua! Papua Merdeka!"

Some protesters filmed the action on their phones, and it was these people the police targeted. As they backed into the crowd, the police and military came forward, guns drawn.

The first shots were fired. People started screaming, running, and getting down on the ground. A couple of protesters were hit, and friends ran to their aid. But the firing was coming back at the police and military, from inside huts and houses, the school, behind trees. The military men gave orders to split into groups and advance on the gunmen. The shooters concentrated on their targets. For once, they had cover while the police and army were in the open. They found their marks, again and again, and the military men couldn't get near them.

The commanding officer could see they'd been drawn into an ambush. He must have radioed for helicopter backup, because two choppers came in from the direction of Tiom.

The choppers had a gunman on each side; they were waiting to get close enough to see us clearly.

Suddenly, a hail of bullets hit the helicopters. The spray of machine-gun fire took out a gunman in one of them straight-away. The chopper that lost its gunman turned around so that the other shooter could aim at our gun placements. The second chopper took a hit, too, from fire coming from the other side of the valley. Although there were spare gunmen in each chopper, it took time to help the stricken co-worker out of his seat, so another gunman could take his place. Critical time.

Our shooters on the hills kept them under unrelenting, continuous fire. By now the first chopper had lost both its shooters, so the pilot decided to turn back. The pilot of the second chopper had taken a bullet and was panicking, trying to lift the vehicle out of the guns' range. The first helicopter completed its turn but in the process, exposed its fuel tank to the machine gun. A hit, and it promptly burst into flames, sending the chopper into a dive towards the ground. The explosion shook the second chopper, and now two guns were focused on it with deadly accuracy. The pilot passed out, and as his hands left the controls, the chopper tipped on its side, bouncing off the mountain and catapulting into the valley below. There was another explosion as its fuel tank ruptured, sending bits of chopper and men flying in all directions.

The machine-gun operators gave a cheer, but their celebrating didn't last long.

Two more helicopters from the direction of Paniai were approaching, and they had seen the fate of the other aircraft. Their guns sprayed the valley as they came in, penetrating the huts and houses and causing pandemonium below. They flew in a formation, with the front chopper shielding the one at the back, as they approached the machine guns.

The freedom fighters focused on the front chopper as they came into range.

The gunman in the helicopter took out one of our machine gunners. His feeder quickly helped him out of their shelter so that the next shooter and feeder could quickly take their places. Enraged, they aimed straight at one of the pilots, peppering him with shells. As the leading chopper went down, the second one came in, guns blazing out both sides aiming at both our guns. This time our feeder in the other gun placement was shot. The shooter behind him grabbed his body and pulled him out of the dugout, as the second feeder took his place. The shooter only stopped firing when his chain of ammunition ran out.

The second feeder was on the job immediately. They'd inflicted carnage on both shooters in the chopper; one man had fallen out the door, the other had been pulled back in by his second officer. The chopper passed the gunner's positions, turned, and came in for another run. Our ammunition was running low now. The village machine gunners prayed to the Crocodile God. They shot at the pilot, the gunners, the petrol tanks, as the helicopter kept changing positions. Something went wrong with the tail blade and the helicopter spun in the air, out of control. It circled towards the ground, the body of the vehicle slamming into the dirt with the full force of its rotation. There was another explosion, then an eerie silence as the protesters surveyed the wrecked village.

Then the wails of the injured started. And all attention turned to them.

I came down from the machine-gun pit, taking charge of the situation. The guns were already being dismantled, ready to be carried away.

"Bring any injured to the schoolhouse! Wrap any wounds in T-shirts or cloth!" I shouted.

I ran to the schoolhouse, a two-room building peppered with bullets. The phone hung from the wall, but it was still working. I called Doctor Liza's number.

"Doctor Liza, we are in Mulia, between Homeyo and Agadagume. We have many people injured. Oh, please, help us!" I said.

"I will come straight away. I have other doctors. Please make sure no one shoots at us," said Liza.

I went outside to shout to everyone. "There is another helicopter coming, carrying doctors. Do not shoot at them. All guns should be moving away from the village now. The army will regroup and come back soon. No more shooting!" I yelled.

The ground soldiers had retreated once the helicopter battle started. They'd gone back down the road to their vehicles behind the landslide. There were burning helicopters and buildings, soldiers and villagers lying dead all around. We gathered the wounded who could be moved, while others were attended to on the ground. It was chaos. I saw a villager lying close to a burning building, so I ran to help him. The young man was unconscious but alive and bleeding, though not too badly, so I picked him up and carried him to the schoolhouse.

The schoolhouse was already full of injured people. I laid the young man on the ground outside and removed his T-shirt to use as a cover for his bleeding leg. People were ripping up curtains and bedsheets to use as bandages and fetching buckets of water to clean the injured as best they could.

It only took fifteen minutes for Liza's chopper to get to here.

The aftermath

T he first thing we saw was a mess of crashed helicopters, smoke rising up from the valley floor, then a scene of devastation. The pilot landed in a paddock away from the fires. We quickly alighted and ran towards the building where people were gathering together the wounded. We were wearing white lab coats with big red crosses on our backs and carrying medical kits.

Dave naturally took charge. Years of being a senior doctor kicked in, and he quickly prioritised the worst injuries, assigning Fred, Mike and myself to different cases. Then Dave looked at another serious patient with gunshot wounds to the head. Ken and Konia helped to lift patients onto desks, and many others helped the doctors by fetching supplies, holding dressings on wounds, or with whatever else needed to be done.

The army had regrouped, reported what had happened back to the barracks, and waited to receive further orders. The order came to round up any civilians left in the village and to find the weapons, particularly the machine guns. Having evacuated their own wounded down the road to Tiom, the rest of the troops marched back into the village. Konia saw them coming, and ran down the paddock towards the trees, and away into the forest. Many of the other men also ran, leaving mostly women and some older men helping the doctors. The troops surrounded the schoolhouse, with an officer in charge of them. He ordered the troops to start taking the villagers away. Dave looked up from his bandaging and spoke to the army officer.

"I'm Doctor David Stone from Australia. I'm requesting that you leave these people here to help me with the wounded," said Dave.

"I am Major Honan, the commanding officer of this unit, and my orders are to arrest all the fighters in this village," said Honan.

"These women and old men were not fighting, they were only protesting, and now they are helping my medical team. Why don't you chase the men with the guns who ran into the forest?" asked Dave.

"My orders are to arrest everyone in this village," said Honan.

"Do you think these girls shot your helicopters? Are you too afraid to chase the men with the guns? How about you leave these people here for an hour and come back to arrest them later?" said Dave, not losing his cool.

The officer left two troops standing guard over the schoolhouse, then went outside to organise the rest of his troops. He clearly hadn't expected to find an international medical team in attendance.

Inside the schoolhouse we were quickly assessing the patients in our care.

"This man has multiple internal injuries. We'll have to evacuate him to Freeport or to Timika," I informed the others.

Fred said, "My patient also has multiple injuries including a punctured lung. He will need evacuating as well."

"My patient has lost a lot of blood from a neck wound, and I think he is terminal. I've bandaged him and will move on to another patient," said Mike.

While Dave reported, "This patient has head injuries and is stable for now, but he'll require evacuation as well. Liza, can you and Fred take those two to Grasberg? If you think they need to go on to Timika, one of you go with them, the other come back in that chopper or another chopper. Ken, please fetch the stretcher from the chopper. Max the pilot can help you to carry it."

So Fred and I evacuated the first two patients to our base clinic. Fortunately, Janette had recruited four nurses in the previous weeks, and at least two of them would be on duty. We could do surgery at Freeport if we needed to. Otherwise, the hospital at Timika was only another chopper ride away.

Dave and Mike struggled on. They prepared the next two cases for evacuation, then decided to work on the lesser injuries themselves in the schoolhouse. They had several patients with bullet wounds in the arms and legs. These cases, they could handle here. They disinfected the desk and themselves, and then their patients. Then they operated to extract the bullets and fragments, sewing up the wounds and incisions. They'd done three of these procedures when they saw the army officer return through the village. His men had rounded up about fifteen villagers and led them out at gunpoint back towards their vehicles. He ignored the doctors as they worked. Maybe he'd had orders to leave them alone. After a couple more procedures, I came back in the helicopter.

"We operated on those two men at our clinic. Fred did a great job, fixing the punctured lung guy first, then the other man. He is staying to organise the clinic for more patients and to watch those first two," I said.

"Great. We have two more who need evacuating. This head injury might need to go to Timika for brain surgery. If you can take care of these two, Mike and I can deal with these other patients here," said Dave.

"Right, I'll take these guys, and I'll send another chopper to pick you guys up and any others who may need to come with you," I said.

Ken helped carry the next patients to the chopper and went with me back to Freeport. We worked into the night, patching up the wounded.

Back at the village an elderly woman organised lining up the dead across the road at the little church. There were eleven dead villagers, and three dead soldiers, with more trapped in the burning helicopters. The fires still burned; all the people left there were helping the wounded – there was no one to put the fires out.

The clinic at Freeport was full. The two doctors' rooms had two patients in each, and Dave was asleep on a bench in the nurses' room. I'd taken Mike back to my room in the exec quarters, and Fred was in his flat. As soon as we woke, we headed back to the clinic to check on our patients. The man with the head injury had already been flown on to Timika with Fred. Mike and Dave had brought with them the man with the neck injury who had not died, but who certainly needed a blood transfusion. These Papuans were tough men. Stoic, they'd made little noise despite horrific injuries, which must have caused a lot of pain.

Fred decided that he wanted to return to Mulia to check on the other injured people. Dave said that he would go with him, and Mike and I could stay with the injured at the Freeport clinic.

We had breakfast in the canteen. Many local workers dropped by our table to thank us for our work the day before.

DAVE

Back to Mulia

F red and I flew back to the village. The landslide hadn't been cleared yet, but the fires were out. The children and old people had returned to the village, and there was activity everywhere. Many of the injured were still near the schoolhouse, beside which a cooking fire had been built. Saucepans, plates and cups had been brought in, along with sacks of rice and baskets of vegetables and bananas.

Women and children were salvaging building materials and rebuilding huts. Some injured men, boys and girls were digging a long pit behind the church – a mass grave. Fred and I greeted the injured men and women, checking for swellings, replacing bandages and dressing the smaller wounds. Some people sat with the dead, washing their bodies and wailing. The priest had arrived, a local man, comforting the relatives of the deceased. There would be a funeral later today. The bodies couldn't lie out in the heat for a long time. Some were wrapped in sarongs, others covered by banana leaves.

A young woman approached me.

"Doctor Dave, please take my phone. I have video on there of the protest, and of the attack. I don't want to be caught with it. Please, put it on the Free West Papua website. Anyone can upload to there. You don't need a password for my phone," said the girl.

"What is your name, dear? How can I get your phone back to you?" I asked.

"I am Jetex, but I'm not from this village. I walked up from Enarotali for the protests, and I'll have to go back soon," she said.

"Liza has a field officer in Enarotali. I can send the phone back there," I said.

"Thank you, but please erase the video first. I don't want to go to jail for making that video," pleaded Jetex.

"I understand. I will download it, then delete it from your phone. You are a brave woman for filming yesterday," I said.

Jetex said, "I met a New Guinean lady who came here and took photos. She said it was important to have evidence of what was happening here."

"She was right. It's against international law to fire on unarmed protesters. The Indonesians obviously weren't expecting anyone to fight back," I replied.

"I am worried for the men they caught and took away. What will they do to them?" Jetex asked.

"I expect the military will question them about who organised the fighting and the guns."

"I hope they let them go. We need the men to work the fields and to fish," said Jetex.

"I will upload your video. It is important evidence. Amnesty International would be interested in seeing it as well," I said.

So Fred and I flew back to Freeport. Fred had a video program on his computer, which enabled him to upload Jetex's short film.

We all crowded behind his desk to look at the footage. The protest was a colourful event, with singing and dancing. The police officers could be seen looking on, and then obviously calling in the army. The army arrived on foot and formed a double line in front of the protest. As the West Papuan flag went up the pole, they opened fire on the crowd. The footage became jumbled then as Jetex ran for cover – it looked like she hid behind a tree. As the shooting was returned by hidden riflemen, the army men also sought cover, and dragged their wounded back with them. The film stopped, then started again. Two helicopters arrived and started spraying the village with machine-gun fire. But gunmen who were dug in up the mountains started returning their fire, and one chopper was seen coming down. Then Jetex must have run away again to be further from the action. From a more distant point, she filmed the second chopper burning on the ground, then a third and fourth joining the battle from the opposite direction. Jetex filmed these choppers also coming down. A final piece of film showed the injured being carried to the schoolhouse with the familiar figure of Konia organising bandages and buckets. It was hard to watch the uncovered injuries, pouring blood, the people covered in dirt, some screaming.

"Right, well, I just have to edit this into a format that is easy to upload. I will leave it just as she filmed it," said Fred.

"It's pretty clear who started the shooting, both on the ground, and from the air," said Liza.

"Yes, we would definitely call this a war crime, if this was a war," I said.

"Upload it, Fred, and if you don't want to endanger your job by saying it was you, you can say it was me," said Mike. "I'm probably safer in Australia than you guys are here. I can afford a good lawyer."

When he had converted the video file, Fred found the Free Papua page, and worked out how to upload. "It looks like we can upload this film anonymously."

So he just added the place name, Mulia, and the date of the protest. The footage alone would tell the story.

We checked on our patients, changed dressings, checked temperatures, pulses and blood pressures. The men were doing as well as could be expected. Janette came in and told Fred and Liza that one of the mining execs had come by to speak to them, so they went out to meet him in Janette's office.

LIZA

Talking to the boss

"I heard that you flew in patients to treat them here. Is this within the protocols that we have established?" asked Jim Sinclair.

"Our guidelines are to treat the villagers at the field offices, unless they are critical and require treatment in a clinic," I replied.

"Are these men in a critical condition?" asked Jim.

"Yes, myself and Doctor Fraser removed bullets from their lungs and abdominal organs," said Fred.

"What, here?" asked Jim.

"Yes, we operated in these rooms. Another man had brain injuries, so we flew him to Timika Hospital. We are not equipped for brain surgery here," I said.

"I didn't think you'd be doing any surgery here," said Jim.

"The equipment we requisitioned was surgical equipment. If there was a mining accident, we want to be ready to keep our miners alive," said Fred.

"But these patients are locals," said Jim.

"It is part of our Community Outreach program to treat the locals. The Indonesians do not provide them with healthcare. Quite the opposite, in fact," I said.

"Alright. I just don't want our company to be sued if anyone dies here," said Jim.

"These people don't have doctors, and they definitely don't have lawyers. Our company pays tax to this government, who in turn does not provide for these people. This government is shooting these people from helicopters, so the least we can do, as decent human beings, is to treat their wounds. We are all getting rich out of this mine, and these people are being slaughtered. As a doctor, I have taken an oath to protect human life. That's not just rich white lives, that's all lives," I said.

"I agree with everything that Doctor Fraser has just said. And you will find that the other Doctor Fraser, and Doctor Stone, who flew in from Cairns to help, feel the same way," said Fred.

"How did the other doctors know to come here?" asked Jim.

"We have a lot of bilingual workers at this mine. It was reported to us that the locals would have a protest, and in this country, that usually precedes a bloodbath. At the recent Lake Paniai massacre, the wounded were left to die. We did not want that to happen to our local villagers," I said.

"I see. If you could write a report about this event, we will include it in our annual report. Thinking about it, it does a lot to justify the additional expense of extra medical staff and equipment. Thanks for your good work," said Jim, as he left.

ARTHUR

Back to the forest

After the Solomons cruise, we headed straight for Manila. We bought a copy of the Indonesian newspaper, the *Jakarta Post*, but there was no news from Papua. I'd been reading the PNG *Post-Courier* and the *National*, since I knew that Kayla wrote for them. But these papers had very little news from West Papua either.

I emailed *National Geographic* the article and thought about Kayla – a lot. Dirk, Franz and I discussed our finances, and whether it would be safer to operate cruises out of Bali or Port Moresby.

Han met us in Manila where we bought another load, including five machine guns this time and a few rifles and ammo.

Surprisingly, *National Geographic* wrote back and said they were interested in the story. But they said they wanted me to write more about Kayla and how she fitted into the story.

I rang Kayla to tell her the good news.

"*National Geographic* want to print the story, but they want to know more about you, Kayla," I said.

"Wow, Arthur, that is fantastic. Some photo-journalists try for years before they get a story accepted there!" said Kayla.

"So, what shall I say about you? How will you fit into the story?" I asked.

"Well, we could tell the truth and say you met me on a fishing cruise. You showed me your photos, and I helped you to identify the animals and plants, and told you some of the local legends," said Kayla.

"What should I say about your background?" I asked.

"Well, you could say that my name is Kayla Yari, and my uncle is a government minister. I studied journalism at the Port Moresby University, then did a cadetship at a local radio station. I had submitted some political articles to *The National* and had some printed. When a full-time job came up at the paper, I applied and got it. Some people said I only got the job because of my uncle," Kayla said.

"Look, Kayla, some people say anything. They knew your writing, because they had printed some of your articles already," I said.

"That's right. I wrote political articles, about our church's work with the Papuan refugees. I interviewed the Archbishop, a couple of priests and refuge workers. I also covered a volcanic eruption in a mountain village, and I drove up with a car full of food, water and medical supplies," said Kayla.

"That takes commitment. You didn't shy away from serious issues, you went to a disaster area and took much-needed supplies," I said.

"Yeah, the newspaper wasn't sure that a woman could cover political stories, but I already had. They sent me to cover the tsunami and flooding in the Solomons, and then they sent me to see if I could cover the Paniai massacre. Our journalists only occasionally get visas to cross into Indonesia. I didn't get one. But I told my editor that I was planning on going anyway. He was OK with that and even gave me some hints about how to get away with it," said Kayla.

"Wow. So your boss encouraged you to cross the border illegally?" I asked.

"Sometimes it's the only way to get a story. He was right that the Indonesian cops would leave a black woman with no shoes alone. He said I was probably more likely to pull it off than a man," said Kayla.

"Kayla, you've really got a lot of guts," I said.

"Arthur, growing up here, we hear stories about Papua, but we are not allowed to go there. It's like a forbidden fruit. I've wanted to go there since I was a little girl. The way our priest talked about the Lorentz National Park, he made it sound like paradise – a place where the Asmat could live their traditional lives, at one with nature. You're so lucky to have seen it," said Kayla.

"Well, we are going in a different way this time. We've seen how well guarded the pipeline that comes from the mine to Amamapare where the ore gets loaded into the ships is. We don't want to drive past there packing our load. So I'll drive up and pick up Rudol and Nollen, then we'll sail up one of the quiet rivers and hike up through the national park. The road to Timika was the weakest link in our chain, so we're going to minimise that risk this time," I said.

"Arthur, you know I really worry about you. I want you to be as safe as you can. Come back and see me when you can," Kayla said.

"Kayla, I think about you a lot when I'm walking through the forest, and camping in my sleeping bag. You're the most interesting woman I've ever met. I can't wait to see you again," I said.

"Well, stay alive, and make some time to see me between your adventures," said Kayla.

"I will. As soon as we've paid off the boat and we're just going to do fishing cruises. I will have time off between trips. We hope to do more trips out of Port Moresby, and I'm thinking of basing myself there. I can't just live on the boat," I said.

"Good luck, Arthur. Papua Merdeka," said Kayla.

"You are my reason to come back. I'll see you soon," I said.

I finished writing the article, giving Kayla credit for the identification of all the species and the folk stories that went with them. I made it sound like I was the expat in a strange place, and she was the local who could explain the details to me. It gave balance and local knowledge to the story.

I did think about her a lot. She was so intelligent and brave, and she looked great in a swimsuit.

We didn't have any cruise bookings, so we headed straight back to Papua. But this time we used a slightly different route. We collected our guides, then sailed with them to one of the rivers in the national park. This meant we didn't have to carry guns past Timika town, where we were most likely to be questioned by the police or the army.

This was a safer way into Papua. We sailed to Amamapare just after dark, when the Customs guys had knocked off for the day, but this time only I disembarked. I was the photographer after all and had the best reason to be there out of the three of us. I could show anyone who asked the email from *National Geographic*.

I drove the jeep up to Mopozap to find Rudol and Nollen.

When I got there, it was quite late. I found Rudol near his cooking fire – he seemed surprised to see me. He found Nollen, and they both joined me in the jeep.

"We didn't expect to see you again," said Rudol.

"Why not?" I asked.

"You have not heard about the battle? There was a protest at Mulia and the army started shooting. But we had guns to shoot back. They sent helicopters, and we shot them down, four of them," said Nollen.

"You shot four helicopters down?" I asked.

"Yes, but we lost eleven men. Nollen was there," said Rudol.

"Nollen, you were there for the fighting?" I asked.

"Actually, I had taken the school kids to the next village. But I came back to help the injured. We are all out of ammunition," said Nollen.

"What did the Indonesians do?" I asked.

"They wrecked the village. They went away, but came back, and rounded up fifteen men and took them to jail. We think they might have Kupsy," said Nollen.

"Oh Jesus. I thought he was too young to fight," I said.

"He was supposed to take the old people away. And he did, but some of them wanted to come back to fight, so he came with them. He was helping carry the wounded, and the army took him away," said Nollen.

"Shit. Well, at least he is alive," I said.

"Your friend, Doctor Liza, she and other doctors came and helped the wounded. They took some away to hospital," said Nollen.

"Good old Liza," I said.

"We were worried that the army might have you too. They came here looking for you," said Rudol.

"What?" I said.

"They came here, they questioned me. I said, you just took photographs. They asked lots of questions, again and again," said Rudol.

"Shit. We'd better get going," I said.

I drove into Amamapare with the headlights off and was relieved to see that the army weren't at the boat ramp. As soon as we boarded the boat, Dirk took off.

"Wayan Chan came to see us. He said the army were asking after us. We gave him five times his usual bribe to not tell them that we were here," said Dirk.

"Jesus," I said.

"Rudol said that the army had gone into Mopozap and asked about us there too. Nollen said there's been a battle, up north in a place called Mulia. They shot down four helicopters. The Indonesians are furious. The villagers lost eleven men, and lots more were injured. Liza brought some other doctors down to treat the wounded," I said.

"Bloody hell. Four helicopters? With those two machine guns? Jeez, they can shoot," said Dirk.

"Apparently they are just about out of ammo. And the village is wrecked," I said.

"Have you got any idea how much four helicopters would cost?" asked Franz.

"They've got to be at least half a million dollars each," said Dirk.

"Shit. They'll be furious," Franz said.

"Right. Maybe this had better be our last run," I said.

"Maybe," said Dirk.

"Maybe we shouldn't do this run?" asked Franz.

"The men are out of ammo. We've got five more guns and fifty more rounds," said Dirk.

From looking at Google Maps, it appeared that Sungai Muras Besar was the river that was navigable the furthest into the national park. At 50-foot long our cruiser was a lot bigger than a canoe and a lot bigger than anything Rudol and Nollen had ever been on before. The Muras Besar river started wide, then split into two narrower tributaries, which later rejoined some kilometres upstream.

Our plan was to keep sailing until we reached the rapids. There were many small tributaries, but Dirk had printed out a map of the river, so we had a pretty good idea of which branch to take.

We sailed up the river, eventually finding a suitable mooring spot. It was after midnight but we didn't feel like sleeping. We hopped in the inflatable and headed further up the river. Dirk had a torch on a headband – a piece of equipment from the mine – which was our only light. We zipped along until we came to some big boulders.

We tied up the inflatable to a tree on the bank. By now we were tired; even so, we thought we'd walk as far as Jita and rest there. We all moved quietly in single file, not talking, with Rudol leading the way, which he did without a light. There were bats and possums, nocturnal frogs and insects, all making their own noise in the forest. We walked until we reached Jita.

A couple of hours before dawn we set up rudimentary camp on the edge of the village.

After a few hours' sleep, Rudol woke the group and suggested that we set off again. We ate some cold food, then hit the trail. Rudol had been into the village and when he came back, he said that the army had been there asking questions.

"How many army?" asked Dirk.

"Only two," answered Rudol.

"Good," replied Dirk, as he transferred his handgun from his pack to his belt.

Franz and I did the same thing. Two guys, we could handle. Lots of guys, and we were fucked.

We walked on in silence. We stopped and ate in silence. I didn't take any photos. Just before dark, we stopped to camp. We were all exhausted.

"One of us should keep watch for a few hours, then someone else. I'll go first, I'm a bit wired and probably won't sleep straight away," said Dirk.

So Dirk kept watch until he felt sleepy, then he woke Franz. The remainder of the night was split up into shifts.

Just before dawn, we got up, ate some cold breakfast, and hit the track again.

After an hour, Rudol signalled for us to stop. We froze in our tracks. Ahead, and to our right from the top of a ridge, were the sounds of men's voices. Rudol showed with his hands that we should retrace our steps, back along the creek bed, then take the track where the creek had forked to the west. We quietly did this. In the next valley there was no real track, but we scrambled through the undergrowth towards the north as fast as we could, to be ahead of the Indonesian voices.

At the top of this valley was a small waterfall where we had to scale a near vertical cliff face, throwing our packs ahead of us as we went. Once into the upper valley, Rudol motioned to us to follow him to a place under an overhang in the steep sides of the cliff. A rope bridge passed overhead. Rudol had calculated that the other men were walking east to west and would cross at this point. We had a little time to grab some bushes and vines to hide behind, then crouch still as the Indonesians crossed the rope bridge.

There were eight of them, dressed in casual uniform, carrying small packs with rifles protruding from them. Every second man carried a chunky two-way radio on his belt. They crossed the bridge in pairs, possibly unsure of how strong the ropes were. When they'd all crossed, one of them radioed to someone else. The reply did not sound like a strong signal, it was quiet and full of static. The report was short. They walked on without a backward glance.

Rudol then led us up the cliff, back to the valley that we had been in first. The creek was much smaller in this valley, and a distinct trail ran along next to it. This was the easiest path to the north. The larger stream where we'd just been had cut steeper drops into its valley. Avoiding these would make for an easier, faster journey.

We walked again until dark. Now we were in the mountains and the familiar path wound up the side of a big ridge. We camped in a tiny patch of trees that clung to the mountainside on a small shelf. We were almost there, but walking at night on these slopes was dangerous. We would stand out against the bare rock to anyone looking – just as the two Indonesian soldiers stood out when they walked down the path towards us. Chatting away, they had obviously not seen the encampment yet, but if they got closer, they certainly would.

Dirk quietly took a rifle from his pack. Franz and I also quietly unpacked rifles, loading them in readiness. Already lying down, we aimed towards the soldiers, waiting as they came into range. There did not appear to be other soldiers behind them, or if there were, they were following a long distance away.

Dirk fired once, then Franz fired, and Dirk fired again. The two soldiers collapsed and fell down the cliff, without having time to reach for their guns or radio. I didn't even fire my gun.

Wordlessly, we packed up our camp, and kept walking towards the Ples Tambu.

In a couple of hours, we were there. We woke a woman who was sleeping by the fire, and she woke a young boy. The boy disappeared behind a pile of logs which had been stacked in front of the entrance to the cave, made to look like they had fallen from higher up the mountain.

Shortly Semu appeared and greeted us.

The passage into the cave had been made very narrow, so that we had to squeeze through, and drag our packs behind us. Then Semu guided us about 100 metres into the cave, to a room not visible from the entrance. Here, he lit a small fire, and we sat around on our packs. We told Semu about our journey, and how we'd shot the soldiers.

"Yes, many Indonesians have been shot now, and many of our own men too. Did you hear about the battle in Mulia?" asked Semu.

"Nollen told us about it. Four helicopters! Your men can really shoot!" I said.

"We have almost no ammunition left. Did you bring more?" asked Semu.

"Yes. We brought five more M60s, and some other rifles, and ammo for all of them," Dirk said.

"All of the guns made it back to either here, or to a safe place near the lakes. The Indonesians are very angry, looking for the men and the guns. They have flown past every day," said Semu.

"Do you think they know you are here?" I asked.

"We are not sure. After the battle, many men walked to here, carrying guns. We did not know all of them. When a few of them left, Konia told us that he did not personally know two of those men, they were not from his group," said Semu.

"Could they have been army men? Are there Papuans in the army?" I asked.

Semu said, "We are worried that they may have been local men from the Special Forces, the Kopassus. We heard there were local men in the Special Forces."

"Yes, the national park is crawling with army men now. We passed many, but we had to shoot those two on the mountain path, or they would have caught us," said Dirk.

"How close to here was that?" asked Semu.

"Two hours walk away, but to the south," Franz said.

"You men had better stay here for the night. We can completely seal off the cave, we will do it now. They will come looking for those men. They are to our north and our south now," said Semu.

We traded the guns, and Semu and some other men carried them further up into the cave. We remained in this section of the caves – the 'guest room'.

Exhausted, we fell asleep, each thinking about how we could get out of this mess.

ARTHUR

Plans to evacuate

Next morning, we discussed our situation and made new plans.

"There is a way," I said.

"What way is that?" asked Dirk.

"If we walk out, the army have a good chance of finding us. But if we fly out —" I said.

"How are we going to fly out?" asked Franz.

"Liza's flying doctor service," I said.

We dug through our luggage for the satellite phone. Our packs had been knocked around on this trip and were wet from climbing up the waterfall. We'd tried to waterproof the guns and sleeping bags, everything really, but water had still seeped in. The bag containing the phone had been wet, and the phone was unresponsive. Franz put it near the fire to try and dry it out.

"How are we going to call Liza now? Smoke signals?" asked Dirk.

"Liza has a field officer in Ilaga. It's only an hour's walk out of here, to the northwest. That's where she picked up Konia," I said.

"Yes, you are right. I'd rather risk an hour's walk than a couple of days' walk," said Dirk.

"Especially a shorter walk away from where we just shot two men, rather than straight back past them," added Franz.

"Yes. That's an important consideration," I said.

We cooked up breakfast – dried fish, rice and vegetables – our first hot meal in a couple of days. There was a small pile of firewood against the wall of our cavern. Hot tea seemed like a luxury after no fires for days.

Semu returned as we were finishing our meal. We offered him dried fish and rice, which he ate happily. He told us that we should wait for at least a day, as the Indonesians would be searching for us. After that, we were free to go. So we went with Semu further into the cave, through the water, to the upper cave that Swando's tribe used as a long house.

Swando was there with his men, just inside the mouth of the cave. Their fire was inside, the smoke rising to the cave's ceiling from where it was sucked up through cracks. If this smoke escaped, it would look like volcanic emissions, rather than a cooking fire.

One man had his arm in a sling, which must have been the work of Liza or her doctor friends. Some of Swando's men had fought at the battle in Mulia. We sat and talked about the ongoing war with the Indonesians. Dirk, Franz and I came to realise that we had been accepted as fellow freedom fighters, whether we identified that way or not. Later in the morning, we heard a chopper flying past. In the afternoon, another flew past in the opposite direction. It might have been the same chopper, we didn't get much of a look at it.

We went back down the cave to the 'guest room' to spend the night, grateful for our packs and sleeping bags in the coolness of the cave. We also slept better knowing we would be let out, that we were not prisoners.

In the morning, Dirk, Franz and I left the cave with the hunting party. Rudol and Nollen stayed at the Ples Tambu; they would return to Mopozap in a few days when there would be less soldiers in the forest. We set off with the hunting party in the direction of Ilaga. After a while they stopped, pointing us to the right track. Then, they headed off down a creek, hunting for food.

We reached Ilaga without seeing any soldiers, and soon found the missionary, Johannes. We introduced ourselves and asked if we could phone Liza at Freeport.

"Liza, thank God I've got you," I said.

"Arthur, is that you? Yes, I got myself a satellite phone. What has happened now?" asked Liza.

"Well, we heard about the battle at Mulia, and the villagers are so grateful that you helped them. But Semu and Konia think that the Ples Tambu has been infiltrated by the Special Forces," I said.

"Shit. Are you there now?" asked Liza.

"No, Dirk, Franz and I walked to Ilaga, and were hoping that you could pick us up. The national park is crawling with Indonesian troops, and we're worried that they'll shoot us. And we have to find Konia, or one of the leaders, to evacuate the cave and save the village," I said.

"OK, I'm on my rounds today, at Jila. I'll pick you guys up next in Ilaga, then I've got to drop in to Tiom, then we'll return to base," said Liza.

"Thank you, Liza, you'll save our skins," I said.

"See you soon." Liza signed off.

Johannes said, "Right, I'll have to hide you guys with Yosia. He got injured in the battle at Mulia and has come home to recover. We're hiding him in a hut down near the playing field, so any army guys that come through don't see his bandages and know he was fighting."

"Thank you, Johannes. God bless you!" said Franz.

"They have been marching through here almost every day. They check the long house, but that's about it. Stay inside and keep quiet. You'll hear the chopper when it lands," said Johannes.

We walked down the hill to the playing field, where Johannes said the chopper would land.

We entered a small hut with an old woman sitting outside. Inside was Yosia, who had his head and arm bandaged. He was lying on a cane bed, flicking through a *Reader's Digest*.

Johannes said, "Yosia, these men have come from the Ples Tambu. They are friends of Konia and Swando. Be very quiet now."

"Hello, I'm Dirk, this is Arthur and Franz," said Dirk, pointing us out. Yosia reached out to shake our hands. It was his left arm that was bandaged.

"Are you the white men who have been helping Konia?" asked Yosia, putting his book down.

"Yes," I said. "We've been trading with Konia and Semu. Did you fight at Mulia?"

"Yes," said Yosia. "Konia helped carry me back to the schoolhouse, after I'd been shot. But I shot lots of Indonesians. I had to reload my rifle three times."

"Good for you!" said Dirk. "We heard you guys shot down four helicopters!"

"The men on the machine guns did an amazing job. Some were killed and wounded, but we kept shooting and smashed those helicopters," said Yosia.

"We brought up five more M60s and more ammo. But we think we might have to evacuate the Ples Tambu," I said.

"What?" said Yosia, "But we have so many things stored there."

"Konia thinks that the cave might have been compromised by the Kopassus," Dirk said.

"Bloody hell," said Yosia.

We sat for a while, listening. The jungle sounded quiet outside. Quiet was good.

"I'm just praying that Liza finds us before the army does," said Franz.

Dirk said, "But who are you praying to, Franz?"

Franz said, "I'll pray to anyone up there who'll listen."

Yosia replied, "We pray to many gods, including your Jesus God."

Franz asked, "Do you really believe in Jesus, or do you just want to learn to read and write?"

"Our gods are more powerful than Jesus anyway," said Yosia.

"How can you tell?" I asked.

"When we pray to the sky gods for rain, or for the rain to stop, they usually do it," said Yosia.

"When the priest or Brother Johannes prays to Jesus, someone usually dies. Jesus can't stop them from dying. Jesus also won't bring food or rain or more animals to hunt," said Yosia.

"Who do you pray to for these things?" Franz asked.

"For good hunting, we will pray to our ancestors. If you listen to them, they will tell you which way to go to find the animals," said Yosia.

"Who do you pray to for the dying then?" I asked.

"If you want them to die quick, you pray to the Crocodile God. If you want them to live, pray to the ancestors," said Yosia.

"This sounds fair enough. I prayed a lot, and I don't know if my prayers were ever answered," said Franz.

"What were you praying for, Franz?" I asked.

"I used to pray to pass my exams at school. Then I mostly prayed to find a woman," said Franz.

"And it didn't work, this praying?" asked Dirk.

"Well, I did OK at school, but I never did find a good woman," said Franz.

"Weren't there any at your church?" I asked.

"I wanted one who was more exciting than the girls at church," said Franz.

"Fair enough. My parents used to ask God to make them rich again," said Dirk.

"Did that work?" Franz asked.

"I don't know. They are rich by most people's standards, but after they had been 'rich colonials with servants' kind of rich, I don't think that 'living in a big city with professional jobs' rich was rich enough for them, if you know what I mean," said Dirk.

"Yeah, I think we can learn a lot from Rudol and Nollen's people. A roof over your head, food to eat, a family, it's all you really need. What a pity that they are being forced away from this kind of life," I said.

"Well, hopefully we can help them in some way, to protect their lifestyles and their land. I hope these people are really safe in the national park, and that the Indonesians don't just burn and steal the land here as well," said Franz.

"Well it looks like you were more successful than Franz in picking up a girl, Arthur," said Dirk.

"Oh, you mean Kayla? She isn't that religious. She just hangs out with the youth group to be social," I said.

"Kayla writes really political stuff. I read her columns. She would write about the battle at Mulia, and that kind of stuff," said Franz.

"Have you got her number?" asked Dirk.

"Yeah I do have her number. She has helped me to write an article for *National Geographic*," I said.

"If we are going to evacuate the village to PNG, we are going to need help on the other side of the border," said Dirk.

"I'll call Kayla. She'll help. She reckons there is a group of West Papuans in New Guinea who help refugees who have crossed the border. Let's see if that phone works yet?" I said.

I dug the satellite phone out of the pack, but it wouldn't charge.

"Probably the battery needs to be recharged," said Dirk.

After a few minutes of silence, we heard the chopper. It got closer, landing in the playing field.

We ran out to meet it. Only Liza hopped out. She gestured for us to get aboard. The pilot left the engine running. We climbed in and buckled up, my first flight since the accident.

We put on our headphones as Max took off.

LIZA

Freeport, or 'the base'

We stopped briefly in Tiom where only I hopped out. I had to check on the three wounded patients recovering at the clinic there. Even better, one of the older men had a visitor, Konia.

"Hi, Konia," I said.

"Doctor Liza! You have done such a wonderful job with our men. Ruggithorn here is feeling so much better. We thought he was going to die," said Konia.

I checked out Ruggithorn and the other two men, changed some dressings, and thought about our next move. I should take Konia with me back to Freeport. It would be easiest if we held a meeting to plan the evacuation.

"Konia, could you come to Freeport for a meeting with me? I've got a few people you should meet with. There is something going on and you need to know about it. I could get the chopper to drop you back here?" I asked.

"Me, Doctor Liza? Who do you want me to meet?" said Konia.

"It's just Dirk, Franz and Arthur. They were at Ilaga when I dropped in, so I picked them up," I said. We were in a hospital ward, and I wanted this to sound casual.

Konia nodded. He understood. "Yes, I'll come with you. I'd like to meet your friends."

We returned to the chopper, Max fired it up, and we all headed back to Freeport.

With the clinic closed we decided to have the meeting there. It was hard to hear what was being said in the chopper.

At the clinic, we met in the waiting room. The doctors, Janette, Dirk's gang and Konia.

"Right," said Arthur. "We have to evacuate the Ples Tambu, maybe walk all the villagers across the border."

"You're right. I think we were infiltrated just after the battle at Mulia, and a Special Forces agent or two has helped carry guns back to the Ples Tambu. The Kopassus will be planning an attack," said Konia.

"What will the Kopassus do?" asked Dirk.

"If that Colonel Yuda is in charge, they'll shoot everyone from helicopters. Every last person, man, woman or child," said Konia. "He did the same at Paniai Timur, and at many other massacres across West Papua. They will bomb the Ples Tambu. Wipe it off the map."

"We must avoid that happening at all costs," I said.

"Yes, we must evacuate the Ples Tambu as soon as possible," said Arthur.

"Maybe we need a distraction," said Dirk. "Something serious happening somewhere else in the opposite direction."

"That is a good idea," said Konia. "If we planned an attack, say on the airfield at Paniai, it would draw the army and the Special Forces to the west. The Ples Tambu is east of here, and so is

Papua New Guinea. If there is time before the monsoon starts, we can walk the mountain paths through the jungle to the border and take all the villagers to safety."

"I'm all for evacuating the village," I said. "But I don't really want to know about the 'distraction attack'."

"You'll need to get a bunch of four-wheel drives for the M60s," said Dirk. "Reinforce the roof and windows, and you can drive those big guns in and really move them around. They won't want to hit you with anything too hard, because they'd be wrecking their own base. If you knocked out their control tower, they'd be stuffed," said Dirk, who'd obviously been thinking about this.

"Good idea, Dirk," said Konia. "I brought a bag of gold down from the village that will help me get that done quickly. We can buy cars in Timika. I must get to Paniai as soon as possible."

"Well, what do you know? I need to visit my clinic in Enarotali today. Max, can you fly us there, or should I ask another pilot?" I asked.

Max had been observing our meeting, while drinking a coffee and eating a burger.

"I'll take you there, Liza. We can take any bird that is fuelled up," said Max.

This was the sort of medical emergency that might stop other medical emergencies from happening.

KONIA

Paniai Lakes

Doctor Liza flew me to Enarotali from where I made my way to Paniai Timur to see some of our leaders who lived there. I'd taken one of the big gold bags with me to Tiom and buried it behind a friend's house, taking only a small amount of it with me in my dilly bag.

We had a meeting at the Paniai Timur church to discuss the distraction attack and the evacuation. I was surprised to see Kupsy, who'd been released from police custody. The other leaders agreed that we needed to go ahead, so we started to plan which groups would do what. Dirk had come along with me and offered to lead the evacuation. But we decided Kupsy should do this as he'd walked that track before.

The leaders thought Dirk would be better off buying the five jeeps that we were going to need for us – a white face would cause less suspicion than a black one. The car dealers in Timika were all white men, so they'd probably do a white man a better deal, too. Five of us went with Dirk to Timika.

One of the other leaders sent men to the Ples Tambu with instructions to carry out the guns. We were going to need them.

Dirk had brought a satellite phone with him so we could communicate with the others. Liza's system of satellite phones actually helped us as much as her medical services did. Suddenly we had phone communications between the villages, which we'd never had before. We could contact multiple villages and call many men together, without having to walk from one place to the next to spread the word.

Our men worked like an army of ants, walking along the mountain paths to the Ples Tambu or down to us at Paniai.

We had many places where we could hide things at nearly every village in our region, from caves to sheds to holes in the ground. It had been really difficult for us to buy weapons and ammunition, so whenever we did manage to get some, we made sure that they didn't get stolen by the police or the army.

I also spread the word about possible infiltrators from the Special Forces. No groups were to take on any new men or women unless they were well known to at least one trusted group member.

Dirk's shopping mission went amazingly well. Dirk told the car dealer that he was a miner who'd discovered a new gold seam, and the men with him were the workers at his new mine. The car dealer bought the story. He was happy to accept gold nuggets as payment for his fleet of second-hand vehicles, plus the men got to test drive them. Usually a white dealer would never allow a local man to test drive a vehicle, unless he was sitting next to him, that is.

Dirk and his men made their next stop the sheet metal works. A couple of our men worked there. Dirk not only purchased the metal, but they also cut and welded it for us after their work knocked off. Dirk had the idea of welding the bipod assembly onto the hood of the jeep, for stability while driving. If we could fire those machine guns accurately while moving, we would have a great advantage. The M60 slotted in or out of the bipod assembly. We could drive, and fix the engine, without having the gun attached.

Dirk organised a big shed in Paniai Timur to store the vehicles.

Because they knew him and he had walked that track before, Kupsy was chosen to lead Swando's tribe out of Papua. He was given a trail bike and lessons on how to ride it so he could get back to the Ples Tambu as quickly as possible.

"Dirk," I said, "You have become a valuable member of our movement. Thanks for all you have done for us."

"Konia, at first I hated you guys, then I came to really admire you," said Dirk. "Now, I'm part of the fight for freedom, and it is the biggest adventure of my life."

"Stay safe, my friend. I might not see you for a while," I said as we shook hands.

"Take care of Swando and all his people," said Dirk. "I feel a bit responsible for bringing attention to his village."

"Not as responsible as I feel," I said. "I just hope that Kupsy gets there before the Kopassus do. I'm going to head up there now, too. Kupsy should have got the guns and the gold moving. I'm going to make sure that they all leave, and that they don't stay behind trying to defend the place. It would be suicide."

"Be careful on that bike. If it gets too steep, get off and push," said Dirk.

"I will, my friend," I said, and gave him a hug. We were all taking big risks. Who knew what the future held?

LIZA

Planning for the big one

So it was going to happen again. Another battle. At least Fred and I would be ready this time and would know what to expect. I called Mike and Dave in Cairns. Mike could come but Dave couldn't. He'd been sick himself, with heart trouble. He'd flown to Townsville for a double bypass operation.

Arthur and Franz went down to Amamapare to find their jeep. So they could experience the track down the mountain and because they were planning to drive back up it, they organised a lift with a truck driver. The HEAT, or Heavy Equipment Access Track, was only used to transport things that couldn't be air-lifted. A cable car took workers from the mine down to the Ridge Camp and Tembagapura. Apparently, there were places along the track where winches had to be used to get up or down very steep sections. The track was completely unusable in the wet season.

Arthur and Dirk each got new satellite phones, so Arthur took the opportunity to call Kayla. She was co-ordinating things on the PNG side of the border and was trying to get a media pass to cross the border herself.

Arthur and Franz were hoping to join the evacuation of the Ples Tambu, and cross to PNG as well. They had given up on getting their boat back for now. I think they were hoping to get back to it by sea, in the night, sometime in the future.

Flying back from Tiom Clinic, the first rain of the season pelted down. The rain had come early. I hoped the evacuation would take place before the monsoon really hit us hard.

ARTHUR

Another way in

Franz and I got a lift back to Timika in a truck that went down the mountain via a walking track that had been bulldozed to the width of a vehicle. The track switched back and forth on itself as it descended the mountain from the volcanic plateau. In places we needed to stop and use the winch on the bull bar to lower the truck down the steep slopes. Worryingly, there were a few vehicles at the bottom of the cliff that hadn't made it. It was a hell of a drive.

By the time we reached Timika it had started raining, so the truckie offered to take us all the way to Amamapare. There we found our jeep and retraced our route back through Timika towards the hell road. Timika is a pretty big town, and to the north are some ritzy suburbs with a golf course and big houses for the 'management' classes. There are tropical trees, mostly flowering ones, forming controlled jungles for a few kilometres.

We stopped just short of the hell road, under a huge poinciana tree, and watched as six or seven army vehicles waited at the bottom of the road for vehicles to come down. There weren't a lot of places to pass on this track, so it was one-way traffic down the steepest bit.

Franz and I looked at each other.

"I don't want to use that road if it's wet," said Franz.

"And I don't want to use that road if it's crawling with army vehicles," I said.

"There has to be another way," said Franz.

We broke out the maps from the glovebox. There were a series of tracks running along the foothills of the mountain range, east towards the national park. We would follow those.

We drove for a couple of hours along these tracks, although we did notice the military on the move on the bigger roads. They were headed up towards the mine.

Franz called Liza while I drove.

"Liza, Franz here," he said.

"Franz, are you on your way back here?" Liza said.

"No, there's been a change of plans. The mountain track is wet, and crawling with the army, so we're heading straight to the village, going in through the north of the national park," said Franz.

"Will you be able to find your way there?" asked Liza.

"We've got maps, and Arthur's photos, so we've got a good chance," said Franz.

"Right. Well, I expect I'll be kept busier on the Paniai side, so good luck. And keep in contact, Franz," said Liza.

"Will do Liza. Good luck to you too," said Franz.

"Mate, can you drive while I check through those photos?" I asked Franz.

We pulled over and swapped places. The four-wheel drive was running well. I had downloaded most of the photos to Liza's computer up at the base, and just kept the photos I needed. These were the mountains, the rivers, the bridges and the big features that pointed out where we were on the track to the Ples Tambu.

Without our guides, these photos might very well help us find our way in.

Rudol and Nollen had said the army went in past their village, parking their jeeps near their local river. We had to go a different way.

We drove over many small one-lane steel or wooden bridges – about seven or eight of them. As we got closer to the national park they became more rickety. We drove between farms and fallow land, some planted with timber, hardly seeing another vehicle. When we arrived at the national park there was an entry gate and a sign in a few different languages saying that hunting was forbidden.

We drove in, shutting the gate behind us, and feeling safer already. It was probably a false sense of security.

We drove as far as we could, until the track ended at a cliff with a river running far below. Franz parked in some bushes. We found the trail, along the cliff to the north running down a crazily steep slope. We headed down. The winding track took us lower towards the water, but still a fair way up. Around the next bend was a cable bridge, which we crossed, before making our way up into the forest again. Eventually, after traversing more bush, we came to another river. We'd smelled village fires along this track, but we hadn't had time to stop and talk. We needed to get to the Ples Tambu before the Kopassus did.

The next bridge we came to was quite elaborate, with a narrow footpath and handrail ropes.

I flicked through the photos on my camera.

I said, "We've seen this one before, only we didn't cross it."

I showed Franz a shot of this bridge, taken from a simpler bridge we'd crossed downstream. I had to zoom in, as this bridge was in the distance in the photo.

"We must have crossed this river further downstream to get to Mopozap," agreed Franz.

"We'll come to the track north soon. We can't be far from where we passed before," I said.

We hurried on, through thick jungle, ascending and descending some killer hills. From a high pass we could see the mountains beyond and the lush river valleys stretching away to the south.

As night fell, we reached a small village near where we'd stayed before. We camped for the night but didn't light a fire.

Yuda goes off at Kopassus

C olonel Yuda was pacing the office and hitting things.
"Unbelievable! Where did the Papuans get those M60s from? Four helicopters downed! Millions of rupiah!" said Yuda.

I just kept quiet. There was no point in talking to him when he was like this.

"And now that bitch doctor up at the mine has set up communication stations in all their villages, so they can talk to each other. Bugger her! We'll see how she likes having Major Honan stationed up at Grasberg, keeping an eye on her. He won't stand for any of her bullshit!" said Yuda.

He was on a roll now.

Honan had been here to receive his orders, and Yuda had told him that he could shoot any locals who weren't mine workers, on sight.

"Have you received the report from the helicopter mechanics yet?" said Yuda.

"No, sir. Their last email said two to three more hours," I reported.

"I wish those mechanics would get a move on! I want to go up there and shoot that village. How long does it take those pricks to fix a few choppers?" said Yuda.

The pilots and paratroopers were all on standby. As soon as the choppers were ready, they could leave. I just hoped I would have to stay here to do communications. I didn't want to go up to the Ples Tambu. It is a very bad omen to attack a holy place like that. They say that tribe has a leader who is like the Holy Buddha. We really shouldn't go and shoot a holy man. The locals hate us enough already.

ARTHUR

Finding the Ples Tambu

We set off walking again before dawn. After an hour, we crossed the path of a couple of men.

Franz said, "Hello, my friends. Are we headed the right way for Ilaga?"

A tribesman replied, "You've just passed Kelkinoga village. The next big village is Ilaga."

"Thank you. I'm Franz, and this is Arthur. We are heading up to the Ples Tambu."

"I'm Jack from Kelkinoga. You will be quicker to walk past Ilaga. When you come to the fork in the path, take the right trail rather than the left. The left goes to Ilaga."

"Thank you, Jack. God bless you," said Franz.

"Look, I'll come with you. You'll need someone to hold the cable when you climb. The bottom end has broken, and a man needs to weigh it down," said Jack.

"Thank you very much, Jack. We came a different way before," said Franz.

Passing his friend his dilly bag, Jack explained where he was going. Then he took off at a cracking pace back the way he'd come. We walked together for about an hour, past the turn off, and in another half an hour reached the bottom of a cliff where a metal cable hung down.

A steel cable about four centimetres in diameter hung down the cliff face. It had frayed away from its mooring, but it looked strong, disappearing up over a ledge.

"You and I hold it while he climbs," said Jack to me, gesturing to Franz.

Franz secured his backpack and tucked an extra T-shirt into his belt to wipe his sweaty hands on. This would be rock climbing without any safety equipment.

As Franz climbed, the tail of the cable tried to swing around, but Jack and I secured it, making Franz's climb more stable. Franz made it onto the ledge.

"It looks like it goes up to another ledge above me," yelled Franz.

"Right. I'll come up to that ledge with you!" I yelled. "Here, Jack, take this bottle of vodka for going out of your way to help us," I said, handing over my bottle.

"Thank you, Arthur, and good luck at the Ples Tambu," said Jack.

Jack secured the tail of the cable as I made my ascent.

Franz went up to the next ledge and yelled back at me, "This is the top, Arthur. You're halfway there!"

I waved down to Jack, then pulled myself up the cliff to the next ledge. The cable finished, wrapped around a huge bolt drilled into the cliff a little further up. We looked around and could see what we recognised as the track up the hill towards the Ples Tambu. We were not far from where we'd shot the Indonesians. We were almost there.

When we reached the Ples Tambu the place was in a frenzy of activity. Men, women and children were carrying things, from logs to chickens with their feet tied up. We saw Konia shouting orders at people, and Semu carrying a huge billum bag with carvings in it – the carvings from the mouth of the men's cave.

"Franz! Arthur! You made it here in time to help. Have you got space in your backpacks?" asked Konia.

"We have, actually. What do you want us to carry?" I asked him.

Konia shouted at a woman, and she came over carrying a very fresh leg of pork. They must have recently slaughtered a pig to take the meat with them. I wrapped it in my raincoat, and tucked it in my backpack, and the woman came back with another one for Franz to carry.

Konia told us, "Most of the gold and the guns have been taken away to different places, the guns to Paniai. We have to leave very soon. The last things are just being packed."

Franz and I sat down and broke out some of Liza's caffeine pills. We were going to be walking a whole lot more, so we were going to need them.

DIRK

Out of the frying pan

Our five vehicles were ready, with a group of men trained up to man each one, including a driver, a primary shooter and feeder, and a secondary shooter and feeder in the back seat.

Paka was our local leader. He divided up the groups and assigned us each a vehicle. I was a team leader, and therefore driver of one of the vehicles.

Paka had brought some two-way radios. He instructed all the men to make sure they knew how to use them. With one in each vehicle, we could make sure we had a co-ordinated attack. Enarotali air strip runs east–west right through the centre of the small town. The control tower and waiting shed were about half-way along the strip, on the south side. The strip was fenced with an old rickety structure that was falling down most of the way around. Our vehicles would be able to knock it over easily. Only a few commercial flights per week came in or out of Enarotali. The army also used it for their two small planes, and helicopters also landed at a spot near the shed.

The army base was a kilometre further out of town, to the east. There was a bridge over a creek on the road between the army barracks and the air strip. This would be one of our targets.

Inside the big shed, which held our gun and ammo collection and where our jeeps were parked before the mission, Paka conducted a briefing to everyone assembled there in their groups. There was a table full of food and drinks, while a pile of camouflage T-shirts and shorts lay on the floor near the table. Some men and women were finding clothes to fit from the pile.

Paka called the meeting to order. "Papua Merdeka! Today is a very important day. Today we turn the tables! Today we attack the Indonesians, instead of them attacking us!" he said.

There was riotous applause and yelling.

"Today we attack the air strip," said Paka. "To prevent army planes from taking off and landing on this strip, we plan to wipe out the control tower and burn it down. One group will destroy the bridge between the army barracks and the air strip. They will then stay in position to slow down the army as they come down that road. When they are overwhelmed, they will retreat to the airstrip.

"We believe they will attack us from the air as well as from land. The other armoured vehicles will be at various points around the airstrip. I've marked these on this blackboard.

"Rifle men and women will use the cover of the drainage ditches on either side of the runway. Your entry points are marked on this map, too. Your targets will be the ground troops. Remember that they might come from either direction. Our trucks will deliver you to the north side of the runway and will wait to pick you up. If any fighter doesn't make it to a truck, there are safe houses in Timika town, marked with an X all around the airstrip. Your cue to retreat is when you run out of ammunition. Bury your guns at the safe houses. We cannot afford to lose them.

"Armoured vehicles will aim primarily at incoming aircraft and vehicles. Feel free to drive all over the airstrip. The more the enemy shoots at the landing strip, the less they will be capable of landing planes on it. Draw their fire, you are protected more than the rifle men and women will be. Try to make your ammunition last. Retreat to this shed, or any other place where you can keep hold of your vehicle.

"If the army feel overwhelmed, they will call in the Kopassus. The Special Forces have many helicopters and paratroopers. If the paratroopers drop in, try to shoot them in the air. This is when they will be easiest to target.

"Doctor Liza from Freeport Mine will fly in to help any wounded. We must not shoot at the Freeport helicopter. The army or Kopassus might aim for them, and in this case, we must try to protect them.

"Rifle men and women, if one of our vehicles approaches, you will help them to unload any wounded, and you may be called to replace them. You have all been shown how to operate those larger guns.

"We can retreat in any direction. This is our home. The army will only retreat towards the barracks. The front of their troop carriers are a target, but the back of them are open, and a very easy target.

"We want to make a big impact today. We will drive these imperialists from our homeland. Papua Merdeka!" said Paka.

The assembled freedom fighters yelled "Papua Merdeka!" Then they headed to their trucks and jeeps. We had a bread truck, a fruit truck, and a couple of rental trucks. We didn't look much like an army, we looked like a bunch of local workers. Except for those of us in the armoured vehicles.

As the sun rose, orders were given to move out.

We jumped into our jeep.

FRANZ

The Ples Tambu

Arthur and I got to the Ples Tambu as the villagers were preparing to evacuate. Konia and Kupsy were organising the operation; their men had already carried out the guns and the gold. But we had a couple of problems.

Johannes, the missionary from Ilaga, arrived not long after us, offering to help.

"Johannes, I'm so glad you're here," I said. "We have an old blind man and a pregnant woman who are not going to make the walk out."

"Right," said Johannes, "I can take them back to Ilaga with me, but we'll have to leave straight away."

"I will tell Konia," I said, and I ran off to find him.

"Konia, Johannes has offered to take Semu's wife and the old man to Ilaga," I said.

"They will need a man each to help them, neither can walk properly," said Konia.

"I will go with them," I said, without even thinking about it.

"The ancestors bless you, Franz. Papua Merdeka."

I ran back to the group.

"Arthur, I'm going to help Johannnes take Semu's wife and the old man back to Ilaga," I said.

Arthur looked at me and said, "God go with you, Franz. I hope to see you again in New Guinea. We've got to go."

I hurried back to Johannes. He'd found Semu's wife and the old man.

"Let's go. I'll take Are Kapa, you take Juvelyn," said Johannes. He led the old man with an arm around his waist, and I helped support the very pregnant Juvelyn. We walked slowly and silently, making our way along the path to the west.

We'd been walking for maybe half an hour, when we heard the sound of helicopters.

"Quickly," I said, "under the trees!"

"Get in close," said Johannes.

I pulled the tarpaulin from my backpack and threw it over us. We huddled under the tarp, perfectly still.

We heard about ten helicopters fly overhead towards the Ples Tambu. I prayed the others were well away from the place.

Into the fire

My team of five jumped into our jeep and headed to the airfield. We were Team Three. Team One headed straight to the control tower. With a short blast of the M60, they took out the two security guards who watched the tower at night. The day staff hadn't arrived yet. Someone from Team One threw a Molotov cocktail in through a broken window, and the small building went up in flames. Another home-made bomb went into the waiting shed next to the tower.

The two-way radio, crackling with static, came to life with, "Well done, Team One. Team Two, you are go for the next target."

Team Two were already driving to the end of the runway where the two small army planes were parked. Short bursts of machine-gun fire broke the cockpit windows, then two team members hopped out of the back doors of the vehicles, and lobbed Molotov cocktails into the cockpits of both planes.

We waited for the retaliation to come, listening attentively to our radios.

"Bridge Team are go," said Paka over the two-way.

"Roger, on our way," came the reply. The Bridge Team were on foot and carried homemade explosives; they had been dropped close to the bridge. I heard an explosion in the distance, and the Bridge Team reported on the radio, "Bridge is down, proceeding to airstrip."

"Roger. Now all teams wait to engage," came the radio call.

A lone fire alarm sounded at the airstrip shed.

The police, first on the scene, were met with some rifle fire while they were still in their vehicle. They turned it around, making a hasty retreat while obviously calling for backup.

Next came the trucks. The army didn't take long to make an appearance. The first truck stopped at the bridge, troops pouring out of the back. Our Bridge Team had retreated, though it would have been a good place to attack. Paka didn't want fighting on one of the streets in town; he wanted to minimise civilians being shot, or their homes or shops being burned or bombed. He wanted the fighting to occur on the airstrip, so we had to draw them in.

"Control to armoured Vehicle One," said Paka on the two-way.

"Team One here, go ahead," said the team leader.

"Drive down to the bridge and draw their fire, pull them into the target zone," said Paka.

"Roger," said the team leader.

Our first vehicle drove down to the bridge where it was met by a burst of rifle fire. They must have done a U-turn and come straight back, pursued by three or four truckloads of soldiers. Then the battle really began. As Vehicle One entered the airstrip, Vehicle Two was waiting, facing the gates.

"Vehicle Two, engage!" came the order from Paka. The machine-gun operators in Vehicle Two mowed down the first row of Indonesian riflemen. The men behind them ran for cover behind a few parked cars, which Vehicle Two peppered with bullets.

"Vehicle Two, retreat. Save that ammo," came Paka's order.

Next came the Pindad Anoas. These armoured personnel carriers have six wheels and could make it over the remains of the destroyed bridge. Four of them drove onto the airstrip in close formation and started towards Vehicles One and Two.

"Four Pindads on site, boss," someone radioed in.

"Aim for the wheels, my fighters," came the command from Paka.

Chaos broke out. We all started moving, as a sitting target is easier than a moving one, but we didn't want to get stuck in the entrance of the airstrip. As Vehicles One and Two retreated, the other three of us came forward, and the Pindads came out onto the field. Fighters with rifles were taking potshots at the wheels. We took a shot when we could, but we were saving our ammo for the air attack.

The Ples Tambu

Today, we finally fixed all our helicopters so they were operational. I don't know which are worse for breaking down, the American Apaches, or the Russian Mil Mi-35s. I'd already had orders to lend two of the Mil Mis to the Timika regiment, because they'd lost four birds in a recent skirmish at Mulia. So we were down to six choppers, and our men were not happy.

Two of my undercover operatives had infiltrated the Mulia subversives. They went for the protest, took guns from fallen fighters, then followed one of their leaders back to their secret cave in the national park. Sergeant Hantu reported to me the exact location of this 'ples tambu'. I'd been waiting to bomb the crap out of it for a few days.

At dawn we headed south from Jayapura to the mountains, which were covered in wretched thick clouds. We made our way to the national park and located the target. There were a couple of naked tribesmen firing at us with rifles, but they were no match for our mighty Hellfire missiles. We launched some missiles and 240 mm rockets, blowing their precious cave to rubble and raining debris down on their huts below. It was terrific.

Then Wira radioed in, "Corporal Wira to Colonel Yuda."

"Yuda here. Go ahead," I said.

"Colonel, there is an attack occurring at Enarotali Airstrip. The Paniai regiment have requested immediate Kopassus backup," said Wira.

"Attention all aircraft. This is Yuda, we have to change course immediately to Enarotali at Paniai. The airstrip is under attack. If you need to refuel, do it at the Enarotali Barracks. Change course immediately for Enarotali," I said.

Our fleet of mighty birds turned to the west and flew at speed to the Lake District. Those Lake People are troublemakers. I thought we'd taught them a lesson by burning the place down. But it seems they needed another one.

DIRK

Firestorm

It was madness. The Indonesians in the Pindads were chasing us every which way. Our armoured jeeps allowed us very little vision, except from the front. Plus, we were trying to save ammo. The Pindads fired at us, and tried to ram us as well, but our vehicles were faster. Our ground shooters aimed at their tyres, and at the Indonesian foot soldiers who must have been ordered to follow the light tanks in.

Then their choppers arrived.

"Attention all fighters, incoming choppers. Time to aim high," came the radio call from Paka.

The Indonesian choppers were armed with big guns and rocket launchers, so the noise became deafening as larger bullets and bombs hit and bounced off our vehicle.

Boom! Suddenly there was a crater in the airfield right in front of us. I drove straight into it, with no time to brake or swerve around it. Our speed took us down and up the crater, rocking us around. Then I saw the planes and made a quick decision.

The Indonesians probably didn't mind destroying the bitumen, but they might not be so keen to destroy their own planes. The Molotov cocktails had caused some damage in the cockpits, but they could be repaired. I headed for a spot between the two planes, then parked.

"Aim high, Lawa!" I said to my gunman.

"Will do, Dirk," said Lawa, from the seat beside me. With the stability of being parked, Lawa could use his gun much better. When a chopper approached, Lawa aimed true and made a direct hit on the pilot. The chopper rose for a moment then fell to the right, smashing into the airfield with a loud explosion as the fuel tank took a hit.

"Lawa hit a chopper," I reported.

"Well done Vehicle Three!" said Paka.

But we had no time to congratulate ourselves. There were two Pindads driving straight for us. I sped out from my spot in between the aircraft, hooking back towards the planes and parking right beneath one of the wings. There were two other armoured vehicles pursuing the light tanks, all of us driving with low visibility, and bullets flying everywhere. Another chopper came towards us.

Boom! Another vehicle was hit, but it was a Pindad, not one of our jeeps. The Indonesians had hit their own ground crew by mistake.

Lawa kept shooting upwards as the second chopper came into range. He made some hits on the chopper, but it kept flying. The pilot must have made the decision to return to base, because it rose, banking back towards the barracks. There were still four choppers and three Pindads chasing us around.

Vehicle One decided to park under the other Indonesian plane, which the Indos must have been told not to fire at.

One of the choppers was flying low, following a ditch at the side of the airfield. They were mowing down our rifle men and women, some of whom were running from their cover. Vehicle One was aiming solely at that chopper.

"Lawa, aim for that Apache that's following the ditch, now," I said.

Lawa turned and concentrated on the Apache. Between the two of us, we brought down that chopper, headfirst into the ditch. As they came closer, we saw the red berets of the Kopassus officers in the cockpit. I was glad to see them hit the ground.

Looking around, I saw one of our vehicles on its side, and a Pindad crawling back towards their base on flattened tyres. Another Pindad was heading straight for us. It was time to move. I shot out from under the plane, driving like a crazy man. The runway was peppered with craters, and the remaining vehicles bounced around in pursuit of each other.

"The choppers are retreating," came Paka's call on the radio. They must have only been prepared to lose two out of their six choppers. Choppers are expensive, like planes.

I had a Pindad right up my arse, firing at the back of my vehicle. I just wanted to get back to the cover of the plane, but at least one of my tyres must have blown, and I was crawling along, running on the rims. We ground to a halt, but Lawa kept firing on the Pindads whenever they came in front of us.

"Vehicle Three to control. We are stuck, our tyres are gone," I radioed in.

"Cover Vehicle Three," came Paka's order. Our remaining vehicles circled us, drawing the Pindads in and out of our vision. Lawa fired when he could. Then he stopped firing. He'd been shot. Raims, his feeder, reached across him and opened the door. Raims shoved him out on to the tarmac and slammed the door. Rusam jumped over from the back seat and took his place.

I was shocked, but I made the call, "Vehicle Three to Control."

"Control, go ahead," said Paka.

"Our first gunman is down, second gunman in place," I said.

I was hit too, but I was the only driver in the car.

"A second Pindad is retreating. There is only one Pindad still operational," came Paka's call.

I couldn't see it. I had to turn our vehicle around. Riding the rims, and trying not to run over Lawa, I did a three-point turn. Now we could see the remains of the battle. We still had three working vehicles, but there was trouble in Vehicle One.

"My gunman has been hit too. We must break to change over. Please cover us," said the driver of Vehicle One.

The other two vehicles were driving like maniacs, trying to lure the Pindad away from Vehicle One. Vehicle One drove back to the plane, stopped and dropped their wounded gunman out the door. Then they resumed the fight. It was difficult for Rusam, my second gunman, to get a shot in. He didn't want to hit our own men who were circling the Pindad.

Rusam took shots at the big wheels of the Pindad whenever he could until finally the Pindad's tyres were shredded. The Pindad turned to crawl back to the Barracks.

"The last Pindad is retreating," reported one of our vehicles.

"Retreat to the shed, all vehicles," came Paka's call.

"Vehicle Three to Control, I've been hit, I'm not sure I can make it that far," I said.

"Try to get as far as the mechanic at Gereja St. We've radioed Doctor Liza at Freeport. Try to hold on," said Paka.

While I was talking, my remaining three passengers opened their doors and unhooked the metal plates which had covered their doors and the windscreen, dropping them on the runway. As I crawled along the quiet streets of Enarotali, Raims held a blanket to my chest. Rusam unhooked the M60 and brought it inside the car. We looked like a normal car again now, and I drove into the garage of the mechanics just before I passed out.

LIZA

After the fire

I took the call from a man named Paka. He said that there'd been serious fighting at the Enarotali Airstrip, and many were now wounded.

Mike, Fred and I jumped into a chopper with its giant red cross on a magnetic sheet covering the bottom of it. Max, our pilot, flew us west to Enarotali, next to the big Paniai lake. From above, the airstrip looked like the moon, covered in craters. There was a jeep on its side, and a tank which had been blown apart, and two smashed choppers.

Some locals were trying to right the jeep, taking bits of metal shielding off it. Others were carrying wounded towards a removal truck. A fruit vendor's truck was just driving off but turned around and came back. We landed near the trucks, on a side street north of the airstrip, where the perimeter fence had been flattened.

There were many wounded.

"I'll check the fruit truck," shouted Fred, as he ran towards it. Mike and I climbed into the back of the removal truck. People were pointing at an unconscious man who was bleeding heavily. He had multiple wounds, and I quickly applied pressure bandages to his chest, arm and head. Mike went to another patient. We asked the least wounded to help us hold things down as we patched people up. Once we had the major bleeding under control, I ran to the second truck. Fred had a lot of patients here, and I helped as best I could.

Then the truck driver said, "We've got to go. They're coming back."

With that I jumped out of Fred's truck and back to Mike's, just as a mechanic drove up with an injured white man – Dirk.

He looked bad. Unconscious and with a chest wound, I helped to load him into the truck, before speeding off.

Someone had tied a blanket to his chest. I removed it, bandages at the ready, but I wish I hadn't. There was a gaping hole beneath his shoulder, to which I immediately applied my largest pressure pad and bandage. If he was going to live, he needed a blood transfusion.

"It's Dirk," I said to Mike, "and he looks bad. Really bad."

"Shit," said Mike. "Can you help me with this one?"

I stepped over other patients to where Mike was bandaging a man with wounds to his lower torso and legs. The man was convulsing or having a seizure of some kind.

"We've got to get him on his side," I said.

As we both rolled the man onto his side, he started coughing out blood.

"That's good, it will clear his lungs," said Mike. We both kept bandaging his bullet wounds.

"Is there a wound on his back near his lungs?" I asked, not seeing any on his front.

"Yes. It looks like this guy got sprayed with bullets from behind as he was running away," said Mike.

At least he was breathing. He stopped convulsing and we managed to bandage his worst wounds.

The truck stopped in a large shed, and I heard our chopper land outside. The second truck came in as well. We had nineteen wounded between us.

"What have you got Fred?" I asked.

Fred replied, "I've got five who are going to need to go to Freeport or Timika."

"How many of ours need airlifting, Mike?" I asked.

"Four here are critical" said Mike.

"Max!" I said to the pilot. "Can you call for two more choppers right now please?"

"I'm on it," said Max.

I picked up the satellite phone. "Doctor Liza Fraser here, is that Timika Emergency Department? … I'm bringing in three patients with head injuries. Please be ready on the chopper pad … Thank you."

"You go with those three, Liza. Mike and I can take these six in the next two choppers. Can you meet us back at Freeport?" said Fred.

"Yes," I said. "We can do the surgeries there. Then we can head back here to deal with the lesser injuries."

Max and some of the freedom fighters helped me carry the first three out.

Walking alone

Johannes and I got to Ilaga in a couple of hours, supporting the old man, Are Kapa, and the pregnant woman, Juvelyn, as we walked. We expected the helicopters to pass over us again, but they didn't.

There were army troops on the ground who came through the village as we were making both patients comfortable. Johannes threw me a cassock like the one he was wearing. I quickly threw it on over my shorts, taking my shoes off to be barefoot like Johannes.

"Who's this?" demanded an army captain who had come over to question Johannes.

"This is Brother Francis from my church," said Johannes.

"Show me your passport," declared the captain.

"Brother Francis left his passport at the main church at Jaya-pura, just like I did. Our Bishop thought that it was safer if he looked after our important documents. It's not like we really go anywhere," said Johannes.

"Where have you been working? You weren't here last time we came through," said the captain.

"I was at a small village higher up the mountain, but a pregnant lady needed medical help, so I brought her down here," I said.

"What village was this?" asked the captain.

"It doesn't really have a name, but the head man is called Semu," I said.

"Alright, Brother Francis, we'll contact the Bishop in Jayapura about your papers," said the captain.

The army men continued on their way north of the village. Johannes let me know when they'd gone.

He said, "You'd better see if you can catch up with the evacuees from the Ples Tambu. If that army captain does check, there won't be any record of you at the Bishop's. He'll definitely come back again. I'll look after Juvelyn and Are Kapa. The Indonesians don't have any records about how many locals live here. They don't have birth certificates or licences, they're almost like fauna to the Indonesians."

"Thanks Johannes," I said. "I'll go straight away. If you can report back to Liza what has happened, that would be great."

"Yes," said Johannes. "I'll give her a call. And I'll call the Bishop in Jayapura too. He'd be very interested to know that the army have invaded the national park and bombed a village. He considers the area to be his responsibility. That's why we brothers are here, unarmed, to teach and help the locals. Godspeed to you, Franz."

Leaving Ilaga, I retraced my steps back to the Ples Tambu. When I got there, the place was wrecked. The helicopters had bombed the women's village and the lower entrance to the cave. I stopped to rest, looking around for any food that could be salvaged. I found some green bananas, which I was busy hacking off the bunch when I heard muffled shouting coming from inside the cave.

I went to the pile of rocks and began rolling and pushing them away. I shouted back and was answered by a voice that sounded like Semu. He was trapped in the cave. I couldn't leave him trapped in the cave, especially if both entrances were blocked. I would stay and help dig him out, but it was going to take some time.

After a few hours, I stopped and made a fire. I was hungry. I still had that leg of pork in my backpack. After I'd set up the fire and put the pork into the coals, I resumed digging, using fallen logs to help move some of the larger rocks out of the way. I was getting closer to the top of the entrance.

Semu's voice was louder now. He could see light! I kept throwing rocks, though my hands were cut and bleeding. Semu, who was in the dark, was also digging from inside the cave. I'd raised a lot of dust too, breathing it in. The sooner I got Semu out, the quicker I could leave this place.

Finally, I saw his hand, covered in dust and blood. We both dug with renewed vigour. We made a space big enough for him to crawl through on his belly.

Remarkably, Semu was unhurt except for some grazes from the digging. He was covered in dust, as I was, so for once we were the same colour – mid-grey.

Semu said, "Thank you for coming back. I thought I would die in the cave."

"Did you stay back alone?" I asked.

"My friend Duddy stayed with me. We wanted to make it look like our people were still here, that our village was not deserted. We had a rifle each and were shooting at the helicopters. We were at the top end of the cave. They shot Dud and were lining up to shoot me too. I ran into the cave as they dropped a big bomb destroying the top entrance. Dud was buried. I came down to try to get out this entrance, but they'd bombed it as well. I thought I'd never get out," said Semu.

"I walked Juvelyn and Are Kapa back to Ilaga. The army came there. Johannes gave me a cassock to wear, telling the army that I was Brother Francis who'd come to help the pregnant lady. The army didn't care about Juvelyn or the villagers, they were just after us white people. You can probably go there, just stay out of their way," I said.

"I will go in the morning," said Semu, "and you should go too, the other way."

"I will," I said, then we turned to the food on the fire.

By now the pork had cooked, although it was a little burnt on the outside. I cut it up with the machete that Johannes had given me. We had enough for later, so Semu wrapped it in a banana leaf and buried it in the ashes of the fire. We both slept well behind a pile of branches, exhausted.

In the morning, we dug up the rest of the pork leg. I cut it in half, giving one half to Semu. We wrapped each piece in banana leaves and stowed them in our bags, he in his billum, me in my backpack. Then we walked away from the Ples Tambu, in opposite directions.

Goodbye to Dirk

The Emergency team at Timika took my three patients as a priority. Then we flew back to Freeport and began work on our other serious cases.

Mike set Dirk up with a blood transfusion before treating another patient. When I got to Dirk and checked his vital signs, they were not good. He wasn't well enough to even undergo surgery.

Janette and the other nurses were doing a great job preparing another patient with torso wounds for me to operate on.

I opened the man up, removed a lot of bullets and repaired his intestines as best I could. I had to cut out one section altogether, but fortunately we have metres of intestines and I was able to join the undamaged ends together. This man was lucky that the bullets had missed his genitals and bladder. I sewed and stapled him back up, and the nurses applied dressings.

I had another check on Dirk. He was worse than before. He was not going to make it. I held his hands and spoke a few words to him.

"Dirk, my friend, I am so sorry that you are wounded. You were there for us when we had given up hope. You encouraged us to exercise, to prepare ourselves to escape. You built us up and gave us strength. And now, you have helped the Papuans to fight for their freedom. You brought them weapons, and a better chance of fighting against their oppressors. But more than that, you brought them hope. You helped them achieve their first victory. You showed them what real allies will do for their friends. I'm sorry to see you go, Dirk. I am glad and proud to have known you," I said.

Dirk was unconscious, and probably couldn't hear me, but I just felt I needed to say goodbye to him.

Then I rushed off to my next surgery. We still had to return to Enarotali fix up the minor wounds after this, and we were flat strapped.

ARTHUR

The evacuation

I t was raining again.

I didn't know whose backpack had the tarpaulin in it, but it wasn't mine. I was drenched through my boots to my socks, but I just kept walking.

We all just kept walking. Men, women and children, all carrying bags, all tired and wet. At nightfall we'd camp at a village. The local people made us feel welcome. This was so different to the way they'd treated Dirk, Franz and me. Men and older boys were invited to sleep in the longhouse. Women and kids were invited into other families' huts, out of the rain.

The first night, I took out my leg of pork, and handed it to the man who was stoking the fire. He bowed at me, so I bowed back. The pork was cooked and shared by everyone. There were also birds, a snake, and yams. We had a real feast. The villagers sang some mournful songs after the meal, which I recorded using my phone.

Thank God for the satellite phone. I called Liza, and then Kayla.

"Kayla, it's me, Arthur," I said.

"Oh, Arthur," said Kayla. "I'm so glad you're still alive."

"Yes, we got everyone out of the Ples Tambu before the helicopters arrived. We could hear them as we walked. Well, almost everyone. Semu and his friend stayed back to defend the place, and make it look like people were still there," I said.

"Oh, that was very brave of them," said Kayla. "Where are you now?"

"Well, I don't know if this village has a name, but it's a day's walk east of the Ples Tambu. We are following the ridges of the southern range. I'm pretty sure we're still in the national park. Franz walked back to Ilaga with the missionary Johannes, and a couple of villagers who couldn't make the long walk. I hope he'll catch up with us," I said.

"Right," said Kayla, "I have been talking to the Papuan Refugee Organisation over here. We will bring vehicles close to the border to meet you. I hope Franz is OK. How long till you reach the border, do you think?" asked Kayla.

"At the rate we're moving, I'd say another four or even five days. This rain is slowing us down. We've already had to change course a couple of times to get around the creeks that are becoming waterfalls," I said.

"Arthur, we're going to assemble at Tabubil. But if you think you might cross at another place, call us and let me know. We'll be in four-wheel drives, so we can drive overland if we have to. How many people are there?"

"Counting me, we are twenty-seven," I said.

"OK, I'll make sure we have enough vehicles. Good luck, Arthur," said Kayla.

"Thanks, Kayla. I miss you," I said.

"I miss you too. Now be careful and stay in touch," said Kayla, as she hung up.

The next day it rained in the morning but had cleared by the middle of the day. I was walking at the back of the group, in case the people at the front encountered any military. Then I could run off and not endanger the group. We came to a stream that had turned into a torrent; people were crossing in small groups, trying to keep their billums dry. A woman just ahead of me was carrying a baby as well as leading a small boy. She picked him up and handed him to me. The little boy probably couldn't swim and I could see he was scared, so I carried him. We scrambled across as a small group, slipping on the wet rocks, and fighting the current in the swollen creek. By the time we made it to the other side, I'd made a new friend. Sui wanted me to carry him all the time now, or at least hold his hand.

WIRA

Kopassus office

T
hings were crazy around here after Colonel Yuda died. The general called from Jakarta saying he'd send Yuda's replacement within a week.

The other officers returned from the mission to Enarotali with mixed reports. Some said that Yuda had been unlucky. Another said that he'd been mowing down the Papuans in a drainage ditch after having told the other officers to concentrate on the armoured vehicles of the rebels. Whatever, he was now dead at the hands of the rebels.

The officers reported that the rebels had at least five machine guns mounted on armoured four-wheel drives, making them a much more formidable enemy. The officers were happy to retreat to save their helicopters and themselves.

I organised a full military funeral for the Colonel, even flying the army band up from Timika to Jayapura.

After that it was terrible. I'd hardly had a moment's rest and no time off at all.

The phone rang. I answered, "Wira here."

"This is Major Honan. Is Yuda's replacement there yet?" said Honan.

"No sir," I said. "Major Karna is acting in his place, but he is out right now."

"I've had reports back from my scouts that there is a lot of movement in the national park. Not just natives but white men. There was an undocumented missionary in Ilaga called Brother Francis – the Bishop wouldn't give us any information about him.

"There is a yacht moored at the south of the park in the Sungai Muras Besar. There is no one aboard, and we think it could be the gun runners' boat. I've stationed a unit to keep watch on it. Paniai is crawling with rebels and rebel sympathisers. I need more men and more equipment at the barracks both there and here in Timika," said Honan.

"Sir, that is a lot to report. I have taken notes, but please send an email to Major Karna as soon as possible. What do you want the Kopassus to do, Sir?"

"If your men could fly some reconnaissance missions over the park, it would save us a lot of manpower on the ground," said Honan.

"Major Honan, I will report this to Major Karna as soon as he walks in the door" I said.

"Good job, Wira," said Major Honan.

I hoped our new commanding officer would be more like Honan and less like Yuda.

LIZA

The moving base

One of the interesting things about the Free Papua Movement is its guerrilla nature. The groups constantly move around to avoid detection, making them easy to lose track of.

After we'd completed our surgeries at Freeport, Mike and I flew back to Enarotali to treat the lesser injuries. As we approached the town, the satellite phone rang.

Paka was on the line. "Doctor Liza, don't go to that shed where we were this morning. We have moved to a shed at the back of the fruit market. The trucks are both there, we'll flag you down."

"Copy that, Paka, the shed behind the fruit market," I said it loud enough for Max the pilot to hear.

Max rose in altitude and headed to the market. They'd moved already, half a day after the attack.

We soon found them with some of the remaining patients still in the trucks. Others were sitting around, or even helping carry things, bandaged up and limping.

Mike and I made a list of patients that we'd treat in the order of the severity of their injuries. We set up treatment tables in a corner where we hoped to be able to maintain a germ-free environment.

Paka, who was running around organising things, came over to see us when he had a chance.

"Doctor Liza! Doctor Mike! Thank you so much for tending to all of the wounded today!" said Paka.

"We're happy we can help," I said.

"Tell me, how is your friend Dirk?" asked Paka.

"Sadly, Dirk didn't make it," said Mike.

"Were there any other fighters who died?" asked Paka.

"Lawa, one of the head injuries. He never woke up either," I said.

"Lawa was Dirk's gunman. He sat beside him in the jeep. I will let his family know," said Paka.

"We can bring his body back here for burial," I offered.

"We can't begin to thank you enough, Doctor Liza and Doctor Mike," said Paka.

We got back to work, taking out bullets and stitching up patients. These long-suffering young men and women had waited all day for treatment without any painkillers. I shudder to think what would have happened to them before we offered our services.

ARTHUR

In the clouds

W
e were walking higher up the mountains now. We were quite literally in the clouds. But if we couldn't see out of the forest, people in choppers couldn't see us either.

We were on a higher ridge than the one we walked on before. While we were still in forest, we could see farms and roads at the bottom of the ridges. Outside the national park, we were now walking through settled Papua, Indonesian Papua.

Our travel became erratic, sometimes walking at night in the rain, and sometimes during the day in the sunshine. We were avoiding the settlements at all costs; we couldn't allow ourselves to be seen by a police or army officer now.

We came to a river with only a road bridge across it guarded by an army officer.

Swando and I sat with the other men surveying the scene from above, looking down over the river from the forest.

"I have an idea," I said.

"What is your idea?" asked Swando.

"I think we should send a woman to walk over the bridge and distract the soldier. Then we can all swim across to the other side of the bridge," I said.

"That is a good idea," said Swando.

"Who will we send?" asked one of the other men.

"Let's ask Tigi," said Swando, who knew everyone in the tribe well.

Tigi was sent for. Young and buxom, I could see why Swando had thought of her.

"Tigi, we have a secret mission for you. It is dangerous, but it will help the whole tribe," said Swando.

"What is it that you want me to do?" asked Tigi.

"See that soldier down there?" asked Swando, "go up and start talking to him."

"But what will I say?" asked Tigi.

"Ask him the way to Tiom from here. Listen to him, then ask him the way to the church in this village, or the mosque," I said.

I'd seen this scene in at least ten movies.

"If he tries anything violent, your husband is going to walk up and find you," I said.

"But I don't have a husband," said Tigi.

"One of these guys will be your husband," I said, pointing to the younger men. They all put their hands up to be picked.

"OK, I'll do it. As long as I get to pick the husband," said Tigi.

The plan went well and we were over the river in less than ten minutes.

That night, as we set up camp high in the mountains, the clouds swept past, and we could see a view down into the foothills below. There was a small town, lit up with streetlights and lights inside buildings.

"That is Oksibil," said Swando.

"Thank you. I'll tell Kayla. She's in Tabubil now," I said.

I called up Kayla. "Kayla, it's Arthur."

"Good to hear your voice, Arthur," she said.

"We are about thirty kilometres north of Oksibil now. We will cross the border tomorrow," I said.

"Have the helicopters seen you? They have been over Tabubil," Kayla said.

"No. Did they see you guys?" I asked.

"Luckily, we were spread all over town at the time, so we probably blended in with the locals. We weren't travelling in convoy or anything like that," said Kayla.

"Good. But I'm afraid I've got some bad news. Liza called and told me that Dirk was killed in the battle at Enarotali. He was driving an armoured jeep. He was shot. But they managed to ground two planes, two helicopters and a light tank, and they destroyed the airfield. So I guess that's why the army and Kopassus haven't been that busy chasing us," I said.

"I'm sorry to hear that, Arthur," said Kayla. "Dirk was a good man. I'm sorry that he died, even if it was for a good cause."

"I haven't seen Franz either. I was hoping that he'd catch up to us by now, but there's been no sign of him," I said.

"Take care, Arthur, and I'll see you on the other side," said Kayla.

"Yes, I'll see you in New Guinea."

FRANZ

Lost in the wilderness

Shit. Now I'm really lost. I thought I was on the path that Swando's tribe were on, but when I came out of the national park, I just couldn't tell which way they'd gone. The roads were crawling with army vehicles, and choppers were passing overhead, forcing me to seek cover.

I went back into the park, thinking of heading south to find the boat. But I came to a line of cliffs which dropped away for kilometres. There was no easy track south from here.

I thought about it for a while and decided to head back to the Ples Tambu. If I got as far as Ilaga, maybe I could call Liza to send a chopper for me. I retraced my steps to the ridge track, and west to the Ples Tambu. I was hungry now, and tired. I hadn't eaten since the pork ran out.

I found the lower entrance to the cave and crawled in. It was dark, but I had my solar-powered phone, out of range, but still good for a torch. I walked the length of the cave, a few hundred metres, and waded through the flooded section. It felt good to get wet. I took the opportunity to wash my face and hair. I could still feel the scars in my scalp. At the top of the cave, the entrance was also caved in, but Semu had built a fire inside it, and had dug a small hole through the rubble to the outside. I waited there for him, and he returned with some birds. He was surprised to see me.

"Franz! What are you doing here?" he asked.

"I couldn't find them. Outside the Lorentz, that track disappears. There are roads, army everywhere. I didn't know which way to go. I thought about walking to Jita, to the boat, but I couldn't find a track south either. So I came back here," I said.

"Right," said Semu. "I'll cook these birds and think about what to do."

Semu cooked while I dried the things from my backpack. I spread out the tarpaulin and my sleeping bag and made sure my machete was dry.

"Do you still have your gun?" asked Semu.

"No, I passed it to Konia when we met. I thought the freedom fighters needed it more than I did," I said.

"I have some guns," said Semu. "But they are buried."

"If I had a gun, I might have a better chance of walking out of here," I said.

"But you don't know the way," said Semu. Then he said, "I know the way."

"We could both walk out. But what about Juvelyn? I thought you were staying to be with her?" I said.

"I went to Ilaga. Juvelyn is doing well. Are Kapa is also OK. They are learning Tok Pisin from Johannes at the school. They'll be alright. I'll walk with you," said Semu.

After we ate, we dug up the guns. Semu had buried his rifle near the last machine gun, and the last two rounds of ammo. The freedom fighters must have wanted to save one, in case all of the others were captured by the Indonesians. I put them both in my backpack.

"There's another rifle, but it is buried with my friend Dud under there," said Semu, indicating the huge pile of rubble which mostly blocked the entrance.

It would take a while to get that gun out.

"Can you ride a motorbike?" asked Semu.

"I can, but I haven't done it in years," I said.

"Kupsy rode one here, when he first came to warn us about the Kopassus. He left it and walked out with some guns. It is at the bottom of the hill with the vine."

After we'd eaten we headed off, scrambling down the slope. Sure enough, there was the bike with the keys in the ignition. It was a 1000cc Kawasaki, and it still had a quarter of a tank of petrol. With me driving, Semu had to wear my backpack so we could fit on the bike.

"I hope that Tiom has a petrol station," I said.

"Sevis stesin? Yes, I think so," said Semu. He pointed, "that way."

I remembered that Semu had been out walking with Konia and Kupsy, so he did know the land beyond the national park. Better than me anyway.

LIZA

Meeting Major Honan

Janette came into my office at Freeport.

"There is a Major Honan here to see you, Doctor Fraser," she said.

"You can send him in, but he'd better be quick. I'm busy."

Major Honan came into my office. He was quite tall for an Indonesian and wore his dress uniform.

"Major Honan, I'm Doctor Fraser. Please take a seat," I said, indicating a chair.

Honan sat down. "Doctor Fraser, I have come to ask you some questions."

"Well, as long as you're quick, because I am very busy," I said.

"Have you recently operated on some Papuan rebels and delivered some to the Timika Hospital?" Honan asked.

"I have treated some Papuan locals. I have a field office in Enarotali. They called me and asked for medical assistance," I said.

"Are you harbouring any rebels here in your clinic?" asked Honan.

"Major Honan, I am a doctor, and I am politically neutral. My job is to look after the health of the mine workers, expats and locals. I also offer health services to the local people in our region, since your government doesn't," I said.

"Are you criticising our government, Doctor Fraser?" asked Honan.

"No. Are you criticising our health service, Major Honan?" I asked.

"I have heard reports that some of your workers are supporting rebels against the Indonesian government, Doctor Fraser. I am stationed here at Freeport now to monitor your activities. Do you know Dirk Feldmuller, Arthur Neilson and Franz Seevink?" asked Honan.

"I have read Amnesty International's report called 'Just Let Them Die', referring to your army's treatment of local civilians. These actions are against international law as laid out in the Geneva Convention. I believe that your military is responsible for war crimes in this area, and, quite frankly, I am getting sick of mopping up after you. I don't have any more time to waste with you, Major Honan. If you wish to argue further, please take it up with my manager, Mr Sinclair," I said, standing up.

"Thank you, Doctor Fraser," said Honan. He stood up and left.

Bloody hell. That man was the last thing we needed around here. We still had five inpatients requiring post-operative care. That creep better not come around here trying to arrest them.

I rang up Sinclair to give him the heads up and told him what Major Honan was after.

"Quite frankly," said Sinclair, "I was a bit pissed off when the army decided to station themselves in Tembagapura last week. They had the nerve to requisition the local hotel and kick our workers out of it. We've had to ask our workers to double up in their flats, and these are people who've just knocked off after twelve-hour shifts," said Sinclair.

"How dare he come in here trying to frighten me in my office. I quoted Amnesty International's report and the Geneva Convention to him."

"I wish he'd take his troops and bugger off back to Timika," said Sinclair. "This town is hardly big enough to service the mine. There's no room for the army up here as well. Anyway, we built this place."

"What the hell are they doing up here?" I asked.

"From what I've seen, they're stopping everyone and asking them for ID or papers. What a joke! None of the locals we employ even have birth certificates. We paid to educate them. We taught them to drive and we bought them their licences. They are our workers and it's our town," said Sinclair.

"I'm glad we're on the same page," I said. "See if you can't use your influence to get them to leave."

"Yes, I'm just thinking about who to call now," said Sinclair.

"Thanks so much. Bye, Jim," I said.

I stood outside my side door and I lit up a cigarette.

It looked like Sinclair had his own reasons to get the army off our plateau. We've got our own security, and they're armed to the teeth. I'll bet they are eyeing off the army right now, counting men and weapons. They are there to protect a fortune in gold, and they've got video surveillance, electronic security systems, armoured vehicles, and access to our fleet of choppers. When I visit the local clinic, I walk out through a bullet-proof gate, after scanning my ID and being visually checked. We live in a fortress. Those army jerks aren't getting in here any time soon.

God, I hope that Arthur and the villagers are alright. I wonder if they've made it to the border yet?

Mike came in. "Hey, Dave had his surgery down in Townsville today. Shall we ring him up?" he said.

"Good idea. I just had to speak to that creepy Major Honan, but I told him what I thought of his attacking the villagers and leaving them to die," I said.

"Good on you, darling," said Mike. "You shouldn't have to deal with those monsters."

"Jim Sinclair wants them out of here too. It seems they kicked all the extra workers out of the motel and requisitioned it for the army. Sinclair said that the mine built the town, the mine owns the town, and the army should go back to Timika," I said.

"That's good. It means our patients are safe here. When they are well enough to travel, we can fly them right over the heads of those army dicks," said Mike. "Hey, have you heard from Arthur?"

"No, not yet," I said. "And I'm worried to ring him in case they are somewhere trying to be really quiet."

"Right," said Mike. "He'll call us if he needs us, or when the mission is successful."

I called Dave in Townsville.

"Hello, Doctor Dave," I said.

"Liza! Thanks for calling," said Dave. "They told me that the surgery went well."

"That's so good to hear, Dave. Mike and I have been thinking of you today."

"I've been thinking of you guys too. In fact, I've got four Townsville doctors to join our International Aid program. They have been fascinated by my stories of patching up the freedom fighters. And one doctor is in administration. He thinks he can access funding for us as well," said Dave.

"Four more doctors! Dave, that's terrific," I said.

Mike took the phone and had a few words with Dave too, about when they'd both be back at work.

I started thinking about what the canteen was serving for dinner, and then I wondered what Arthur and Swando's tribe would be eating, and where.

Reaching the border

We were so close now I could almost smell New Guinea.

But there was a problem. The village we were staying in was tiny. The villagers told us that army helicopters were sweeping the border two or three times a day, and always at different times. There was no fence, but the forest had been largely cleared along the border, meaning there are few trees to hide under. Swando wanted to cross at night, but the ground was slippery, and there were cliffs to get down which would need vines or ropes. And we had women carrying babies travelling with us, and I was carrying little Sui. On the open cliffs, we'd be easy targets. Those bastards could still kill the whole tribe.

We decided to wait where we were and make plans. We talked about breaking into smaller groups. We just didn't know what would be best.

Swando, Konia, Kupsy and the men had a meeting. Were there enough vines for everyone to make the descent? Who would help the children and elders? Who would carry what? How long would the walk take? The men told us to send the weaker members down first, then follow them. We couldn't risk shouting to each other or wasting time by hesitating.

In the end we concentrated on one rope at a time. There was a waterfall that a few people could hide behind, but they would get very wet if they did. Each man was assigned a small group to assist. I would help Sui, his mum and baby sister.

FRANZ

The hell ride

I t had been a long time since I'd ridden a dirt bike. And I'd never driven one this powerful.

I stopped at the petrol station in Tiom, where a local man happily filled up the tank in return for a small nugget. He called me 'brother', which is when I looked down and realised, I was still wearing the cassock.

Brother Francis, the rebel biker, I thought.

After we'd filled up, we left the road. Semu pointed out the trail and which turns to take. The roads followed the valleys, and we were riding the ridges, under the trees, away from most of the farms and houses. There were still huts up here. Some locals lived in houses, some in huts. Some came out to wave at us as we zoomed by.

We covered a lot of ground. The rain had turned the track to mud, covering us in it. For once in my life I was glad I wore glasses, because I could wipe the mud off them. Semu wiped his eyes on the back of my cassock!

At the really steep sections I hopped off and pushed. Or I lowered the bike, sliding in the mud myself. I couldn't afford to have an accident now.

I rejoined the road to cross a river. There was an army grunt stationed at the bridge, so I thought I'd better slow down to talk to him.

"Hello, officer," I said.

"Hello, brother," said the officer. "Do you have your papers on you?"

"I'm terribly sorry," I said. "I don't have them on me. I'm Brother Francis, I'm taking to take this man to Oksibil for medical treatment."

"What is he called?" The officer asked me.

"He is called Duddy," I said. It was the first name other than Semu that came into my head. They might be on the lookout for Swando or Semu.

"Alright, brother, you can pass," said the soldier. This religious outfit was coming in really handy.

As night was falling, we got to the village where the crossing was planned. They were still here!

ARTHUR

Franz and the last gun

We heard a motorbike approaching, so I hid my white face in a clump of banana trees.

It was Franz and Semu! I ran down to meet them.

"Franz! Thank God! I was worried you were dead. And you too, Semu! You're alive too!" I was stunned and speaking drivel.

"Did you bring any guns with you?" asked Konia, getting straight to the point.

"Yes," said Franz. "Semu and I dug up the last machine gun and we brought a rifle too."

"That's good," said Swando. "Very good. We have to cross this valley in daylight. The locals tell us that a helicopter patrols at different times every day."

"I can operate the gun," said Konia. "But I need someone to be my feeder and backup operator."

"Then I will lead the crossing," said Kupsy. The two brothers weren't supposed to be on a mission together, in case they were both killed.

"I can be the feeder," offered Franz.

"No, Franz, you have made your contribution already," said Konia. "You should make the crossing with Arthur. You are both at a great risk. I need a volunteer from among our men."

"I will do it," said Semu. "They destroyed our home. I want a chance to shoot back at them."

Swando looked upset, but he said "You are brave, my son. You stayed back to defend our home, and now you will defend us as we escape the Indonesians."

It was decided.

Franz and Semu unpacked the guns from their backpack. It was covered in mud, like the two of them. Konia, Semu and Franz assembled the gun, made sure it was clean and in working order.

"It's big," said Semu, trying to lift the gun by himself.

"In Vietnam, the American soldiers called it 'The Pig' because of its size," I said.

"We will turn those Indonesians into long pork with The Pig," laughed Konia.

We laughed too. We, who had been so worried about becoming long pork ourselves.

Franz said, "You'll need my backpack to carry the gun back to where you need it."

He emptied out his bag, making a small pile of possessions.

"That stuff can fit in my bag, Franz," I said. "And you might want to change back into those clothes. Your cassock is filthy."

"There is a creek where you can wash, just beyond the bananas," said Konia.

"There is a rocky outcrop where that gun can be set up," I said. "There's a fig tree for cover, and the rock has a good view north and south up and down the valley."

"Yes," said Swando. "That's a good place for it. But when should we go? First light?"

Konia said "Let's wait till the first chopper flies past. Then, we'll have a few hours before it flies past again."

Franz and Semu had a wash – they really did look like mud men, the PNG Asaro tribe who paint themselves with mud and wear a mud mask for ceremonies. Our men had been out hunting, so we had some birds and possums for our last dinner in Papua. The Papuans carried rocks out to the outcrop, building a small wall for the gunmen to hide behind. Rocks from the creek, stepping stones, even the rocks from around our fire all went to make the wall. We slept in a newly built hut from where I called Kayla briefly to say that tomorrow was 'the day'.

ARTHUR

Crossing the border

We didn't have to wait too long. The sun was up at five, and the helicopter flew past at six thirty. That was our cue to go. We walked the track to the cliff line and soon found the first vines. Sui's mum, Gilea, had her baby tied to her back with a sarong. I sent her down the vine first. Most of the village women had never left the national park; some had never left the village. I don't expect many had abseiled down a vine in the wet season, either. I sent Sui down next. Then I made the climb as Gilea held the tail of the vine for me. We walked along the narrow path until the next drop and repeated the process. From one point, I could see down into the valley and that the start of our party had reached the valley floor.

I couldn't see the waterfall yet, but I could hear it. The early rains had filled the creeks that fed the fall, and the water thundered down.

Then there was another sound. The helicopter had turned around and was heading back up our valley towards us. Had we been seen by army scouts?

My group ran for the waterfall. Franz's group behind me did, too. The space behind the waterfall only held so many, and the groups before us had run back to take cover there as well.

Franz reached into my backpack and grabbed the tarpaulin. I followed him back to a crevice in the cliff, and Franz, myself and another man huddled into the crevice and covered ourselves with the tarp. In the valley, our friends took cover behind fallen trees, but they were exposed to the moving helicopter.

We couldn't see much of the action, but we could hear it. The chopper came in low, focusing on our party. They'd already fired on our people down in the valley who were most visible, then they must have come into Konia's range. Our machine gun sprang to life, peppering the Mil Mi chopper on its roof and tail. The chopper lifted itself and turned towards our side of the cliff.

Konia just kept shooting. He was aiming at the cockpit now. But the chopper was focusing on Konia and Semu behind their small stone wall. There was a brief halt in the firing; maybe Konia and Semu were changing rounds? Then the firing continued as the chopper got closer and closer.

Then it happened. Konia must have found his mark. The Russian Mil Mi tipped to one side, crashed into the cliffs, and dropped down to the valley below. There was an explosion. We came out of our hiding places to take a look.

From our position, we couldn't see Konia and Semu. We passed behind the brown waterfall and continued down to the valley.

From there, we could see that Konia was lying forwards over the wall.

Semu sat next to him and gave us a feeble wave.

I reached for the satellite phone.

"Liza, it's Arthur," I said.

"Arthur, did you make it across?" asked Liza.

"We are crossing the border right now. We're about thirty kilometres north of Oksibil. Konia has been shot and is unconscious. Semu has also been shot but he's awake. They are on the top of a cliff, near a big fig tree. There's a crashed chopper in the valley below, which may help you to locate them," I said.

"It will take us some time to reach you, but I'm on my way," said Liza.

"I probably won't see you, but thank you, Liza. Thank you from all of us." I cut it short and continued my climb.

I had to carry Sui, who was crying and scared. Franz was helping an old woman; we were all hurrying to reach the safety of the forest on the other side.

A final job before my days off

It was about 450 kilometres from Freeport to Oksibil. It would take us a couple of hours in the fastest helicopter we had.

Arthur had said they'd camped at a village just before the crossing, so hopefully some of the local villagers could render first aid before we got there.

It was still early in the morning when I got Arthur's call. Max offered to fly me, while Fred and Mike could take care of our patients. Getting used to this now, Max and I carried two stretchers out to the chopper. I dashed back to grab some sandwiches and drinks from the canteen before returning to the chopper pad and getting underway.

Max was chatty on the headphones.

"I don't usually get to fly over this way," Max said. "The national park is really beautiful along here. Look at all the creeks and rivers falling over the cliff line."

I looked down and saw the rainforest between breaks in the clouds.

"You're right, it's absolutely stunning," I said.

Some waterfalls were white, others brown with sediment from the swollen creeks. The forest was tall and many layered, with every shade of green above and below the brown and grey rocks of the cliffs and mountains.

Past the national park, the land was cleared along the valleys for farms, roads and occasional buildings.

"I'm going to follow the ridges that the villagers probably took. No point flying south to Oksibil if they didn't go that far," said Max.

"From what Arthur said, they were trying to make the shortest journey, and stay away from the towns as much as possible," I said.

This was quiet rural land – a mixture of small and large land holdings. But there were still collections of huts among subsistence gardens. These were the places the Asmat would stay.

"Right, we're approaching the border now," said Max. "Keep your eyes peeled."

The border area had been partially cleared below the steep mountains. We turned to the north and followed the border clearing. Max had a satellite map on his control panel; I leaned over the front seats to look at it.

"Down there! Look!" said Max, pointing down the cliffs to the valley. A wrecked chopper lay smouldering, its rotor blades all askew.

"Right, they've got to be up here somewhere," I said.

We saw a fig tree on an outcrop, and a collection of huts surrounded by a garden farm.

"Is there anywhere you can land?" I asked.

Circling, we found a flattish spot close to the cliff's edge. Max put us down slowly on the rocky cliff. As the engine slowed down, we could feel a bit of wind against us. I hopped out and walked towards the village.

A man met us, directing us to a large hut in the village, which must have been their longhouse. These are supposed to be only for men, but in medical emergencies, who cares?

Semu was lying just inside, conscious and moaning.

"Semu," I said, "it's me, Doctor Liza."

"Liza," was all he said. He looked pretty haggard.

I gave him a shot of pethidine and removed the rags that had been tied around his wounds. He'd copped bullets in the shoulder and the neck. Luckily, the neck wound had missed his arteries and windpipe, but he still looked pretty bad. He was hot and his pulse was slow. I disinfected his wounds, then bound them up with pressure bandages. Max had brought a stretcher in and put it down beside him.

"What about Konia?" I asked.

The villagers shook their heads and looked down. I guessed that he didn't make it.

"Can I still see him?" I asked.

I was led out to where some men were digging a large hole under some trees. At the bottom of the hole lay a machine gun. Next to the hole lay Konia.

He was quite messed up. Someone had wiped his face clean, but his dreadlocks were all stuck together with blood. He had wounds across his chest and his arms, and on his forehead. He was wearing the same T-shirt that I had last seen him in.

I said "Papua Merdeka, Konia. Papua Merdeka!"

The people around me understood this and joined in with "Papua Merdeka!" themselves.

I lit up a cigarette, and a couple of the men looked at me with that look that all smokers recognise. I rolled a couple more ciggies and passed them to the grave diggers. I gave them the rest of my pouch, and my lighter too. I had another pouch at the base. It looked like it was a long way to the shops from here.

When the hole was long enough, they would put him in, on top of the gun. If anyone dug it up, they'd see the man, and probably not the gun.

I went back to the chopper, where a local had helped Max to load Semu in the back. I jumped in with him. Max resumed his seat at the front.

As we rose in the air, the little children started waving, and then the adults did too.

I waved back, wondering how many of these villagers grew up here, or were they all on their way to freedom in Papua New Guinea?

ARTHUR

Freedom in PNG

Some of the people in the valley had been hit by bullets, but no injuries were so bad that they couldn't keep moving. Franz ripped up his cassock – which he'd washed in the creek, so it was sort of clean – and we bandaged some arms and legs with strips of it. It was enough to stop the bleeding and keep people walking. We were so close now.

The climb up the other side of the valley was not as bad as the Papuan side. Then under the cover of the trees, into the forest. We kept walking, away from the border, not stopping until we saw a vehicle. It was a four-wheel drive driven by a local man. As soon as he saw us, he hopped out.

"Swando? Semu? Arthur?" asked the man.

"Yes! I am Arthur! Swando is with us!"

"I can take seven or eight," he said. "I'll radio the others. Climb in!"

We could hardly believe it. We put women and children in the first vehicle. The man radioed the others, and soon we heard engines coming from the north and the south. They must have stretched out their convoy, unsure of exactly where we'd be.

The first vehicle pulled off as the next ones arrived. Our tribe were organising themselves into jeep-sized groups.

"I think they are taking us to Tabubil," I said to Franz.

"No, Telefomin," said one of the drivers. "It is further from the border. The Indos are flying over Tabubil, the shits," said the man.

Then Kayla drove up in another vehicle.

"Kayla!" I said. I gave her a hug. Franz hugged her too. We were stunned to see her.

We stood and talked while the vehicles loaded up and took off.

"Leave room in mine for these two," yelled Kayla to the villagers.

Swando had jumped in with his bag of skulls and carvings, along with his wife and some children. Kayla stopped talking and looked out at the trees.

"Arthur, do you have a gun?" she asked quickly.

I reached into the backpack for the rifle.

Kayla snatched it off me and aimed over my shoulder.

Bang! Bang! Bang!

I turned and gasped. A hundred metres away, an Indonesian soldier in camouflage gear clung to a tree then fell down. He was holding a two-way radio.

"Let's get out of here," said Kayla, as she leapt into the driver's seat.

We bounced along through the forest.

"Where's that track?" asked Kayla.

Another vehicle peeled away to the right, and Kayla followed.

"Those damned Kopassus scouts. They don't respect our border. They just fly over and walk in, like they own the place. I wish they'd all just go back to where they came from!" said Kayla, as she drove along.

Franz and I were in shock. Kayla had told Franz and me that she was a journalist, but she was too bloody good with the rifle to be a journalist. How was I going to broach this subject?

"Dirk, Franz and I shot two soldiers near the Ples Tambu, but we were lying down, and had time to aim," I said.

"You're a crack shot, woman," said Franz.

"Yeah, ever since I was a kid my dad took me to the rifle range," said Kayla. "I didn't have any brothers, so I suppose a daughter was the next best thing to a son."

"Do all the women from the church know how to fire a rifle?" asked Franz, still incredulous.

"Don't bet on it, kiddo," joked Kayla.

It was maybe forty kilometres to Telefomin. We stopped at a big farm shed and piled out. Some local women had some cooking fires going. There were long benches and stackable chairs. Women were dishing out food onto tin plates and passing them to our villagers.

"This is a refugee camp supported by our church and the Papuan Refugee Association. We'll stay here today and get everyone registered. Hey, can you not mention that thing with that guy today? If I reported it, it's miles of paperwork, and I could face consequences." said Kayla.

I said, "I don't remember that thing with that guy?"

Franz said, "What thing with what guy?"

"Thanks guys. Do you both need a lift into Port Moresby? I'm going back in myself," said Kayla.

"What will happen with Swando and the villagers?" I asked.

Kayla explained, "There are negotiations going on right now as to where they are going to go. We're trying to find one community that is willing to take the lot of them, so they can stay together. This place is a temporary camp, being close to the border. We usually have family groups crossing together and then we find villages for them to join. It's often just down to how many huts they'll need, or buildings. What you saw today was all our teams. It was good to know exactly how many are coming over and when. Those Kopassus arseholes kill so many on both sides of the border."

Franz said, "We are so glad to get across. The army sent helicopters to the Ples Tambu and blew up both entrances to the cave. Semu and Dud stayed there so it didn't look like the place was deserted and shot at the first helicopter with rifles. Dud got shot and buried in the rubble at the top of the cave. I had to help Semu dig his way out the lower entrance. The machine gun had been buried further inside the cave, so we dug it up to bring with us.

"Semu told me that Kupsy had ridden up on a trail bike to give the early warning, and they started carrying the stuff from the cave straight away. The motorbike was still there, so we did the hell ride to catch up with the rest of these guys. There were army troops and helicopters all over the place, so we kept off the roads. And I was still wearing the cassock that Johannes leant me," added Franz.

"We were just so stunned when Franz and Semu caught up with us. We had begun to think that the army might have got them," I said to Kayla.

She'd only had the barest details of our trip, so it was good to fill her in.

"When we saw they'd brought the guns, we were so relieved. Otherwise crossing the border seemed like a suicide mission. The locals told us that the helicopters flew over a few times every day, and they clear-felled much of the border strip so they could hunt people down easier. We had kids to carry, old people and women with babies, so we weren't travelling very fast," I said.

"Konia and Semu volunteered to man the gun, while the rest of us came across. They got that chopper, but they both got shot. Arthur called Liza to pick them up, although we don't know if they were still alive," said Franz.

"They have scouts everywhere," said Kayla, "That's why this morning's chopper turned around and came back. One of them saw you guys and radioed in. They've killed dozens of our people, maybe hundreds."

"I hope Liza picked them up. I can ring and see," I said.

Liza picked up after a few rings.

"Hello, Liza here."

"Liza, it's Arthur. We made it across."

"Arthur, that's great to hear. The whole village?"

"Yes, we're all here in a refugee camp in Telefomin. Did you find Konia and Semu?"

"Semu is doing OK. Fred is just operating on him now. Konia didn't make it. They shot him in the head and the chest. He would have died quickly. The villagers were burying him under a clump of trees when I got there. And they buried him on top of the big gun. I suppose they didn't want to be found in possession of it," said Liza.

"Oh, I am sorry to hear that. I'll pass the news on to Kupsy. It's good news about Semu, though. Swando will be glad to hear it," I said.

"I'm glad you and Franz are safe, Arthur," said Liza.

"You rescued us too, thanks, Liza. Papua Merdeka," I said.

"Papua Merdeka!" said Liza.

I had to deliver the good news and the bad news before we left for Port Moresby.

ARTHUR

Drinks for Dirk and Konia

Swando was happy to hear about Semu, and grateful that Liza had rescued him and taken him back. To him the Ples Tambu was home, so Semu would be close to home and to his wife in Ilaga.

Kupsy was pretty devastated about Konia, but also philosophical about death. They both knew the risk when they joined the OPM. They would rather die fighting for freedom than get shot trying to defend their land unarmed, like their father and uncle had.

Kayla introduced Kupsy to all the refuge workers.

"This is Kupsy, he's an OPM fighter. He and his brother led this village across the border after Kopassus targeted their home in the Lorentz National Park. His brother Konia died, but not before he'd shot down a helicopter to let this tribe cross the border," said Kayla.

One of the refuge workers said, "We are pleased to meet you, but sorry to hear about your brother."

Kupsy said, "I'll return to the OPM and rejoin my group. I can take back any messages you have for the organisation."

One worker said, "I'm Paul, a group leader here. If you can wait a few days, we can send you back with a small team of our men who have a mission across the border. You can stay here until then."

Kupsy said, "Thank you. I will return with your men. My group will miss me and will want news about the evacuation of Swando's tribe."

"Are you heading back to Port Moresby, Paul?" asked Kayla.

"Yeah, there's a meeting of the Papuan Refugee Association that I've got to go to tomorrow. Actually, it could be good if Kupsy came along to that," said Paul.

"We're going to drive down today, and maybe have drinks for our fallen friends tonight. Arthur and Franz lost their friend Dirk at the battle at Enarotali, and they were friends with Konia too. Maybe Kupsy can come along for drinks with us and go to the meeting with you?" asked Kayla.

"OK, I'll take Kupsy down and back, if that works. My wife won't mind if he stays with us. We've got room. Kupsy can tell the PRA about the OPM's recent activities. If we can get better communications set up, we can save more lives, at least, at the border," said Paul.

We said goodbye to the villagers and jumped in Kayla's 'Fowil Draiv'. Kayla drove carefully down the winding mountain roads from Telefomin to the coastal plain. It was a 780-kilometre drive, so it would take most of the day. Franz and I offered to take turns driving, if she'd give us directions.

We stopped for dinner at Orloli, which was about halfway. Kayla bought us some vodka and beers at a bottle shop there, as the shops would be closed by the time we got to Port Moresby. New Guinea did feel free compared to Papua. The towns weren't patrolled by gun-toting soldiers and police. People walked, rode bicycles and wore whatever they liked. Hitchhikers tried to pull us over. We had to stop for cows and goats and snakes on the road.

It really hit me now that Dirk was dead. Would the mine send his body back to his parents in Amsterdam? What would happen to his place in Bali and all his things? Would he have written a will?

Franz had a bit of a nap in the back seat, so Kayla and I took turns driving, not saying much. I suppose we each had a lot to think about.

Port Moresby is a big city. Kayla drove the last bit, as the traffic really was crazy. The noise of the city woke Franz up, and he cracked a warm beer for himself, and one for me.

At Kayla's place, she got some orange juice out of the fridge, and poured us vodka drinks.

"To Dirk and Konia," toasted Franz.

"Dirk and Konia," Kayla and I responded.

"I can't believe we lost them both within a few days of each other," I said.

"I guess this is a war, a guerrilla war, hidden from the world," said Franz.

"Oh, I'm going to write about it in my newspaper," said Kayla. "I'm a correspondent for the Papuan Liberation movement."

"Yes, I've read your columns, Kayla. You wrote about the Paniai massacre, it was on the front page," said Franz.

"I'll write about the battle at Enarotali too, but I don't think I can write about the evacuation of the Ples Tambu. I can't give away too much about the refugees' pathways, because so many people need to use them. You've seen how hard it is," said Kayla.

"Liza could probably give you an account of the Enarotali battle. She flew in there to help the wounded. She flew into Mulia too," I said.

"Yes, I'm wondering if Liza or one of her friends put up the video footage of that battle on the internet. I'll have to call her for an interview," said Kayla.

Paul dropped Kupsy at Kayla's place, just as we were pouring the next drinks.

"I'll just drop him and go, Kayla," said Paul. "My wife is expecting me. I can pick him up later tonight, or in the morning."

"The morning is probably good. I've got couches and a spare bed here," said Kayla.

"I've got a spare bed at my place too," added Franz.

"Righto, don't drink too much," said Paul, as he left.

"Wow, Paul told me a lot about the Refugee Association," said Kupsy. "I didn't know there were tens of thousands of us over here."

"Yes, there are heaps of refugees, and plenty of young people prepared to go back and fight, too," said Kayla.

"Konia and Dirk are both martyrs to the cause, and we won't forget them," said Franz. He was looking a pretty sad now.

"I'll put some music on," said Kayla. She played a CD from a local band. Kupsy looked amazed to hear a band singing in Tok Pisin.

"I can't believe a black woman lives in such a nice house," said Kupsy.

"I've got a good job at the newspaper, Kupsy. They pay me well, and I can write about the independence movement in Papua too. New Guineans are interested in what's going on next door. We hate the Indonesians too, though maybe not as much as you do," said Kayla.

"And who is this band? I didn't know our musicians made recordings?" said Kupsy.

"This is George Telek's song 'Free West Papua'. Telek first recorded with the Australian band, Not Drowning, Waving. I can play you some Papuan hip-hop too, but I thought this was better music for memorial drinks," said Kayla.

We listened to Telek sing:

San I go daun, san I Kamap,

Na wari stap yet Long West Papua.

O I laikim fridom, fridom, long West Papua,

Ol wantok bilong yumi.

Ol I ronawe nabaut, Na hait long bikbus,

Ol I laikim fridom, Husait bai helpim ol.

Ting-ting bilong ol,

Na bilip bilong ol long independence

Wanpela taim.

"I don't understand a lot of Tok Pisin, but I can understand that song," I said.

"Many words sound like English words, and Telek's written that song in simple words so it's easy to learn and sing," said Franz.

We had a few more drinks and listened to some sad music. One song featured a female voice, singing a haunting melody in a soft voice.

"What's this song, Kayla?" I asked.

"This is 'Sweet Lullaby'. She is singing her baby to sleep," said Kayla.

It was so beautiful, it almost made me want to cry.

"It was a big hit for Deep Forest in 1992. But the singer never got paid. A woman called Afunakwa from the Solomons sang it to a musicologist back in 1970, and the French band found the recording twenty years later. The song is in Baegu language."

I looked at Kayla, and said, "It's lovely, and very appropriate for Kupsy, who has lost his brother, and his father."

"I will have to go back, and see my mother," said Kupsy.

Franz had noticed an old guitar among piles of newspapers and CDs. He strummed along to the tune.

"Oh, that reminds me of youth group at church. So many of us played guitar," said Kayla.

"Did you ever learn to play the national anthem?" asked Franz.

Kayla found another CD and put it on. She played a recording of the West Papuan anthem, which had many verses. Kayla translated as each verse described the physical features of the land.

"I hadn't heard the West Papuan National Anthem before," said Arthur.

"When little kids sing it, they just sing the first, sixth and seventh verses," said Kupsy.

"To me, it's weird that it's in Indonesian. But I suppose it was written after the Indonesians took over, and that became the language taught in most schools," said Franz.

Franz played some more songs, followed by Kayla's Papuan hip-hop. We moved on to the beers, which were now cold in the fridge.

"So, you're heading back across the border, Kupsy?" asked Franz.

"Yeah, Paul said there was a small group of men heading across in a few days, who I could join," said Kupsy.

"I wonder if we could come to that meeting tomorrow?" I asked.

"You're not going back there, Arthur," said Kayla. "They know you and you won't be safe there."

"Oh, I'm not walking back in," I said. "Franz and I left our boat moored in a river in the national park. We need to sail back and pick it up. We'll be looking for crew members so we can sail one boat there, and two boats back."

Franz said "We can't run our fishing cruises without our boat. We might have to sail in at night. It would be quicker to fly a chopper in, but choppers are loud and boats are quiet."

"There will be Asmat lowlanders in the Refugee Association. They will know the rivers," said Kupsy.

"God, you boys are just terrible," said Kayla, shaking her head.

The inquest

J akarta District Court, Jakarta, Indonesia.
Inquest into the death of Dirk Feldmuller, Engineer, of the Netherlands, at Enarotali Airstrip, Papua, in November 2019.

Mr and Mrs Feldmuller sat in the courtroom accompanied by their adult son, Dirk's brother. They had a lawyer with them too, a Dutch guy. Mr Feldmuller wore a tailored suit, and had his grey hair combed into place neatly. His speckled skin betrayed a youth spent in the tropics, his later years in the cold old country. Mrs Feldmuller wore a patterned silk dress and jacket, with a golden cashmere wrap that caught the colour of her greying blonde hair. Tall and slim, she wore a string of enormous pearls that looked like they could have cost at least a $1,000 a pearl. They both had the intelligent blue eyes which Dirk had shared. Dirk's brother looked like a tamer version of him, the curly blonde hair cut short, and dressed in a schmick grey suit. I'd only ever seen Dirk in hi-vis work clothes, or casual shorts and singlets. He'd worked in the cold mountains of Grasberg, but flew out to his town-house in Bali.

The barrister representing Mr Feldmuller's family, Mr Alexander Mulder, rose.

"Could the witness please introduce herself to the courtroom?"

"My name is Liza Fraser. I am a doctor from Cairns, Australia, working at Freeport Grasberg Goldmine," I said.

"How did you know the deceased, Mr Dirk Feldmuller?" asked Alexander.

"Mr Feldmuller worked as a mining engineer at Freeport, but I came to know him after the incident. I'm under a suppression order from Freeport regarding the incident. Can I speak about it in court?" I asked.

"This is a closed courtroom, so suppression orders intended for the media do not apply here. You may speak about the incident if it is relevant to this inquest," said Alexander.

"It is. Mr Feldmuller and I were among a group of seven Freeport workers who went down in a helicopter crash as we flew out from the mine. The pilot and one miner were killed, while Dirk, Ken Knight, Arthur Neilson, Franz Seevink and I survived.

"We were rescued by Asmat highlanders, led by Swando and his son Semu. They took us to their cave home, known as the Ples Tambu or Taboo Place, in the mountains of the Lorentz National Park. We could not attract the rescue helicopter sent by Freeport due to heavy cloud cover and monsoon conditions. We lived with the Asmat tribe for a few weeks before a rescue party reached us. In that time, Dirk and myself came to learn about the tribe and their connection to the Free Papua Organisation, known as the OPM. We learned about how the Americans ran our billion-dollar mine, and paid tax to the Indonesians, who provided very little by way of services to the Papuans, and actively stole their land and shot their men," I said.

Coroner of Inquests, Mr Leonard Midoro, interjected.

"Kindly refrain from criticising the Indonesian government in your statement, Doctor Fraser."

"Is this inquest looking for the truth, or do you want me to spout propaganda about my employer and your government?" I asked.

"We are here to seek the truth about Mr Feldmuller's death. Please keep your evidence relevant to that topic," said Midoro.

"My evidence is relevant," I said. "Dirk and I listened to Konia from the Free Papua Organisation, who told us of the history of Indonesian massacres of their people, particularly when they protested the terrible pollution our mine caused to their rivers and land. In 1977, when the OPM attacked the mine's pipeline, eight hundred villagers were slaughtered by the Indonesian Army and police. More recently, there have been massacres in the Papuan capital, Jayapura, in 2006, 2008, 2010. Our chopper was heading there when we came down. The Paniai Lakes had massacres in 1967, 1969 and in 2014. In their report about the most recent Paniai massacre, Amnesty International said that the Indonesian police and army's response to wounded Papuans was to deny them medical aid and just let them die."

"As a doctor, I decided that I would endeavour to extend the mine's medical services to our regional villages, where otherwise there was no service of any kind. The Catholic Church provides education and medical services to the Asmat people further south in the national park. I had been working in Timika Hospital and Tiom Clinic, but I've now extended services to eight other villages and towns including Enarotali at Paniai."

Alexander asked, "How did Mr Feldmuller come to be at Enarotali?"

I had to think about what to include and exclude here. This was a court of law, and Dirk's parents deserved to know how and why he died. But I did not want to implicate my friends, further than they had already implicated themselves, in anti-government actions.

I said, "Dirk became active with the Free Papua Organisation because he sympathised with the villagers whom we lived with, and the guides who walked us out of the forest. Some of our staff speak fluent Tok Pisin, and Asmat dialect, so we remain alerted to regional medical emergencies."

"Which people do you refer to, exactly?" asked Alexander.

"Franz Seevink speaks Asmat and pidgin. Ken Knight and I both speak Tok Pisin. Konia from the OPM told us that our village, the Ples Tambu, had been infiltrated by the Kopassus, the Special Branch of the army, and was to be targeted for aerial bombardment, despite it being under the Catholic Church's protection in the national park. Konia and the OPM leaders from our area decided to launch a distraction attack on the Enarotali Airstrip to draw the army helicopters away from the Ples Tambu so that the villagers could escape the massacre.

"Konia, Arthur and Franz volunteered to help walk the villagers to the Papua New Guinean border. They helped children and old people to make the arduous walk hundreds of kilometres through the mountains," I said.

"Were these people armed?" asked Alexander.

"Konia and Arthur's group were unarmed," I said, "but Franz lost the group and returned to the Ples Tambu after it was bombed. He helped dig Semu, the younger chief, from the rubble of their cave. This pair had a gun, which they carried with them as they caught up with the rest of the villagers at the border."

"Was this gun used?" asked Alexander.

"Yes. When the villagers attempted to cross the border, the Indonesian Army shot at them from a helicopter. Konia used the gun to shoot down that helicopter, and was himself shot dead in the process. I was called to assist another Papuan who had been shot and seriously wounded in this attack. I saw Konia just before he was buried. His father and uncle had also both been killed by Indonesians as they attacked and stole their homes in Wamena."

"How did Mr Feldmuller come to be in Enarotali?" asked Alexander.

"Dirk attended a meeting of the Free Papua Organisation when the evacuation was planned. He volunteered to be part of the distraction raid at Enarotali. They needed a white man to buy the vehicles they required. The car dealers in Timika wouldn't sell multiple vehicles to a Papuan man. These vehicles were modified into armoured cars mounted with machine guns. There were also few drivers among the OPM fighters, so Dirk put his hand up to be a driver.

"The OPM leader from Enarotali rang and told us that there had been an attack, and that there were multiple casualties. I flew in with Doctor Carmichael and we found Dirk among the wounded. We flew him back to Grasberg to our clinic, but he was too unwell to operate on. Dirk suffered a large chest wound, after having been fired at by tanks, helicopters and ground soldiers. I stabilised Dirk and made him comfortable during his last hours. Freeport flew Dirk's remains back to Amsterdam, despite the fact that he hadn't worked for the company for a few months. He had worked there for five years prior to that."

Alexander asked, "What did Mr Feldmuller do in the months between working at the mine and the time of his death?"

I thought about this before answering. Mr Feldmuller senior and his wife were looking on with interest. Dirk must have told them something, but definitely not everything.

"Dirk started a fishing cruise business with Franz and Arthur, running short cruises out of Bali and Port Moresby. They called it 'Fish Lombok dot com', and they seemed to be doing well. I had been thinking of taking a three-day cruise, after having seen Arthur's photographs on their website. Arthur told me that they were fishing in the rivers of the Lorentz National Park, with the intent to run cruises there in the future, when they came across members of the Free Papua Movement, and decided to help them."

Oh God, that didn't sound very believable, even to me.

The Coroner, Mister Midoro, then asked, "I put it to you that Dirk Feldmuller and his associates were running guns for the Organasi Papua Merdeka. Would you say this was correct?"

I thought about it for a few seconds. Nothing worse could happen to Dirk, but Arthur and Franz could still get in a lot of trouble over this issue. I decided to lie.

"Not to my knowledge. I know that Dirk, Arthur and Franz left the mine after our helicopter accident. I stayed because I need the money to pay off my student debts. And because I wanted to help the Papuan people by extending medical services to those who have none. I believe that Dirk and his associates ran a legitimate fishing business. Arthur told me that he had returned to Papua to photograph the national park for *National Geographic* between cruises, and that they were scouting for unspoiled fishing locations. I do not believe that Dirk and his friends sold guns to the Free Papua Movement."

Alexander and the Feldmullers looked visibly more relaxed. But the Coroner was getting all fired up.

Midoro asked, "Where did Dirk Feldmuller meet with the OPM? Did he help plan their attack?"

I had my lies sorted out now. Feign ignorance. Admit nothing. Incriminate no one who was still alive. Including myself.

"I don't know, how could I be expected to know this? I am a doctor, flying in for ten days on, ten days off. I work my guts out when I am here. I am responsible for twenty thousand mine workers and their families in the mornings, and in the afternoons I fly to village clinics for childbirths and accidents. I am on call twenty-four hours for when a mineshaft collapses and I have to amputate a worker's leg which is caught under huge rocks. I get phone calls from my fieldworkers to come and help the wounded when the Indonesian Army decides to undertake another massacre.

"I was surprised to see Dirk among the wounded at Paniai. I was surprised to get a call from Arthur to fly to the border to help Konia and Semu. The facts I have told you, I have pieced together from what I hear from my patients, the ones who are still capable of speaking. I don't like patching up intelligent young leaders like Konia, only to find him shot to pieces, lacerated by machine-gun fire. I was extremely saddened to find Dirk among the wounded at Enarotali, never to regain consciousness. If Dirk was involved with Konia and the Free Papua Movement, good for him. I am not a member of their organisation. As far as I am aware, Konia was the only member of the OPM that I treated. I don't like cleaning up after the Indonesian Army's massacres. If Papua had journalists and tourists, they could tell the world about these ongoing atrocities that I have to deal with in my work."

Coroner Midoro didn't like where this was going. He said, "Thank you for your evidence today, Doctor Fraser."

The Feldmullers smiled at me as I left the courtroom. I walked through the cleaner part of Jakarta to an older, dirtier district where I was staying at a cheap hotel. It was stinking hot, and the streets smelled like fried street food and garbage. I crossed over a stream that held more rubbish than water. The streets were full of rubbish, plastic bags blowing in the wind.

Alexander sent me a text when the inquest was over. "Meet me at the bar at the Hilton. Feldmullers would like to meet you, six pm."

I wanted to meet them, too, so I texted back and went about getting ready. I only had the one suit to wear to court, but I could shower and change my blouse. I brushed out my hair; the evening was cool enough to wear it down.

The Double Tree Hilton was a big rectangular high-rise, set among large pools and two big trees. The bar was by an enormous pool, benefitting from the slight breeze across the water.

Alexander had changed into a more casual suit. He stood up to greet me.

"Liza, you did very well today. Come and meet the Feldmullers, Gerhard and Marguerite, and their son Johan," said Alexander, introducing me.

"Pleased to meet you," I said, "but so sorry about the circumstances."

"It's good to meet you, dear," said Marguerite. "It sounds like you were one of Dirk's friends."

"Yes," I said. "We grew close as a group after our crash and rescue experience."

"I felt that you knew more than you wanted to say in court. To protect Dirk's friends?" asked Gerhard.

"Yes, there is a lot more. Did Dirk tell you much?" I asked.

"He told us how the mine left you there, and how your husband Doctor Mike and his friend Doctor Dave sailed from Cairns and hiked in through the national park to find you. He told us that the Asmat kept you prisoner, and that Doctor Mike bought him and his friends in exchange for guns. After that, it got sketchy. We thought he was just running tours as well," said Gerhard.

"Dirk really wanted to help the Papuans," I said. "He respected them – their toughness and their belief that they could fight and get their land back. I think that Dirk, Arthur and Franz did run guns up to the Ples Tambu. Konia and his brother Kupsy brought their crews through the village on their walks, carrying guns and gold. The OPM used the cave as a secure place to hide their resources and people.

"After Dirk had brought the Papuans a couple of machine guns, they held a protest at Mulia, and the army attacked. They shot down four helicopters, so understandably the army officers were furious. A Kopassus scout followed the freedom fighters to the Ples Tambu. Konia realised that they had been compromised, after not recognising one of the men and asking the others about him. I'd been attending the wounded from the Mulia protest, and I picked up Dirk and his friends from the village near the cave. Konia had been visiting a wounded protester. With Konia, we held a meeting in my office, while army creeps surrounded our mining town of Tembagapura.

"Dirk volunteered for the Paniai attack, while the others helped the villagers and themselves to flee across the border. The villagers risked being massacred by aerial bombardment. The army were looking for Dirk and his friends, and would have locked them up or worse if they found them. We helped to save the whole village of Asmat highlanders, whose culture had changed little since colonisation. But we lost Dirk and Konia. I'm so sorry that Dirk died. I did all I could for him. But he died doing what he believed in and helping others much less fortunate than himself."

"We thought that Dirk might have been up to something like that," said Marguerite. "In a letter, he wrote that now he understood how we felt when the Indonesians took our plantation back in the sixties. We wanted to visit our old place, but the Indonesians wouldn't even let us have a visa for Papua province."

"Konia and Kupsy's farm was probably tiny compared to your plantation, but it was all they had. The army killed their dad and stole their farm twice. It's hard to live amid that kind of ongoing injustice without wanting to do something about it. Dirk made a difference to the cause. With machine guns, the fighters could retaliate against the army helicopters. At Enarotali, near the Paniai Lakes, the helicopters retreated after they shot the first one down. The Papuans have a chance to fight back with those machine guns, but the Indonesians won't give up the province and the mine without a big fight. Freeport is Indonesia's number one taxpayer. The tide is turning, but the Free Papua fighters still have a long way to go."

"Thank you for telling us about Dirk, and about yourself," said Johan. "You're a brave person to do what you do."

"Dirk was so brave, and always so positive. When we were losing hope, he made us exercise so we'd be fit for mountain walking when we escaped. He told Arthur that the tribe would cut him into long pork if he didn't heal his broken leg. He gave up his seat in the rescue helicopter and walked back through the national park with our guides, Rudol and Nollen. He wanted to see the great rivers and climb through the waterfalls. He'd hassle

Franz about his Christianity, and question Rudol about praying to the ancestors and the Crocodile God."

"The Crocodile God?" asked Gerhard.

"The Asmat prayed to him for a quick death, either for their prey, their enemies, or themselves. I hope that the Crocodile God was with Dirk in the end," I said.

"And the ancestors too," smiled Marguerite.

LIZA

Dropping Semu home

It was a month later when Arthur and Kayla's article was published in the *National Geographic*. I loved reading it so much that I ordered a few copies to drop off around the villages. Brother Johannes, and Rudol and Nollen would love to see themselves in the photos.

Semu had been at the clinic for a while. His chest wounds became infected. It was a case of trying different drugs to clear them up. I planned to take Semu back to Ilaga, where his wife Juvelyn was with their new baby.

It wasn't a busy day, so I asked the pilot if we could do a flyover around the Ples Tambu first. I wanted to see how much damage the aerial bombardment had done, and I was sure that Semu did too.

Our pilot today was Patrick.

"G'day, Doctor Liza," said Patrick.

"G'day, Patrick, this is my patient, Semu," I said. "We'll be dropping him back to Ilaga today, but we'd like to do a flyby around his old home, the Ples Tambu, as well. It's not far from Ilaga and I have the co-ordinates here if that's OK."

"Righto," said Patrick, "It's not a village anymore?"

"Well, you know how each village has a Haus Tambaran for worship and ancestors' relics and stuff. The Ples Tambu was a whole secret village. Their people had discovered a large habitable cave many years ago, which the men lived in, while the women lived in huts near the lower entrance. Anyway, the Indonesians bombed it about a month ago, and all the villagers had to leave. Semu was injured then, but his wife was evacuated to Ilaga where we are dropping him."

"It sounds like you know a lot about the local people," said Patrick.

"Well, I've looked after them, just like they look after me. Semu's tribe took care of a group of us when our chopper crashed not far away. It's still there, by the way. They brought us to the upper entrance of the cave. Now this place is secret, by the way, so if you could not write about it in your log, that would be great," I said.

"If we're just flying by, and not landing, I am not legally required to enter it in my flight log," said Patrick.

"Perfect!" I said, and I gave the thumbs up to Semu. Semu gave me the sign back, and we all laughed.

Patrick took off and followed the mountain ridges to the east. It was rainy season now, so the waterfalls and rivers were all fully flowing. We were fortunate to have a fine day, though the clouds looked like they might blow in later for an afternoon thunderstorm.

"OK, Ilaga is down there," said Patrick. "But this Ples Tambu is a little further along."

We saw the smoke rising from the cooking fires of Ilaga, and the top of the long house, the biggest hut, emerging from the trees. We followed the mountains towards the Ples Tambu.

Then Semu started pointing and shouting. Semu pointed out the remains of the women's village. A mountain of rubble piled up where most of the huts used to be, with a few broken huts poking out of the rocks at the edges. It looked like a natural disaster or an earthquake had hit.

Patrick slowed down and lowered us closer to the site. Semu pointed to a slight opening near the top of the mountain of rubble. "This must be where Franz helped to dig Semu out," I said. "The other entrance was around to the right, and high up the cliffs."

"We can build stone huts next time," said Semu.

I saw rubble, but he saw building blocks.

The Ples Tambu was in a valley high among the peaks, so Patrick lifted the chopper and followed the mountain ridge. We passed a small waterfall; I wondered if it was connected to the reservoir of water in the cave. Again, Semu spotted it first, and pointed it out to Patrick.

Patrick rose up and hovered near the upper entrance. We could see where Semu had made a slight opening in a pile of rubble that fell all over the ledge and had obviously tumbled to the valley far below, knocking down some trees. The Indonesians had sure used some serious firepower on the Ples Tambu.

"Which way to the crashed chopper?" asked Patrick.

"I think it's further along this ridge, where the edge gets more jagged. But we don't have to go there," I said.

"No, I want to see it," said Patrick. "I knew John, and I want to see where he ended up."

I hadn't thought that the pilot would be personally involved too, but of course he was. The pilots also swapped each other out, and they all maintained the choppers as well as flying them.

They all trusted each other to do a good job. Their lives all depended on it.

Patrick flew higher again, to be at the level of the peaks, and get a good view. He spotted the wreckage, down a steep jagged valley. We lowered down to have a look at it, all wrecked and smashed up.

I saw John's body, or what was left of it amongst the wreckage. Birds or animals had picked some of his bones clean. He didn't look pretty.

"Rest in peace, John," I said.

Patrick took some photos of the crash site, then we rose and turned, and headed for Ilaga.

Brother Johannes was waiting at Ilaga with Juvelyn and the new baby. Patrick turned the engine off, and we hopped out of the chopper.

Semu ran to Juvelyn and embraced her, looking lovingly at the baby.

"Boy or girl?" asked Semu.

"It's a boy, we'll call him Mtengwe," said Juvelyn.

So, one day, Swando's village would be called Mtengwe's village again.

ARTHUR

Epilogue

Living in Port Moresby involves one meeting after another. Refugee association meetings are interesting and have taken me all over Port Moresby and the other towns. I've also met officials from the Catholic Church to get the rundown on what they are doing and where. The *National Geographic* article was printed, and I visited *The National* newspaper to meet some of Kayla's workmates.

Kupsy went back across into Papua with some other OPM activists after they did some training with the Refugee Action Group. Kupsy and his new friends were kitted out with satellite phone and solar chargers, so communications could be maintained. He was keen to see his mother again and tell her the news about Konia.

I could have made some money doing journalism, but I've made so much more running cruises. I needed our boat back.

I'd been getting on really well with Kayla so it made sense to move out of Franz's place and in with her. She's great. She works so hard and is full of ideas about how to get things done. And she's a real lateral thinker.

Franz and I had new business cards printed. We decided to base ourselves in Port Moresby rather than Bali, as the Indonesians couldn't make our lives quite so miserable here.

We couldn't really work in the monsoon season, so we went about planning our future business. A new name, new routes. We looked into hiring a boat, but it took all the profit out of the venture. We had to get our boat back. Or at least try.

Kayla knew our boat was near Jita, and that the Catholic Church ran a school in Jita. So she visited her friend at the Archdiocese offices in Boroka. St Mary's cathedral is a wonder of 1970s architecture, with a big white body and a conical tower, painted inside in ochres, like the high roof of a tribal long house. The church offices were close by.

"Cathy, this is my partner, Arthur," said Kayla, introducing me.

"Arthur," said Cathy. "You're the first white man I have met who has survived the border crossing!"

"Hello, Cathy," I said. "Franz made it across too, but we are just glad that most of the villagers made it across."

"Your actions helped prevent a massacre. The people of the Ples Tambu have been resettled in a south Papuan village. Our parishes try to help the refugees to settle in. It's all about saving souls," said Cathy.

Kayla said, "Arthur wants to make contact with the missionary in Jita, to find out about his boat, which he left near there."

"Well," said Cathy, "I have his contact details right here."

Cathy rifled through her desk drawer and located a file-card box. She flipped through it and took out a card.

"Old-fashioned, I know," said Cathy, "but it works when the electricity or the internet go out."

"Oh God," said Kayla, "especially in the monsoon. When I was a student, I lost so much writing when a storm hit and the computer died."

"Here's your man. Darius O'Kane. He is a priest with a teaching degree." Cathy wrote his contact details on a blank card for me. Then she picked up her desk phone and called him.

"Father Darius," said Cathy. "It's Cathy here from the Archdiocese of Moresby … I've got my friend Arthur Neilson here. He'd like to meet you."

Cathy waited for his response and passed the phone over to me.

"Hello, Father Darius, I'm Arthur," I said.

"Hello Arthur, how can I help you?" said Darius.

"Father, I am a co-owner of a boat, a fifty-foot cruiser moored not far from your village," I said.

"Oh yes, and how did it manage to get there?" Darius asked.

"My friend Franz and I have been running fishing cruises in Indonesia, and around PNG, up to New Britain and the Solomons. We were scouting for good fishing spots in the national park, but left Papua via an overland route," I said.

"And now you want it back?" asked Father Darius.

"Ah, yes, but there are one or two problems," I said.

"Would those problems be anything to do with the Indonesian Navy vessels that have been moored around here recently?" he asked.

"Yes, those are exactly the problems that I am worried about, Father."

"Right," said Darius. "Well the good news is that the large navy vessel that was here a month ago only stayed for a week. A medium-sized ship took its place for two weeks, and now it's been replaced by a smaller boat in the last week. We only have a small market, and their supplies must only last so long. Also, I think the sailors get bored. In a small village, there is not much for them to do, and they can't swim because of crocs and sharks."

"I would be so interested in finding out when they finish keeping watch and change to regular patrols. Surely they don't have the manpower to stake out every fishing boat in Papua?" I said.

"I would be more worried if they were to impound your boat," said Darius.

"But that would be stealing!" I said.

"I wouldn't put it past them," said Darius.

"I'd really like to know if they reassess their presence and reduce it to patrols. You can email me at arthur@fishpng.com," I said.

"Arthur, if you are coming across to us, we have some people who would really like to come back with you. How many can you fit on the boat?" said Darius.

"With three crew, we took eight passengers on cruises," I said.

"Yeah, but it looks like a pretty big boat," said Darius. "How many could you fit in for a ten-hour trip across the border?" asked the priest.

"Well, it's not so much about how many will fit in, but about how much they all weigh," I said. "Our boat is a fifty-footer and will only take about twenty-five people maximum, especially if we are foolish enough to sail during the monsoon."

"OK, good. The monsoon might be enough to send the Indonesians looking for a safer moorage here too. Our jetty is only accessible to them at high tide, but they have driven some poles into the mud to tie up to. They are frustrated that they can't buy planks here, but our people don't want to sell their timber," said Darius.

"We will have a small inflatable, but it only takes about five people at a time. There may be some Asmat men heading back there with us," I said.

"Right. Well, stay in contact, and I'll talk to my people about what they are planning too," said Darius.

"So glad to have met you, Father Darius," I said.

Franz had a Papuan Refugee Association meeting at his place, or rather, a Refugee Action Committee meeting. The larger group organised rehousing and registrations for refugees. This smaller group was another matter.

Franz had met his friend Malcolm at the Royal Papua Yacht Club. He'd asked about hiring a yacht to train new crew members. Malcolm got him a good deal because he was training new workers rather than taking out tourists.

Franz had a crew of five young Papuan men – Lungstar, Mathew, Sikin, Luke and Juxman – all keen to learn how to sail a cruiser.

I came out on their third training sail to see how they were going. Franz actually made a really good teacher. He got the first two men to take the boat out, then bring it in again. Then the next two did the same thing. Then the fifth man teamed up with one of the others, and took the boat out and in. They all did a good job.

"Wow! You men all did really well," I said.

"That's good," said Franz, "because Malcolm and the yacht club guys are probably watching us."

Next we went out into the open water, and each of the men took a turn at the wheel and checking the navigation equipment.

Franz patiently explained to Sikin how the computer program worked. He hadn't really seen a lot of computers before.

We'd been sailing close to the coast, and as I watched Franz with Sikin, I understood that Franz was teaching him to see where the boat was in respect to the coastline. Franz asked the skipper at the time, Juxman, to turn to port and starboard, so that Sikin could see how the screen showed the landscape move in relation to the boat, which stayed in the middle of the screen. It came naturally to Franz and me; we grew up playing computer games. These guys hadn't, and had only just begun to understand maps, so this was a great way to teach them.

On the way back into port, Franz told the skipper that he could see a huge storm cloud off to one side, and asked him to steer around it. When we encountered big waves, Franz showed the men how to sail across them, rather than alongside the waves, which could tip the boat.

Franz was thorough and patient, and the men all learned quickly. They were a good crew.

"Our next sail is a night sail so they can get used to those conditions," said Franz.

"You've done a great job with them, Franz," I said.

"Yes, they are nearly ready for our first mission," he replied.

"That's good, because I've made contact with Father Darius in Jita. He's been keeping an eye on the navy boats for us. Apparently, they had a big ship there for a week, then they swapped out with a smaller boat, and now there is a smaller one again. I'm hoping they'll think it's a waste of time to keep a boat there permanently and will switch to a patrol. Then we're in with a chance," I said.

"It's good that they didn't just impound the boat," said Franz.

"Well, it's a bit big to tow, and I've got the keys to the engines," I said.

"It must be difficult to hot-wire boat engines," said Franz.

"Not to mention, illegal," I said.

"I've had one bad-weather sail with the men," said Franz, "but I wouldn't mind a practice run with a storm."

"Yes, a big storm might provide a good opportunity to get in there and out again, with minimal chance of getting followed," I said.

The freezer was chock full of frozen fish, so I fried up enough to make us all a feed. I showed some of the Papuans how the gas stove worked, how to heat the oil and how to fry the fish. All of these skills were important. We had to make sure that these men could operate the boat, even if something happened to Franz or me.

A few mornings later, Father Darius rang.

"Arthur," he said, "the Indonesians are packing up their boat today. They've just filled up with fresh water from our tank and bought all the fresh food at our little market. They are heading off."

"That is fantastic news," I said. "A patrol will be much easier to avoid than a boat stationed there."

"I've also sent that information up the river, to our other missions," said Darius. "I've already got one family here, and I'm expecting a few more to join us in the coming days."

"Right," I said. "How many days until you round up all the passengers, do you think?"

"It's hard to say," said Darius. "Maybe about three days. There are people coming from Tiom and from Paniai. I'm not sure how close everyone is, but I'm getting news as they arrive at the various missions."

"Thank you. I'll pass the word on to our crew. They are sailing like professionals now. The mission should go well," I said.

I told Kayla, who was quite excited.

"I think that the Papuan Refugee Association might have a few OPM activists who want to cross back into Papua with you guys as well," said Kayla.

"Great," I said. "We'll be people smuggling in both directions."

"Well, you've seen how difficult it can be to cross the land border," said Kayla.

"Hopefully, this mission won't get that ugly," I said. "If they send a helicopter after us, we'll be in trouble."

"That's true," said Kayla. "Let's pray for bad weather."

Our prayers to God and the ancestors were soon answered. The monsoon struck with force. A category four storm had formed over the Arafura Sea, and most boat owners sought safe moorage, even bringing their boats up onto land using the giant lift at the yacht club.

Our crew set sail on an 'overnight exercise' from the yacht club, picking up six OPM men from a small jetty near Goroka. They were carrying large backpacks. I asked what they contained.

"Drones," said one of the men. "We've learned to use drones to track ahead and keep an eye on the enemy."

"Great," I said, "drones could come in very useful."

Darius called to tell us that the patrol boat was visiting mid-morning, and that it was the South Papuan Border Patrol. It could well be Wayan Chan from Amamapare. Both our boat, and this thirty-foot hired cruiser, could go faster than Wayan Chan's old tugboat.

We set off at midday intending to arrive at Jita by midnight, returning that same night to arrive by the following lunch time.

Some of our crewmen chewed teeth-staining betel nut to stay awake. Franz and I drank energy drinks to get the same effect, but without the red teeth.

With seven crew and six passengers, the boat sat quite low but was still able to make full speed.

Wayne was the leader of the OPM group who'd hopped on in Goroka, a suburb of Port Moresby. He introduced himself to all the crew, and introduced his team.

Wayne approached me and Franz to tell us about his mission.

"Arthur and Franz, it's good to meet you," said Wayne.

"G'day Wayne, Papua Merdeka!" I said.

"I've got to fill you in on our mission, so you've got the full picture," said Wayne.

"Fire away!" said Franz. "So to speak."

"Ha ha, no, we don't have any guns," said Wayne, "but we've got some explosives. Father Darius has a speed boat ready for half our team. We will sail to Amamapare and set them off near the pipeline and the port. This action will draw attention away from the Jita operation. Darius has enough refugees to fill up both your boats, so we wanted to maximise your chance of getting back across the border. Our other three will rendezvous with us later."

"Oh, I had hoped that only the bigger boat would carry the refugees. That's alright, we'll have four crew for the bigger boat and three for the smaller one. Even in the dark and storm, we should be OK," I said.

"And we've brought fuel for the other boat, in case it's low," said Franz.

The storm was indeed building up. The waves were big, but Sikin was doing a good job of cutting through them. We rostered each man for an hour at the wheel.

Our course kept us away from the coastline, so we couldn't be seen. We didn't see any other boats on our radar; no one else was stupid enough to go out in a category four storm.

We crossed the border and made our way around the south Papuan coast. To get to Jita we could take any one of three rivers; the Akimuga, Muras Besar, or Toorpedobot. The three rivers had branches that joined in a delta swamp area where seven or more rivers split and rejoined on their way to the sea.

We aimed for the Muras Besar. We were sailing north now, but the storm was howling in from the west, regularly pushing us off course. In the darkness, it was hard to see anything up on deck, but two crew members were keeping watch in their weatherproof jackets.

The coastal swamp loomed like a big dark mass, and soon we were in it. As the river narrowed, we followed the twists and turns of the Muras Besar.

We soon saw the lights of Jita up ahead, which meant that we must be getting close to our boat.

Sure enough, around the next bend, there it was – the *Pukpuk*, which means crocodile, the name we had given it. It was dark, and the inflatable wasn't tied to it. These were good signs.

We pulled up alongside so I could jump across to the *Pukpuk* with a rope. I tied the *Pukpuk* to the hire boat just long enough for Sikin, Juxman and Luke to pass the fuel tanks and jump across as well. Franz took the hire boat straight to the jetty at Jita. We were two crews now. He must have started loading passengers immediately. We filled up the fuel tank, then followed Franz to the village.

The OPM guys had jumped in a speedboat and took off past us, flat stick.

The *Pukpuk* took a little while to warm up, not having gone anywhere in over a month, but was soon running smoothly. We met Father Darius at the jetty.

"Arthur, it's good to meet in person," he said.

"Father Darius, thanks so much for helping us out."

"Look, I'm afraid we may have too many for the boat to carry," said Darius.

"Just start loading them on, and when we get to the capacity line, we'll stop," I said.

"Alright. I have prioritised the passengers, and the rest might have to go next time, or find another way," said Darius.

Sikin and I helped quite a few small families into the boat. These were mostly mums and kids, and some male passengers with injuries. These were the people who had survived the last round of fighting but didn't want to see any more. They carried only billums, blankets and food.

We packed them in to the bottom of the boat. By the time the capacity line reached the water level, we had ten adults, twelve children, and four crew.

We were headed back down the Muras Besar when we head the sound of a distant explosion. I switched the two-way radio to channel ten, a rarely used channel, to reach Franz.

"Where are you guys?" I asked.

"We are near the mouth of the Mandeville river," said Franz.

"We are still in the Muras Besar," I said.

"We picked up something large on the radar, coming from the southeast. We're going to hide in the river mouth until it goes past," said Franz.

"Right, we will take the next branch that heads to Toorpe-dobot and the Blumen. The big boat may well check the Muras Besar on its way to Timika," I said.

A couple more explosions followed.

Luke spotted a creek in the left bank, and we headed straight into it. The satellite navigator showed us among the networks of creeks and islands, and we wove our way through the muddy swamps, towering with mangrove trees.

"A big navy boat is coming from the east, on my radar now, so I'm switching mine off so they won't pick it up," said Franz on the two-way.

"Right, I'll do the same," I said.

Then Sikin said, "I could send up a drone. Will they pick that up?"

"How small is it?" I asked.

"Small, it fits in this little backpack," said Sikin.

He unpacked a drone, which was only about thirty centimetres across. If the radar couldn't pick up a dinghy with an outboard, it wasn't going to pick up a drone this size.

"OK, send it up," I said.

I felt like a sitting duck, hiding behind a mangrove island with the engines and navigation turned off. Sikin sent up his drone which, although tossed by the winds a little, sent back a good picture of what it saw.

A navy destroyer was charging along the coastline, going nearly double the speed we were capable of. Sikin sent the drone higher and higher, to where we thought we could see the hire boat a few river mouths along from us.

The navy boat passed Franz's boat, and ten minutes later, passed us as well.

"Right, bring that drone back in, Sikin, and we'll get going," I said.

Franz hopped on the radio, "We have set sail. See you there."

We powered down the river and into the Arafura Sea. The full boat handled pretty well, but the storm still raged on and the waves were all over the place.

We steered out to sea to the south, then east towards PNG. The storm came in patches now, but seas were still choppy. The buckets had been passed around down in the hold, as passengers got seasick. The Papuans had made themselves comfortable, sitting in rows on the bunks. There were children sleeping in the top bunks. Crossing the border at around dawn, we were so relieved to see in a new day in New Guinea.

Franz and I stopped in Daru, where Jenella's family lived. The PRA had a refugee camp here as well. We met an activist with a bus at the quiet jetty there.

Franz said, "Arthur, I promised God that I'd become a Brother if we made it back from that mission alive."

I said, "I also promised Kayla that I wouldn't cross the border into Papua again after this mission. But I don't mind if our boat goes. It looks like we've got some good sailors trained up now, for both the fishing cruises and whatever else."

Acknowledgments

This book is dedicated to all the Freedom Fighters in West Papua. May your battle for independence be victorious. May those in exile return to their countries with freedom. May all Indigenous people everywhere win the right to govern themselves and their land. Papua Merdeka! Free West Papua!

Thanks to the Papuan Freedom activists all over the world: Benny, Maria and Calvin Wenda and their family, and Buchtar Tabuni; writers like John Waromi and Aprila Wayar; journalists like John Martinkus; academics like John Saltford and Mike Leach; lawyers like Veronica Koman and Emanuel Gobay; and theologians like the Reverend Benny Giay.

The Free West Papua Campaign has support groups in Australia, PNG, the USA, the UK, Melanesia, Micronesia, Denmark, the Netherlands, Poland, Vanuatu, Tonga, Fiji, Solomon Islands, East Timor, Samoa, Polynesia, New Zealand, Scotland, and Indonesia. In Australia, there are campaign support groups in Darwin, Wide Bay, Sydney, Brisbane, Northern NSW, Coffs Coast, Newcastle, The Cove, Gold Coast, Ballarat, Townsville, and Hawks Nest.

I'd like to thank John Birmingham, Dirk Flinthart, Susan Prior, William Cutts for his book describing his missionary work in Papua, and Fiona Bazley Hodges. Thanks to my Papuan friends, to Russel Norman, the staff at the Children's Hospital, and to the rescue helicopter and ambulance staff. Thanks to my lecturers Carole Ferrier, Cliff Watego (RIP), Richard Fotheringham, and Veronica Kelly. I'd like to thank my dad Gerald and mum Josephine for teaching me about fishing and travelling. Thanks to David Terare, to my guides Stanbuli and Kingi, and to the musicians George Telek, Trio Ambisi, Edo Kondologit, and Afunakwa (Deep Forest). Finally, I give thanks and love to my husband, Edward, and my daughters Veronica and Jessica.

About the Author

Mandy Curties Partridge studied her BA at The University of Queensland and her MA at Griffith University. Mandy co-edited the UQ newspaper *Semper Floreat*, where she met writers like John Birmingham, Dirk Flinthart, Helen Dale, Peter McAllister and Howard Hunt. Mandy worked in theatre and circus, and wrote *Alice's Excellent Adventure*, and *Death Wears a Red Nose* for the West Australian Circus School, and *Mistress Mandarella's New Boots* for the Brisbane Powerhouse. Mandy's first book, *Acrobalances*, was published by Nick Hudson in 2015. Mandy represents her city as the Brisbane Town Crier and loves researching and public speaking. She has travelled to many countries on six continents and considers this to be as essential a learning experience as university study.